PENGUIN  CL

CUP OF GOLD

Born in Salinas, California, in 1902, JOHN STEINBECK grew up in a fertile agricultural valley near the Pacific Coast—and both valley and coast would serve as settings for some of his best fiction. In 1919 he went to Stanford University, where he intermittently enrolled in literature and writing courses until he left in 1925 without taking a degree. During the next few years he supported himself as a laborer and journalist in New York City and then as a caretaker for a Lake Tahoe estate, all the time working on his first novel, *Cup of Gold* (1929). After marriage and a move to Pacific Grove, he began to publish California fictions, *The Pastures of Heaven* (1932), *To a God Unknown* (1933), and short stories of the working classes. Popular success and financial security came only with *Tortilla Flat* (1935), a novel about Monterey's *paisanos*. A ceaseless experimenter throughout his career, Steinbeck changed courses regularly. Three powerful novels of the late 1930s focused on the California laboring class: *In Dubious Battle* (1936), *Of Mice and Men* (1937), and the book considered by many his finest, *The Grapes of Wrath* (1939). In the forties he became an amateur marine biologist, as depicted in *Sea of Cortez* (1941), and wrote about the war in *Bombs Away* (1942) and the controversial play-novelette *The Moon Is Down* (1942). *Cannery Row* (1945), *The Wayward Bus* (1947), *The Pearl* (1947), *A Russian Journal* (1948), and *Burning Bright* (1950) preceded publication of the monumental *East of Eden* (1952), an ambitious saga of the Salinas Valley and his own family's history. Later books include *Sweet Thursday* (1954), *The Short Reign of Pippin IV* (1957), *Once There Was a War* (1958), *The Winter of Our Discontent* (1961), *Travels with Charley in Search of America* (1962), *America and Americans* (1966), and the posthumously published *Journal of a Novel: The* East of Eden *Letters* (1969), *Viva Zapata!* (1975), *The Acts of King Arthur and His Noble Knights* (1976), and *Working Days: The Journals of* The Grapes of Wrath (1989). The last decades of his life were spent in New York City and Sag Harbor with his third wife, with whom he traveled widely. He died in 1968, having won a Nobel Prize in 1962.

SUSAN F. BEEGEL is editor of a scholarly journal, *The Hemingway Review*, and adjunct professor of English at the University of Idaho. Coeditor of *Steinbeck and the Environment: Interdisciplinary Approaches*, she is the author of two additional books and more than fifty articles on various aspects of nineteenth- and twentieth-century American literature and history. A research associate of the Williams College–Mystic Seaport Program, she has a special interest in maritime studies and literature of the sea.

JOHN STEINBECK

Cup of Gold

A LIFE OF SIR HENRY MORGAN, BUCCANEER, WITH OCCASIONAL REFERENCE TO HISTORY

Introduction by SUSAN F. BEEGEL

PENGUIN BOOKS

PENGUIN BOOKS
Published by the Penguin Group
Penguin Group (USA) Inc., 375 Hudson Street, New York, New York 10014, U.S.A.
Penguin Group (Canada), 90 Eglinton Avenue East, Suite 700, Toronto,
Ontario, Canada M4P 2Y3 (a division of Pearson Penguin Canada Inc.)
Penguin Books Ltd, 80 Strand, London WC2R 0RL, England
Penguin Ireland, 25 St Stephen's Green, Dublin 2, Ireland (a division of Penguin Books Ltd)
Penguin Group (Australia), 250 Camberwell Road, Camberwell,
Victoria 3124, Australia (a division of Pearson Australia Group Pty Ltd)
Penguin Books India Pvt Ltd, 11 Community Centre, Panchsheel Park, New Delhi – 110 017, India
Penguin Group (NZ), 67 Apollo Drive, Rosedale, North Shore 0632,
New Zealand (a division of Pearson New Zealand Ltd)
Penguin Books (South Africa) (Pty) Ltd, 24 Sturdee Avenue,
Rosebank, Johannesburg 2196, South Africa

Penguin Books Ltd, Registered Offices:
80 Strand, London WC2R 0RL, England

First published in the United States of America by Robert M. McBride & Co. 1929
Published by Covici, Friede, Inc. 1936
Published by The Viking Press, Inc. 1938
Published in Penguin Books 1976
This edition with an introduction by Susan F. Beegel published 2008

3 5 7 9 10 8 6 4

Copyright John Steinbeck, 1929
Copyright renewed John Steinbeck, 1957
Introduction copyright © Susan F. Beegel, 2008
All rights reserved

ISBN 978-0-14-303945-7
CIP data available

Printed in the United States of America
Set in Sabon

Contents

Introduction

John Steinbeck's *Cup of Gold* is, in the words of one early reviewer, a "rather weird" novel. Published in 1929, when Steinbeck was just twenty-seven years old, his first book rings with the clashing blades of dissonant elements. *Cup of Gold* is an historical novel, a fictive biography that follows the career of the actual Sir Henry Morgan (1635?–1688), England's infamous "King of the Buccaneers," with considerable fidelity. Yet the book is indebted not only to history, but to "boy's own" adventure stories as well as to dramas of the screen and stage—to the swashbuckling romance as well as the brutal reality of the pirate tradition. And *Cup of Gold* is also a literary fantasy wherein the wizard-bard Merlin can instruct the historic Henry Morgan and the Grail quest of Arthurian legend can inform a story set largely in the seventeenth-century Caribbean.

The novel's experimental style reflects its dueling genres. Inspired by a medieval revival fashionable in the 1920s, Steinbeck juxtaposes modernist prose and naturalistic observation with archaic speech and highly wrought figurative language. *Cup of Gold* combines a realistic method with allegory and parable. The book can be read as an ordinary man's tragic quest for fortune, fame, and love; an artist's failed quest to find his Muse; or Europe's bloody quest to realize an American Dream in the New World. It can be a cautionary tale about the piratical ethics of American business and its corporate robber barons, or about the similarly piratical ethics of a new American imperialism. And finally, *Cup of Gold* is an autobiographical novel, the story of young John Steinbeck's quest to find his vocation. Perhaps the best way to make sense of this dissonant symphony is to investigate each of its unusual elements.

STEINBECK AND THE HISTORIC HENRY MORGAN

The basic plot of *Cup of Gold* is reasonably faithful to the actual life of Sir Henry Morgan, arguably the most famous pirate in English history. The novel traces Morgan's rise to fame and fortune—his boyhood in the Welsh mountains, his departure for the West Indies, his entrapment in indentured servitude, his slow acquisition of wealth and the means to buy a sailing vessel, and his eventual fulfillment of his dream "to go a-buccaneering and take a Spanish town." Morgan's brutal but brilliant career climaxes with his capture of the "Cup of Gold"—Panama City with its fabled riches. His depredations nearly bring him to the gallows, but instead Morgan claws his way to a knighthood and the lieutenant-governorship of Jamaica, winning the hand in marriage of the previous governor's daughter, his cousin Elizabeth. *Cup of Gold* ends with the ailing knight on his deathbed.

From *Captain Blood* to *Pirates of the Caribbean*, virtually every pirate story in our literature owes something to the life and legend of the genuine Sir Henry Morgan, and *Cup of Gold* is no exception. A gentleman's son from Wales, the historic Morgan probably went out to the West Indies as a soldier in a military expedition against the Spanish. After helping England seize Jamaica from Spain, Morgan based himself in Port Royal. There he created his own flotilla of small vessels and a heterogeneous force known as the Brethren of the Coast—a sea-borne army of English, French, and Dutch adventurers, professional cattle hunters, vengeful Indians, escaped slaves, runaway sailors, convicts, and cutthroats. Responding to no authority but the will and charisma of their leader, the Brethren fought the Spanish solely for prizes and plunder, hence the motto Steinbeck records, "No prey, no pay." Ashore, they were known for rape, loot, and pillage. They took hostages, tortured victims to learn where their valuables were hidden, and held entire towns for ransom, burning them down if the gold and silver were not forthcoming. Between 1655 and 1671, Morgan and his men would sack eighteen cities, four towns, and thirty-five villages of New Spain. Morgan's capture of Portobello against heavy odds was perhaps the most successful amphibious assault of his century, and his sacking of the fabled treasure city of Panama the most notorious.

These activities were a militant form of venture capitalism authorized, for the most part, by the British crown. Lacking a navy large enough to defend her developing interests and challenge Spanish supremacy in the New World, England instead relied on privateering—a legalized form of piracy—to harass the enemy. Men such as Morgan, able to fund their own expeditions and raise their own crews, were given letters of marque to legitimize their depredations and were allowed to keep their booty, often divided with respectable investors who purchased shares in their voyages. To the English, Morgan was, in Steinbeck's words, "a hero and a patriotic man." To the Spanish, however, this ruler of "a wild race of pirates" was "only a successful robber"—if not an infamous terrorist.

The historic Henry Morgan, like Steinbeck's protagonist, married his cousin Mary Elizabeth, daughter of Colonel Edward Morgan, lieutenant-governor of Jamaica and Henry's uncle. As in *Cup of Gold*, the marriage took place shortly after the death of the bride's father, but fact differs from fiction in one important way—the actual wedding happened well before the sack of Panama. Morgan was already a successful and wealthy buccaneer, but the marriage was not contingent upon his triumph, and seems to have been made for love, as Mary Elizabeth had no dowry. This historic union echoes in every pirate yarn featuring a love affair between a buccaneer-hero and the governor's daughter/niece/ward, whether Captain Peter Blood and Arabella Bishop, or Will Turner and Elizabeth Swann. By transmuting the actual Morgan union into a loveless marriage of convenience, *Cup of Gold* departs from both the romance and reality of the pirate tradition, and establishes its own ironic, antichivalric tone.

Problems arose for the historic Morgan when—as in the case of Panama—he continued his marauding without state sanction during a brief period when England and Spain were at peace. For this, he was arrested and taken to London to be tried as a pirate; but when England's relationship with Spain took a turn for the worse, he was released, knighted, and made lieutenant-governor of Jamaica. There Morgan eventually died of the combined effects of tropical fever, dropsy, and alcoholism in 1688, leaving behind thousands of acres of sugar plantations and Mary Elizabeth, named in his will as "my very well and entirely beloved wife."

Cup of Gold's subtitle is "A Life of Sir Henry Morgan, Buccaneer, with Occasional Reference to History," and the novel parallels the life so closely that some early readers skipped over the adjective "occasional" and mistook the fictional work for biography. Steinbeck's brief intercalary chapters on the history of piracy in the Caribbean, his discourses on other pirates of the age such as Pierre le Grand, L'Ollonais, and Edward Mansvelt, further blurred the boundaries of fact and fiction for muddled readers. The *St. Louis Star* referred to "Mr. Steinbeck" as Morgan's "biographer," and proclaimed "[H]ere is presented Morgan's complete life (including his loves) dealing with every phase, whether real or legendary." Berton Braley, who published a doggerel epic titled *Morgan Sails the Caribbean* (1937), acknowledged *Cup of Gold* as a source, treating the novel as nonfiction.

For most of the "facts" of Sir Henry Morgan's life, Steinbeck relied not on primary research in English and Spanish archives, but on a single source, Alexander O. Exquemelin's *The Buccaneers of America*. Originally published in Dutch as *De Americaensche Zee-Rovers* (1678), Exquemelin's work was first translated into English in 1684. While little is known about Exquemelin himself, he apparently went out to the Caribbean island of Tortuga with the French West India Company, and "through necessity" became a buccaneer, serving under Morgan at Panama. Exquemelin's firsthand account of life among the buccaneers was a bestseller in its time and has been in print almost continuously since the seventeenth century. It is a classic sea narrative and the urtext of most pirate stories in our language.

As Darlene Eddy has observed, Steinbeck drew many of *Cup of Gold*'s striking images and realistic details from *Buccaneers of America*. Dafydd's account of the Indian thorn torture, Merlin's musing on the futility of keeping fireflies, Morgan's encounter with a drunken pirate captain who orders him to drink or die, famished buccaneers coming out of the jungle at Panama and gorging on fresh meat, heedless of the blood running down their beards—these are a few of the images Steinbeck took from Exquemelin. More important, *Buccaneers of America* contributed to *Cup of Gold*'s portrait of the grim labor conditions that drove diverse men into joining Morgan's gang of desperados, and to the novel's graphic depiction of their cruelty, greed, and debauchery when unleashed on the cities of New Spain.

Buccaneers of America, however, is also replete with questionable (and damning) statements about Morgan himself. Steinbeck almost certainly knew that in 1684 the historic Sir Henry had successfully sued Exquemelin's English publishers for libel. Yet the novelist chose to retain aspects of Exquemelin's account that contribute more to pirate legend and compelling fiction than to accurate history or biography. For instance, *Buccaneers of America* claims that Morgan began as an indentured servant in the West Indies, although most historians believe that he originally went to the Caribbean as an officer in an English military expedition against the Spanish in Hispaniola.

Steinbeck kept the legend of Morgan's indentured servitude nevertheless, using it to transform *Cup of Gold* into a black inversion of a Horatio Alger story, as Morgan cheats his generous owner and exploits his fellow slaves to make his way from rags to riches. Steinbeck also retained Exquemelin's claim that Morgan tricked his men out of their fair share in the booty from Panama. Historians have doubted this as well, believing that the take from Panama was simply less than expected because the city's real riches, silver ingots from Bolivian mines, had been shipped out before the attack. Here again Steinbeck uses Exquemelin's disenchantment with Morgan to expose the

American success story as a climb up "a ladder to a higher, more valuable crime."

Exquemelin also had some libelous things to say about the historic Morgan's treatment of women captives during the sack of Panama:

> The rovers had a way of dealing with those women who held out. . . . [O]nce a woman was in their hands they would work their will upon her, or beat her, starve her, or similarly torment her. Morgan . . . was no better than the rest. Whenever a beautiful prisoner was brought in, he at once sought to dishonour her.

Buccaneers of America goes on to sketch the bare kernel of a story about Morgan and "a woman so steadfast her name deserves to live." Ironically, Exquemelin does not name this "young and very beautiful wife of a rich merchant," but says that "no lovelier woman could be found in all Europe." Lusting after her, Morgan at first tries her virtue with kindness—with private quarters, a slave, fine meals, visits from friends, and gifts of jewels. The lady, "as chaste as she was well-bred," persists in refusing him and tells Morgan that he will "have to let her soul go free" before he can "work his will on her body." Enraged, he has her stripped, imprisoned, and starved, but she continues to refuse, saying she will never give in so long as she lives. Eventually, Morgan accepts defeat, returning the lady to her husband in exchange for a substantial ransom. Steinbeck transformed Exquemelin's libelous little story into a major plotline in *Cup of Gold*—Morgan's longing for and rejection by the captive beauty La Santa Roja.

STEINBECK AND THE ROMANCE OF PIRACY

Steinbeck was not simply writing a biography of Sir Henry Morgan, or an historical novel based entirely on period materials such as Exquemelin's narrative. He was also keenly aware of the romantic representations of piracy in children's literature and popular culture. A careerist from the start, young Steinbeck was as interested in winning a large popular audience as he was in critical acclaim and academic plaudits. While working on *Cup of Gold*, he gave this advice about writing in a letter to his friend Webster Street: "Always crowd the limit. And also if you have time, try your hand on a melo drahmar, something wild and mysterious and unexpected [. . .]." A story, Steinbeck felt, should be "as racy as you think the populace will stand." He certainly understood and hoped to exploit the broad appeal of pirate stories. *Cup of Gold* seems to project a fantasy of its own hoped-for reception when "a multifarious population" crowds the beach at Port Royal "to see the Captain Morgan who had plundered Panama":

> Great ladies, dressed in the silken stuffs of China, were there because, after all, Henry Morgan came of a good family—the nephew of the poor dear Lieutenant-Governor who was killed. Sailors were there because he was a sailor; little boys because he was a pirate; young girls because he was a hero; business men because he was rich; gangs of slaves because they had a holiday.

Seeking such a reception, Steinbeck turned first to a novel that had held great importance for him as a boy—Robert Louis Stevenson's children's classic, *Treasure Island*, first published in 1881. The years of Steinbeck's boyhood were the heyday of *Treasure Island*'s popularity. In 1911, the year he turned nine, Simon & Schuster issued a deluxe edition with the immortal illustrations of N. C. Wyeth, whose portrait of peg-legged Long John Silver with a parrot on his shoulder now defines the popular idea of a pirate. In *Cannery Row*, Steinbeck remembered "with pleasure and some glory" that Robert Louis Stevenson had lived in Monterey, where Steinbeck's parents owned a summer cottage in Pacific Grove. "*Treasure Island*," he wrote, "certainly has the topography and the coastal plan of Point Lobos"—an opinion he may have formed as a boy playing at pirates and reenacting scenes from a favorite novel in the same terrain.

Set in the eighteenth century, *Treasure Island* tells the story

of young Jim Hawkins, whose mother runs the Admiral Ben-
bow Inn on the west coast of England. An old and dissolute
buccaneer, Billy Bones, comes to stay, and when Bones drinks
himself to death, Jim finds a map in the pirate's sea chest showing the way to buried treasure. Soon Jim sets sail to the West
Indies to seek this fortune, accompanied by two pillars of the
community—Squire Trelawney and Doctor Livesey—as well as
the trickster Long John Silver, a pirate masquerading as their
cook. A narrative of thrilling fights and adventures, *Treasure
Island* is also an initiation story. Coming to manhood in a world
of treachery, violence, and greed, Jim nevertheless finds physi-
cal and moral courage as well as Captain Flint's treasure. *Cup
of Gold* reverses the moral tendencies of the children's story,
yet owes a number of elements to *Treasure Island*—the decision to begin with Morgan's boyhood, the arrival of Dafydd (a
burned-out buccaneer resembling Billy Bones), young Henry's
innocence and vulnerability among the hard-bitten characters
of a seaport tavern as he seeks a passage, and the Irish sailor
Tim, who like Long John Silver simultaneously befriends,
teaches, defrauds, and exploits the boy.

Steinbeck was almost certainly indebted as well to Rafael
Sabatini's *Captain Blood*, a swashbuckling historical novel
that became an international bestseller in 1922. Like *Cup of
Gold*, Sabatini's novel draws from the Henry Morgan story.
In places (notably its description of Blood's clever escape from
the Spanish fleet at Maracaibo), *Captain Blood* so closely parallels Exquemelin's narrative that Sabatini teasingly writes,
"[T]hose of you who have read Esquemeling [alternate spell-
ing] may be in danger of supposing that Henry Morgan really
performed those things which here are veraciously attributed
to Peter Blood. I think, however, that . . . you will reach my
own conclusion as to which is the real plagiarist." Yet not all
of the similarities between *Cup of Gold* and *Captain Blood* are
necessarily due to their common source. As Joseph Fontenrose
points out:

> Steinbeck's Henry Morgan owes several traits to Peter Blood. . . .
> Both Blood and Steinbeck's Morgan, forced into indentures,

become valuable to their superiors (Blood as physician to the governor), gain fame as pirate chiefs, and finally become governors of Jamaica. Each named a ship after his ladylove, Blood's "Arabella," Morgan's "Elizabeth" (and Blood had an "Elizabeth" under his command). In fact, simply considered as a story of buccaneering on the Spanish Main, *Cup of Gold* is fully as entertaining as *Captain Blood*.

Cup of Gold differs from *Captain Blood* in many important ways, however. First published as a series of short stories in the magazine *Adventure, Captain Blood* is literally the stuff of pulp fiction. Despite Sabatini's relative seriousness about historically correct background, Blood is a stereotypical hero— pure-hearted, just, and brave—a pacifist physician wrongfully arrested for treating a wounded man during England's Monmouth Rebellion. Deported to Barbados as a plantation slave, Blood saves his fellow prisoners from wretched conditions by masterminding their escape into piracy. Unlike Steinbeck's ruthless and ambitious Morgan, Blood is a reluctant if brilliant buccaneer, with no desire but to return to respectability as soon as possible, so that he may be worthy of the governor's niece, the lovely Arabella Bishop. After shining in the obligatory series of piratical adventures, Blood regains his good name by saving Port Royal from the French and is rewarded with the governorship of Jamaica and Arabella's hand. *Captain Blood* has a classic happy ending, whereas in *Cup of Gold* Morgan's governorship and marriage are hollow and ironic victories, and the novel's true conclusion is the pirate's lonely death. Nevertheless, Sabatini demonstrated for Steinbeck that the Morgan story contained the necessary ingredients for popular success, if only the young author could unlock them.

Since its infancy, Hollywood had understood what Steinbeck called "melo drahmar" as well as the popular appeal of the wild, mysterious, unexpected, and racy. Pirate movies had it all—high adventure, picaresque heroes, duels and broadsides, exotic locations, opulent costumes, desperate deeds, drunken orgies, and romance flourishing on dark soil. Steinbeck came of age in the era of silent films and the swashbucklers of the time may have influenced his choice of subject. The years 1912, 1918, and 1920 each saw a film of *Treasure Island*, while *Captain Blood* first flickered onto the screen in 1924, in an early version not to be confused with the better-known 1935 rendition starring Errol Flynn.

Then, in 1926, the year Steinbeck began work in earnest on *Cup of Gold*, came *The Black Pirate*, a silent masterpiece that made cinematic history at box offices across America. An epic on the grand scale, *The Black Pirate* was filmed in an early two-tone color process and featured a lively orchestral score by Mortimer Wilson. The movie starred the athletic Douglas Fairbanks as yet another pure-hearted gentleman who after out-pirating the pirates wins the girl and is restored to his rightful position. Fairbanks performed the breathtaking stunts—swinging through the rigging and, famously, sliding down a sail—that have since become an obligatory part of a pirate movie. Billie Dove played the captive Princess Isobel; Steinbeck's La Santa Roja, also Ysobel, may be her namesake. Whether Steinbeck had such films in mind as he wrote *Cup of Gold* is impossible to say, but in a letter dated November 1937 he would remind his agents: "If you get any request for stories for Hollywood remember there is still that old Cup which is the only thing I have ever done that would make a good movie."

Thanks to Steinbeck's first wife, Carol Henning, and her correspondence with bibliographer Robert DeMott, we do know that *Cup of Gold* was influenced by a contemporary play about Henry Morgan—*The Buccaneer*. Written by Maxwell Anderson and Laurence Stallings, popular playwrights best-known as the authors of the World War I play *What Price Glory?* (1924), *The Buccaneer* played for just a few weeks on Broadway in October 1925. Steinbeck never saw this obscure play on stage, but read it in a 1926 collection of Anderson and Stallings's works, *Three American Plays*.

Drawn from Exquemelin's story of Morgan and the resisting female captive, and set almost entirely in Panama City, *The Buccaneer* is first and foremost a romance, and probably influenced the love interests twining through *Cup of Gold* as well as Steinbeck's decision to emphasize La Santa Roja. Like Stein-

beck's Morgan, Anderson and Stallings's buccaneer has left a
woman behind in Wales, rejecting her love and the beauty of
his native land for life as a sea-rover:

> "Very pleasant it is back in Wales with the mountains turning
> gold in autumn and green in spring. A man comes home peace-
> fully every night but Saturday, kisses his decent little wife a fru-
> gal little kiss, and before he knows it, he's dead and done for.
> That's domesticity for you. I decided that I didn't want to die
> that way. I took ship."

Morgan dreams instead of "a perfect city" and "a perfect
woman." On invading Panama, he commandeers for his head-
quarters a hacienda belonging to the beautiful Donna Lisa, who
resists his every advance. Morgan's lust for her slowly turns to
love as her bravery, wit, pride, and virtue win his respect. As in
Cup of Gold, Morgan's capture of Panama and love for Donna
Lisa seem the culmination of his life's quest. "Lady," Morgan
tells Donna Lisa, "it was at your shrine that I worshipped. It
was for *you* I hoped as I cut my way through Spanish lines to
Spanish gold. It was *you* I longed for. I long for *you* now!"
Steinbeck's Morgan too dreams of capturing the perfect city
and the perfect woman, telling his friend Coeur de Gris on the
eve of the attack: "You cannot understand my yearning. It is as
though I strove for some undreamed peace. This woman is the
harbor of all my questing."

In *The Buccaneer*, Donna Lisa slowly comes to love Morgan
for his courage and unconventional ways, and especially for the
exciting life he offers. "To love me is an adventure," Morgan
proclaims. She too longs to "take ship" and escape the stifling
domesticity that is her lot as a woman, and her adventurous
spirit is recapitulated in Steinbeck's La Santa Roja, rumored
to ride astride and handle a rapier as well as a man. When
Morgan sees Donna Lisa, he feels himself struck "by tropic
lightning"; Steinbeck's La Santa Roja also possesses "the harsh
dangerous beauty of lightning."

But unlike *Cup of Gold*, where the captive lady defeats and
humiliates Morgan, and comes to represent all dreams that turn

to ashes, *The Buccaneer* has a traditional happy ending. When Morgan is arrested for piracy and taken to England for trial, Donna Lisa follows, and when he is released and knighted, she agrees to become his wife. "Who'll follow Sir Henry Morgan to the Caribbean and the Spanish Main?" he asks the English court. "Who's sick of living at the rotten center of an empire? Who'll see Jamaica with me, and a thousand ports of call?" No man steps forward, but Donna Lisa does.

Comparison of the romances in *The Buccaneer* and *Cup of Gold* also helps to highlight Steinbeck's bold treatment of race in his pirate story. *The Buccaneer* changes Exquemelin's Spanish lady into an English widow. Blonde and blue-eyed, Donna Lisa is actually Lady Elizabeth Neville, and when she marries Morgan, she becomes Lady Elizabeth Morgan. Thus Anderson and Stallings elide Exquemelin's beautiful captive and the historic Morgan's wedded wife. More than a plot convenience designed to end a romance with a marriage, this strategy seems fundamentally racist, belonging to the anti-immigration and nativist sentiments of the 1920s. Courting Donna Lisa, Morgan says "[M]y heart tells me that if I were to step but a pace nearer you I should catch the scent of Devonshire roses from your hair and the fragrance of English hawthorn from your sweet body. England, madame, is a passion to me, and the stench of foreigners is poison to my blood." Steinbeck's Morgan too imagines La Santa Roja as "a young girl with blue, seraphic eyes" and as "a perfume after filth," but instead encounters a hawklike woman with a bold, black gaze. Here, as elsewhere in *Cup of Gold*, Steinbeck does not shy away from the historical realities of mixed races and cultures in the seventeenth-century Caribbean. Episodes such as Morgan's affair with Paulette—"poor little slave of the jumbled bloods, she was Spanish and Carib and Negro and French"—remind us of his daring when set against the whitewashed pirate stories of his time.

LITERARY INFLUENCES: JAMES BRANCH CABELL AND DONN BYRNE

In *Cup of Gold*, Steinbeck drew not only from the romance and reality of the pirate tradition, but from more ambitious literary models—specifically, from two icons of the medieval revival in 1920s American literature, James Branch Cabell and Donn Byrne. Both writers were widely read and held in high critical esteem during the period when Steinbeck conceived and wrote *Cup of Gold*. To a young writer working in solitude far from the experiments in literary modernism then underway in Paris, Cabell and Byrne seemed to set a standard of excellence. Their embrace of fantasy and romance, their historical settings, their use of allegory and symbolism, and their preference for archaic and figurative language appealed to some of Steinbeck's deepest instincts, and he could not know that both writers would drop out of fashion in the coming years, eclipsed by the rising sun of Ernest Hemingway and his disciples, with their contemporary settings, graphic realism, spare style, and clipped dialogue. The influence of Branch and Cabell, now all but forgotten, is important to a reading of *Cup of Gold*, however, helping to explain much that seems "weird" in this first novel.

Of the two writers, James Branch Cabell was perhaps most important to Steinbeck. Cabell was best-known for a series of fantasy novels set in the mythical medieval country of Poictesme. Of these, the most famous was *Jurgen* (1919), the story of a middle-aged pawnbroker who regains his youth, becomes a knight, and goes questing through many imaginary lands, meeting the sorcerer Merlin and courting fabulous beauties including Helen of Troy and the princess Guenevere of Arthurian legend. The novel uses archaic language—"Thus did Jurgen abide at the chivalrous court of Glathion" and "If she avow such constant hate of love as would ignore my great and constant love, plead thou no more!" The novel is also rich in figurative language: "When Guenevere undid her hair it was a marvel to Jurgen to note how snugly this hair descended about the small head and slender throat, and then broadened boldly and clothed her with a loose soft foam of pallid gold." It is easy, when looking at *Jurgen*, to see how Cabell's work emboldened Steinbeck to insert elements of fantasy and allegory into *Cup of Gold*, especially those drawn from his beloved *Morte d'Arthur*, such as Morgan's own meeting with Merlin, and the novel's overarching structure of a Grail quest. Cabell's success also gave Steinbeck license to indulge in archaic language—"And at last, when thou art girded with honor and repute, thou shalt marry a white-souled maiden of mighty rank"—and revel in metaphor—"Night drew down like a black cowl, and Holy Winter sent his nuncio to Wales" or "the ship ran before the crying dogs of the wind like a strong, confident stag."

But Cabell's *Jurgen*, like *Cup of Gold*, is antichivalric in its tendencies, an essentially ironic and often comic modern novel using allegory and symbolism not to create but to deflate ideals and illusions; not to celebrate the romance of the past, but to expose the mediocrity of modern life by contrast. Jurgen can't quite warm up to the lovely Guenevere—"Why, then, am I not out of my head about her?"—and eventually abandons his questing to return to a life of domesticity with his shrewish wife, Dame Lisa. So too Steinbeck's Morgan will give up buccaneering and his dreams of an ideal love for respectability and marriage to his "hectoring . . . badgering . . . browbeating" cousin Elizabeth. Both novelists, in their way, use the quest motif to record the tragicomic, blundering efforts of (in Steinbeck's words) "a little, struggling life to squirm upward, through the circles toward Gwynfyd, the sheening Purity."

Cabell also uses a kind of stylistic dissonance to reinforce his novel's thematic ironies at the sentence level. An inflated speech in archaic language might end with a modern pinprick: "And so on, and so on!" Or Cabell will deliberately undercut his own metaphoric language, as he does after Jurgen's elaborate description of Guenevere's golden hair: "[W]hen I proclaim that my adored mistress's hair reminds me of gold I am quite consciously lying. It looks like yellow hair, and nothing else: nor would I willingly venture within ten feet of any woman whose head sprouted with wires, of whatever metal." Steinbeck engages in similarly comic deflations, as when Gwenliana ends her lofty and lurid prophecy of Morgan's future—"There shall be fighting and shedding of blood, and the sword shall be thy first bride. . . . The terror will precede thee like a screaming eagle over the shields of men"—with a plaintive, "I could have done better with a sheep's shoulder." Perhaps the most-cited example in *Cup of Gold* occurs when Morgan's father considers the "cruel difference" between himself and his son Henry:

> "[W]hereas he runs about sticking his finger into pot after pot of cold porridge, grandly confident that each one will prove the pottage of his dreaming . . . I believe all porridge to be cold. And so—I imagine great dishes of purple porridge, drenched with dragon's milk, sugared with a sweetness only to be envisioned."

The purple porridge and dragon's milk are apt to disturb readers who miss Steinbeck's Cabellesque method and intention—using ludicrously inflated language to underscore the harshness of everyday reality and the folly of dreams.

Jurgen became notorious—and a literary cause célèbre that could not have escaped Steinbeck's attention—when the New York Society for the Prevention of Vice seized the plates and all copies of Cabell's novel, and charged his publisher, Robert McBride & Company, with violating anti-obscenity law. The trial, held in 1922, vindicated the novel (only very mildly erotic by today's standards) and made Cabell a bestselling sensation and literary cult figure. Steinbeck may have been hoping for a little of the same sort of notoriety when he created the character of Paulette, who possesses:

> . . . hair like a cataract of black water, eyes as blue as the sea, set in oriental slits, and a golden, golden skin. Hers was a sensuous, passionate beauty—limbs that twinkled like golden flames. Her lips could writhe like slender, twisting serpents or bloom like red flowers. . . . Henry thought of her as a delicate machine perfectly made for pleasure, a sexual contraption. . . . He built for her a tiny, vine-clad house roofed with banana leaves, and there he played at love.

Even the facts of Steinbeck's early career demonstrate his affinity with Cabell. Cabell's editor, Guy Holt, named in the *Jurgen* obscenity trial, would become the first editor to encourage young John Steinbeck, while Cabell's publishing house, Robert McBride, would eventually publish *Cup of Gold* after many other firms had turned it down. In the end, Cabell's influence on Steinbeck may have cut both ways. In 1946, Cabell published a pirate fantasy of his own—*There Were Two Pirates*. Cabell's protagonist, based on the historic pirate Jose Gasparilla, ravages the coast of Florida, all the while longing, like Steinbeck's Morgan, for the lost love he left behind in the Old World. Unlike Morgan, however, Cabell's hero—by separating himself from his shadow—is allowed to experience his life as it would have been had he chosen not to "go a-buccaneering," but to remain with his Isabel.

Like James Branch Cabell, Donn Byrne (baptized Bernard Byrne, and sometimes known as Brian Oswald Donn Byrne or Donn-Byrne) wrote serious fiction in the vein of historical fantasy and enjoyed a critical reputation that gave the genre both respectability and marketability during the years when *Cup of Gold* was conceived and written. Byrne published a number of novels very much in vogue in the 1920s. Among those known to have influenced Steinbeck are *Messer Marco Polo* (1921), the story of the thirteenth-century Italian explorer's love for the daughter of Kubla Khan; *Brother Saul* (1927), a fictional account of the biblical tyrant King and his jealousy of and attempt to murder his friend David (echoed in Morgan's murder of Coeur de Gris); and *Blind Raftery* (1928), a tale of a wandering eighteenth-century Gaelic poet and his Spanish wife. Such popular works helped reinforce Steinbeck's decision to choose an historical fantasy about the pirate Henry Morgan for his first novel.

Steinbeck was most interested, however, in Byrne's unique use of language. Born in New York City but raised in Ireland, the Irish American Byrne attended Dublin University and later studied Romance languages at the Sorbonne and the University of Leipzig. Byrne's Irish patriotism and linguistic flair led him to write most of his novels in Irish dialect. *Messer Marco Polo*,

for example, is narrated by a wandering Ulsterman. This gives
Byrne's prose a deliberately poetic quality, as in:

> But the young people would know it was spring, too, by token of
> the gaiety that was in the air. For nothing brings joy to the heart
> like the coming of spring. The folk who do be blind all the rest
> of the year, their eyes do open then, and a sunset takes them, and
> the wee virgin flowers coming up between the stones, or the twit-
> ter of a bird upon the bough. . . . And the young women do be
> preening themselves, and young men do be singing, even though
> they have the voices of rooks.

It also creates some extremely strange dialogue. Byrne's
Marco Polo speaks with an Irish accent—" 'Tis only a saint
can perform miracles"—and even Kubla Khan says things like
"Well, now, laddie."
Contemporary readers may cringe at the thought of the far
more gifted Steinbeck imbibing such syrupy and silly stuff. But
the young writer saw possibilities. In *Cup of Gold*'s descriptive
passages, Steinbeck too would reach—and even overreach—for
poetry—a poetry that immediately surpassed Byrne's and that
would only grow stronger as his career advanced.

> Winter was come sliding down over the world from the Pole;
> and riverward there was the faint moaning of new ice. It was
> a sad day, a day of gray unrest, of discontent. The gently mov-
> ing air seemed to be celebrating the loss of some gay thing with
> a soft, tender elegy. But in the pastures the great work horses
> nervously stamped their feet, and all through the country small
> brown birds, in cliques of four or five, flew twittering from tree
> to tree and back again, seeking and calling in recruits for their
> southing.

Proud of his Irish ancestry on his mother's side, Steinbeck
also experimented with Irish dialect, placing it in the mouth
of Morgan's Welsh father—"What time will you be starting,
the morning?"—and more appropriately using it to color the
speech of the Irish sailor, Tim—" 'Twas when I was a boy like

xxiv   INTRODUCTION

this one here, and I sailing in a free ship that tucked [sic] about
the ocean. . . ."

   Not long after completing *Cup of Gold*, Steinbeck understood that he would need to sweep "all the Cabellyo-Byrneish
preciousness" out of his prose "for good." "I seem to have
outgrown Cabell," he wrote to his friend A. Grove Day, and "I
have not the slightest desire to step into Donn Byrne's shoes."
Already Steinbeck knew that he had "twice [the] head" of these
two early influences. Yet in some respects his protests are dis-
ingenuous. Long after the triumph of *The Grapes of Wrath*
(1939), Steinbeck remained attracted to medievalism as well
as to the comic and satiric possibilities of fantasy, as we see
in *The Short Reign of Pippin IV* (1957). At the time of his
death in 1968, Steinbeck was working on his own translation
of Malory's *Morte d'Arthur*. The "Cabellyo-Byrneish" strain
underlies his canonical works as well. Throughout his career,
Steinbeck would continue to combine allegory and fantasy
with naturalism, to strive unabashedly for melody and sensu-
ality in his descriptive writing, and to value the poetic prop-
erties of dialect, albeit more realistically deployed (as in *The
Grapes of Wrath*). Cabell and Byrne were unusual models for
an American writer serving an apprenticeship in the 1920s, and
Cup of Gold provides an important look at young Steinbeck
experimenting with their methods—methods that would give
his mature work a distinctive stamp.

CUP OF GOLD AND
YOUNG JOHN STEINBECK

Cup of Gold is not solely a historical-biographical-swashbuckling
pirate fantasy with literary ambitions. The novel also has a strong
autobiographical strain. Writing to his friend A. Grove Day on
December 5, 1929, Steinbeck confessed that *Cup of Gold* was
written in part "for the purpose of getting . . . all the autobiographical material (which hounds us until we get it said) out of
my system." Into the story of young Henry Morgan, Steinbeck

wove the experiences of his own young life and of his quest to
become a writer. Those experiences included Steinbeck's own
very real voyage to Panama—a country torn by political unrest
and speaking volumes about American corporate and military
imperialism in the 1920s. His literary quest included an abor-
tive assault on that Cup of Gold for all American writers—New
York City. These autobiographical currents make *Cup of Gold*
not only a portrait of the artist as a young man, but an allegory of the Faustian bargain implicit in the American dream—
whether the dream of an aggressive young nation, Steinbeck's
"Republic of Buccaneers"—or the dream of an aggressive young
individual ambitious for fortune, fame, and love.

John Steinbeck was born to John Ernst and Olive Hamil-
ton Steinbeck on February 27, 1902, in the small town of Salinas, California. His father resembled Henry Morgan's father,
Robert, in being a failure, a dreamer, a gardener in his spare
time, and a compassionate man loved and respected by others.
Having lost his own business, the senior Steinbeck nevertheless maintained his wife and four children (three daughters and
John) in modest comfort through his work as a bookkeeper
for the Spreckels Sugar Factory and as Treasurer for Monterey
County. Olive, a schoolteacher before her marriage, was a
dominant force both in her family and in the community—
known for her energy, her determination, and her ambition for
her children. Aspects of Olive's character mark the pragmatic,
iron-willed Mother Morgan. About his protagonist in *Cup of
Gold*, Steinbeck would write:

> Henry, if you considered his face, drew from his parents almost
> equally. His cheekbones were high and hard, his chin firm . . .
> like his mother's. But there, too, were the sensual underlip . . .
> and the eyes which looked out on dreams; these were Old Rob-
> ert's features. . . . But though there was complete indecision in
> Robert's face, there was a great quantity of decision in Henry's if
> only he could find something to decide about.

Young Steinbeck found something to decide about in the
pages of books. From enchanted boyhood readings of works

including the Caxton *Morte d'Arthur* and Robert Louis Stevenson's *Treasure Island*, books that would leave indelible marks
on *Cup of Gold*, he acquired a passionate love of language and
a desire to become a storyteller as strong as Henry Morgan's
desire to "go a-buccaneering and take a Spanish town." Steinbeck must have felt, very early, the conviction that he could
achieve greatness as a writer if only he could avoid entrapment
in the mundane concerns and expectations of the adult world.
Steinbeck's Merlin, an elderly failed poet who understands the
dangers of the path, looks sadly at his own idled harps and says
to Henry Morgan:

> "You are a little boy. You want the moon to drink from as a
> golden cup; and so, it is very likely that you will become a great
> man—if only you remain a little child. All the world's great have
> been little boys who wanted the moon. . . . But if one grow to
> a man's mind, that mind must see that it cannot have the moon
> and would not want it if it could. . . ."

Before Steinbeck could drink from the moon, there was college. His parents insisted. He arrived at Stanford University
in the fall of 1919 and attended sporadically for the next six
years. Single-minded about his dream, Steinbeck focused largely
on creative writing and literature classes, voracious reading in
Stanford's excellent library, meetings of the English Club, and
his own writing. He may have viewed some of his professors
as Henry Morgan views James Flower—quiet and kindly, ineffectual and inefficient men and women who cried out to be creators and were not, but who recognized in him "one of those
divinely endowed creatures who control[led] the fire" they
lacked altogether. Steinbeck's contempt for Stanford's required
curriculum meant a wealth of incompletes and failures, as well
as quite a few leaves of absence. During these periods, Steinbeck found employment supervising migrant workers on the
Spreckels ranches, where sugar beets were grown and harvested
by gangs of hobos and bindlestiffs, as well as by Japanese,
Mexican, and Filipino labor. His education resembled Henry
Morgan's in *Cup of Gold*, alternating between self-directed

study in James Flower's magnificent library and overseeing the plantation's multiracial work force.

In the spring of 1925, Steinbeck left Stanford without taking a degree or even completing the equivalent of three years' course work. This was failure by the standards of the adult world, and his parents, especially his mother, were understandably disappointed. He had little to show for himself except a sheaf of unpublished manuscripts, including a short story about the pirate Henry Morgan—"A Lady in Infra-Red." But still Steinbeck had the resolve to continue to test his dream, and again like his own young Henry Morgan, he proposed to do that with a voyage. If Panama, that fabled Spanish treasure port, was the "Cup of Gold" for the aspiring seventeenth-century buccaneer, then surely New York City, America's vibrant capital of the arts, was an equivalent Grail for the aspiring twentieth-century writer. Somehow, Steinbeck persuaded his long-suffering father to buy him a $100 tourist-class ticket for travel by freighter from San Francisco to New York. In *Cup of Gold*, Robert Morgan also finds the courage to let his son go, and the novel contains this insight into a father's hope:

> "Why do men like me want sons?" he wondered. "It must be because they hope in their poor beaten souls that these new men, who are their blood, will do the things they were not strong enough nor wise enough nor brave enough to do. It is rather like another chance with life; like a new bag of coins at the table after your fortune is gone. Perhaps the boy is doing what I would have done had I been brave enough in years past. Yes, . . . I am glad this boy finds it in his power to vault the mountains and stride about the world."

STEINBECK'S PASSAGE TO PANAMA

On November 1, 1925, Steinbeck left San Francisco on board the *Katrina Luckenbach*, a 449-foot-long steamship with twin screws, four turbines, and the modern conveniences of electric lights and wireless. With a black hull, red boot-topping, and buff ventilators, *Katrina* was not a passenger liner, but a working freighter owned by the Luckenbach company. She carried about forty crew members and had space for only a few passengers in her two-story deckhouse. Thanks to boyhood summers at his family's cottage on the Pacific shore, Steinbeck had the sea in his blood. "The water slapping smooth hulls was a joy to him to the point of pain," he wrote of Henry Morgan. On the waterfront, "He felt that he had come home again to a known, loved place . . ." At one point during his Stanford years, Steinbeck had even tried to run away to sea and work a passage to China, but could not find a shipboard job. Now he was outward bound on his first voyage. As a tugboat towed *Katrina* out of the harbor and her foreign crew hustled about the deck, Steinbeck must have felt some of the excitement he ascribes to Henry Morgan as the *Bristol Girl* casts off: "They were starting for the Indies—the fine, far Indies where boys' dreams lived."

Katrina was actually bound first to Panama, Morgan's "Cup of Gold." She cruised down the coasts of California, Mexico, Guatemala, Honduras, Nicaragua, and Costa Rica at a top speed of 13½ knots (about 15 miles per hour). This leisurely pace gave Steinbeck time to observe birds and marine life such as the storm petrels and flying fish described in *Cup of Gold*. He also had time to get to know the vessel's crew. Perhaps, like Henry Morgan, he found "wise, kind men . . . [who] taught him what they could," not only about the working of the ship, but about "songs of death and mutiny and blood in the sea," "the peculiar clean swearing of sailors," and tales "of wonders seen and imagined." At least one sailor, resembling the treacherous Tim in *Cup of Gold*, found a way to part a naïve young man from his money. In a 1937 interview about his voyage to New York, Steinbeck told Joseph Henry Jackson that "On the way he learned to his astonishment that plain, ordinary, unloaded dice could be controlled if one knew how. The discovery came to him through the medium of a large and very black sailor and was slightly expensive, but at least it was something to know."

Steinbeck's voyage on *Katrina* also gave him time to form a friendship with a young, California-born artist named Mahlon Blaine. Like Steinbeck, Blaine was headed for New York to seek his fortune. Specializing in the fantastic, the surreal, the sensuous, and even the satanic (illustrations for Edgar Rice Burroughs's *Tanar of Pellucidar*, Gustave Flaubert's *Salammbô*, William Beckford's *Vathek*, Paul Verlaine's *Hashish and Incense*, the Marquis de Sade's *Justine*, and a tome on *Satanism and Witchcraft* are among his best-known works), Blaine would soon make a career for himself as a book illustrator in the style of Aubrey Beardsley. The two shipmates would remain in touch. Four years after the voyage of the *Katrina*, Blaine would illustrate a striking dust jacket for *Cup of Gold*.

Steinbeck left the *Katrina* at Panama City for a stay of several days. According to Joseph Henry Jackson, the writer planned "to absorb color there for a book he had in mind, the romanticized life of the pirate Henry Morgan." But Panama City in 1925 was neither colorful nor romantic. In mid-October 1925, just a few weeks before Steinbeck's departure from San Francisco, the city erupted in violence, as thousands of workers joined in a general strike and marched to protest high rents. The situation deteriorated into widespread rioting when Panamanian police killed a leader of the protests, Marciano Mirones. Would-be revolutionaries flying red flags massed in Cathedral Square, and American tourists told the *New York Times* of hearing a "thunderstorm" of rifle volleys from the protesters, followed by the sound of machine-gun fire as government troops responded. President Rodolfo Chiari asked the United States for military assistance, and on October 12 three steel-helmeted battalions of the Thirty-Third Infantry marched into the city from their barracks in the Canal Zone, dispersing mobs at bayonet point and setting up machine-gun nests to guard government buildings and the president's palace. On October 23, with order restored, U.S. troops withdrew. The *Christian Science Monitor* reported a subsequent wave of arrests, deportations, and evictions of troublesome ringleaders, as well as President Chiari's declaration that the Panamanian legislature did not need to meet because "the recent disturbances . . . might influence the lawmakers toward partial legislation in favor of tenants."

In Panama City between two and three weeks after the withdrawal of American forces, Steinbeck must have heard talk about the riots and seen the anger still smoldering in the eyes around him. In what reads as a racist attempt to trivialize the Panamanian crisis, the *New York Times* quoted an eyewitness, Captain George Zeh: "The nucleus of a revolution is a bottle of rum, two half-breeds, and a negro armed with rifles and machetes." Steinbeck, whose Henry Morgan will lay waste to Panama City with a mob of such have-nots, would not have seen any irony in Zeh's statement. From Steinbeck's visit to Panama, *Cup of Gold* would derive not local color, but a sense of how vulnerable a people "grown soft in their security" might become, and of how the oppressed, once armed, might go "marauding like tigers from a broken cage."

After his brief stay in the city, Steinbeck boarded another freighter to continue his voyage via the Panama Canal. Now his voyage would trace the approximate line of Henry Morgan's historic seventeenth-century march across the Isthmus of Panama. Fifty miles wide at its narrowest point, the Isthmus joins the continents of North and South America, while separating the Pacific Ocean from the Caribbean Sea. From its discovery by Balboa in 1513, movingly described by Steinbeck in *Cup of Gold*, the Isthmus has been used as a shortcut between the Atlantic and Pacific Oceans, a way to avoid a dangerous sea voyage of many months and thousands of miles around Cape Horn, the storm-torn southern tip of South America. The Spanish of Morgan's day appreciated its commercial benefits. Gold and silver from Spanish mines in Ecuador, Peru, Bolivia, and Chile were carried up the Pacific coast in merchant vessels to Panama City, then loaded onto mule trains for transport by land across the Isthmus to Portobello, where a waiting *flota* would carry the treasure to Spain. Henry Morgan appreciated the military significance of the Isthmus, understanding how it could be used for rapid delivery of a strike force from the Caribbean to attack Panama City—the richest port on the Pacific—from its landward side. Steinbeck's freighter would have made the forty-nine mile transit of the canal and its locks in about ten hours, time enough for him to search for glimpses of the jungled and mountainous terrain Morgan's men traversed in 1671.

In 1925, when Steinbeck first saw it, the Panama Canal was a fresh marvel of modern engineering and a symbol of America's buccaneering spirit. In a sense he had grown up with its story. The United States acquired rights to and began construction on the canal in 1904, when Steinbeck was two years old. The brainchild of President Theodore Roosevelt, built with the labor of 50,000 workers from many nations, the Panama Canal cost $352 million dollars to build. Thousands of workers gave their lives; during the American effort as many as 5,000 died due to landslides, construction accidents, and endemic diseases such as yellow fever and malaria. Finished in 1914, the year Steinbeck turned twelve, it was a source of national pride. The United States now dominated the trade of two oceans, exacting tolls from every passing ship, and had become a global naval power, controlling the path between the seas. In Steinbeck's *Cup of Gold*, Balboa dresses in his "scoured armor," wades into the Pacific, and "firmly addresse[s] the sea and claim[s] all the lands it broke on." Teddy Roosevelt, the "New Imperialist," might have done the same.

There was, however, a darker side—a piratical side—to the Panama Canal story—one that Steinbeck probably knew well. In 1903, the United States spent $40 million to purchase the rights to the canal project, ostensibly from a bankrupt French company that had been trying for years to build a canal without success. The money, however, went to a Wall Street syndicate formed by financier J. P. Morgan. Like Steinbeck's Henry Morgan, J. P. Morgan was a man who understood that "honesty—public honesty—may be a ladder to a higher, more valuable crime." Acting on inside knowledge of the Roosevelt administration's interest in Panama, Morgan's syndicate had secretly purchased the French company for a song. When Congress approved construction of a canal through Nicaragua instead, Morgan's group used campaign contributions to help Roosevelt "persuade" legislators to reverse the vote. Thousands of French stockholders lost their investments (in French, the word "Paname" is synonymous with "swindle") as Morgan's syndicate raked in millions of taxpayer dollars. When newspapers broke the story, President Roosevelt himself sued for libel and veteran newsman Joseph Pulitzer was frightened enough to flee the country. When Congress mounted investigations, they lasted long but went nowhere. The analogies between J. P. Morgan and Steinbeck's Sir Henry Morgan, who cheats his own men out of the booty of Panama and uses his riches to bribe the king, would not have been lost on readers in 1929.

"I took the Isthmus," Teddy Roosevelt declared unrepentantly, and a buccaneer named J. P. Morgan, a robber-baron with a famous yacht not coincidentally named *Corsair*, had helped him to do it. Panama at this time was an annex of Colombia, and when Colombia refused to ratify a treaty leasing the Canal Zone to the United States, Morgan's syndicate, with the connivance of the Roosevelt administration, arranged and underwrote a convenient "revolution" in Panama. Colombian troops were bribed to abandon their posts, while Roosevelt, in an example of his famous "gunboat diplomacy," sent the warship USS *Nashville* to sit off the Panama coast and discourage interference. Not surprisingly, the newly installed government of Panama was eager to make a treaty ceding the Canal Zone to the United States on very favorable terms.

These recent events were still resonant as Steinbeck traversed the Panama Canal. In 1921, the scandals had been revived when the League of Nations forced the United States to grant Colombia $25 million and free access to the canal as reparations for the illegal seizure of Panama. In 1925 in Panama City, Steinbeck had learned firsthand that the United States would use military force to prop a puppet government in Panama. Steinbeck's *Cup of Gold*, albeit set in the seventeenth century, is at least in part about twentieth-century American imperialism and the piratical ethics of American business, as exemplified by Panama. In both centuries, a Morgan had contrived to carry the Isthmus by force and to swindle workers and stockholders of their fair share in the profits. Writing about Edward Mansvelt, who formed the buccaneers of the Caribbean into the dreaded Brethren of the Coast, Steinbeck writes obliquely about the violence and greed implicit in the American Dream:

But there was a power of dream in him. Out of his mob of raga-muffin heroes he wanted to make a strong, durable nation, a new, aggressive nation in America. As more and more of the buccaneers flocked to his command, his dream solidified. He consulted the governments of England and France. They were shocked, and forbade him to consider such a thing. A race of pirates not amenable to the gibbets of the crowns? Why, they would be plundering everybody.

Steinbeck's freighter steamed out of the Panama Canal and on through the Caribbean Sea to his next port of call, Havana, Cuba. In 1925, Cuba, like Panama, was a U.S. protectorate, only nominally independent after the Spanish-American War of 1898. Like the English buccaneers of Henry Morgan's time, Americans on the threshold of the twentieth century had invested in driving the Spanish from the New World. Cuba too was associated with the belligerent imperialism of Teddy Roosevelt, who famously led his Rough Riders in the charge up San Juan Hill, and with the militant capitalism of J. P. Morgan, whose steel-hulled steam yacht *Corsair*, commissioned into the U.S. Navy, helped destroy the Spanish fleet at Santiago Bay. In Henry Morgan's day, Havana was the major city of New Spain, a rich and bustling port where Spanish galleons gathered in fleets before crossing the Atlantic. Coming into the harbor, Steinbeck would have seen Havana's sixteenth-century El Morro castle and its fortifications, built to keep marauders like Morgan out. Touring the historic city, he would have absorbed atmosphere useful in his novel to come, enjoying Havana's Spanish architecture, including a 1701 cathedral as well as Old World plazas and drives. In a 1952 memoir titled "Autobiography," Steinbeck recalled taking "a pretty girl around Havana in a carriage" and being "charmed and worldly about broad rum drinks like tubs of soaking fruit."

THE BIG APPLE AS CUP OF GOLD

From there, it was on to New York City, the writer's "Cup of Gold." For Steinbeck, New York had come to be what Panama was to his Henry Morgan, "the harbor of all my questing." So strong was the young man's dream of the fortune, fame, and love awaiting a writer there, that Steinbeck later remembered thinking he could simply step off the freighter and into a fantasy of the celebrity life. In "Autobiography," he wrote, "I don't know what I thought I was going to do with that very pretty girl [from Havana] once I got to New York—marry her, I guess, and take her into my penthouse on Park Avenue, where my guest list had no names but those of the famous, the beautiful and the dissolute." Reality was very different.

> From a porthole, then, I saw the city, and it horrified me. There was something monstrous about it—the tall buildings looming to the sky and the lights shining through the falling snow. I crept ashore—frightened and cold and with a touch of panic in my stomach.

Steinbeck was not destined for a penthouse, but for a sofa bed in his married sister's studio apartment. Of the one hundred dollars he'd had with him on leaving San Francisco, just three dollars remained on his arrival in New York.

Like his protagonist Henry Morgan, who arrived in the West Indies to find himself sold into indentured servitude, Steinbeck was condemned by his empty pockets to hard manual labor, pushing wheelbarrows of cement on a construction project by day, and trying to write at night. But soon things seemed to be improving. Mahlon Blaine, his friend from the *Katrina* voyage, helped Steinbeck find a room in a rundown hotel. An uncle helped him find a job as a newspaper reporter. Steinbeck met and fell in love with Mary Ardath, a showgirl from the *Greenwich Village Follies*. Best of all, Blaine introduced him to the publishing firm of Robert McBride & Company. There James Branch Cabell's editor, Guy Holt, encouraged Steinbeck to believe that if he could supply enough short stories, McBride would publish a collection. He immediately went to work on pieces including the Henry Morgan story from his Stanford days, "A Lady in Infra-Red," the germ of *Cup of Gold*.

Yet it would take New York City just six months to tear the wings off a young man's dreams. The first blow to fall was a "Dear John" letter from Mary, a materialistic beauty who believed he should give up writing fiction for the advertising business and who would soon marry a banker. Mary would become the model for the woman who destroys Merlin's gift in *Cup of Gold*: "She was vague as to the nature of success, but she made it very plain that song was not a structure of success." Days later, Steinbeck was fired from the newspaper job he had been neglecting for his own writing. Unemployed, his rent in arrears, he wrote feverishly until he had assembled enough short stories for McBride. But when Steinbeck returned to the firm with his manuscript in hand, expecting publication of his first book, he learned that Guy Holt had left the company. Instead, Steinbeck found a new editor who not only refused to honor Holt's verbal commitment, but refused even to look at the manuscript. According to biographer Jackson Benson, Steinbeck "went berserk":

> He shouted and raged and threatened to tear the editor limb from limb and started to do so. He was half-carried out of the office, down the stairs, and ejected onto the sidewalk, his manuscript pages slipping from his grasp and floating out in a trail behind him.

New York, like La Santa Roja, had proven to be a fickle muse, not to be taken either by fawning or force. At first seething with the anger and humiliation of rejection, Steinbeck next gave way to anxiety and depression. In "Autobiography," he remembered locking himself in his room for two weeks, living on rye bread and dried herrings, afraid even to go out on the streets. Like Henry Morgan in *Cup of Gold*, he may even have feared himself "sick with mediocrity." Unemployed and with no prospects, Steinbeck had little choice but to return home in defeat. Unable to afford a passenger ticket, he sailed for San Francisco as a workaway on another Luckenbach freighter, assisting the steward in serving and cleaning up after meals.

THE COMPOSITION AND PUBLICATION
OF *CUP OF GOLD*

Most aspiring writers would have given up at this point. Instead, with an iron will unmatched even by his piratical protagonist, Steinbeck took a job as caretaker of a large summer estate on Lake Tahoe, at the foot of California's Mount Tallac. This time he would try a Thoreauvian approach, seeking among the mountains of home a simple, rural muse more akin to Morgan's barefoot Elizabeth than to the hard-bitten, sophisticated La Santa Roja. Having learned the hard way that publishers preferred novels to short story collections, Steinbeck now began the work of transforming "A Lady in Infra-Red" into *Cup of Gold*.

The caretaker's position was ideal for writing. Steinbeck was given a little cabin of his own and the run of the library in the main house. There was a phonograph in the cabin, and as he wrote he often listened to Antonín Dvořák's symphony "From the New World." Written not long after the Czech composer's arrival in New York City, the symphony features a heroic, hard-driving horn movement emblematic of determined ambition, contrasted with a tender, nostalgic largo—making a perfect "score" for *Cup of Gold*. In good weather, Steinbeck wrote outdoors in the woods—the family reported finding cups and glasses under the trees for years after his departure. In the winter, with the family gone, Steinbeck was entirely alone and often snowbound, with little to do but read and write. He would stay in the Tahoe job for two years, and through two long winters, until his first novel was done.

In the summer of 1928, Steinbeck sent a messy manuscript full of typos, crossings-out, and scribblings-in to his friend Ted Miller in New York. Miller, after arranging to have *Cup of*

Gold retyped, agreed to act informally as Steinbeck's agent, taking the manuscript around to publishers. A series of rejections followed—seven in all—and then, in January 1929, Steinbeck received the exciting news that Robert McBride & Company, the same publisher that had turned down his short stories, had accepted his first novel. By now, Steinbeck was down out of the mountains, working on another novel, living in his parents' Pacific Grove cottage, and courting Carol Henning, who would become his first wife. He was grateful for an advance of $250.

At first, he was glad to learn that his friend Mahlon Blaine, by now enjoying considerable popularity as an illustrator, would create the dust jacket for *Cup of Gold*. Brightly colored, Blaine's jacket featured a mustachioed Sir Henry Morgan in the regalia of a seventeenth-century nobleman, including a plumed hat, cloak, lace collar and cuffs, knee britches, silk stockings, silver-buckled shoes, and sword. Morgan clutches an immense golden chalice, and is joined by two barefooted pirates with gold earrings and neckerchiefs, pistols tucked in their sashes. But when Steinbeck saw the cover, he was badly disappointed. He thought the colors were "ghastly," and the jacket more appropriate to a boys' adventure story than a work of art. That, however, may have been the publisher's intention. Perhaps because of its exciting dust jacket, *Cup of Gold* sold best at department stores during the Christmas season. Biographer Jackson Benson writes, "One wonders how many little boys were lost in the swamp of Steinbeck's prose as they tried to follow Henry Morgan's trek across Panama."

The book was published in August 1929, a little more than two months before the stock market crash of October 1929 began America's slide into the Depression. McBride did not bother to send Steinbeck an advance copy; the author saw his first novel for the first time in a department store. He complained bitterly about his publisher's failure to market *Cup of Gold*—book clubs turned it down, few review copies were distributed, and bookshop orders were not filled. Still, *Cup of Gold* enjoyed modest but respectable sales, with 1,533 copies sold from its first issue, more than the sales of Steinbeck's next two novels combined.

CRITICAL RECEPTION

Cup of Gold received only a handful of reviews (helpfully collected in Luchen Li's *John Steinbeck: A Documentary Volume*), but almost all of its first critics found something to admire in the novel: "Mr. Steinbeck's graceful manner lifts the yarn above the adventure groceries of this degenerate age," they wrote. "Thoroughly masculine and should find much favor with those male readers who used to delight in those bloody tales of piracy and rebellion." "A meaty pleasing yarn wherein action sets the pace and clever writing plays the tune." "Mr. Steinbeck's fantasy is enjoyable reading."

Yet for the most part, the same critics were thoroughly confused by the novel's dueling genres and styles, and by its failure to meet their conventional expectations. The *New York Herald Tribune* expected "a novel of adventure," probably something on the order of *Captain Blood*, and was disappointed to discover that "the tale lacks the color and spirit traditional to its genre, perhaps because the author has preferred to tinker with a realistic method." The *St. Louis Star* expected a children's pirate story like *Treasure Island*, and was shocked by *Cup of Gold*'s passion and brutality: "While most previous stories, whether historical or fictional of Morgan's life, were written for the consumption of school boys, here is one that is decidedly not for juvenile perusal." The *Ohio State Journal* expected a biography, but found "little of fact or history," and resented the novel's "shimmer of imagination." The *New York Post*, also expecting a biography, objected to the intrusion of "fantasy," but particularly disliked the novel's blend of "two schools of style . . . the modern naturalistic and the period manner" which "do not harmonize." Only an anonymous reviewer for Stanford University's newspaper, perhaps someone who knew Steinbeck, came close to capturing the spirit of this "fanciful, rather weird, and sometimes historical novel":

> *Cup of Gold* is the picture of a dreamer—of a dreamer who eternally searched for some ephemeral happiness. Cities and coun-

tries richer than man ever dreamed of fell before his armies. He
had women, gold, ships, power. But peace was not there and
Henry Morgan was a lost soul looking for something he could
never find. And thus he died.

These early reviewers were the first and last critics to read
the novel as the work of an unknown writer. *Cup of Gold*
failed to garner Steinbeck any significant attention from the
literary world and was soon out of print, only to be reissued
in 1936 after the author's bestselling success with *Tortilla Flat*
(1935) made his name. Now *Cup of Gold* would assume critical importance simply because it was written by John Steinbeck. Published by P.F. Collier, the 1936 edition opened with
a preface by Lewis Gannett, who lauded Steinbeck's talent as
"among the most beautiful and most significant . . . in American literature today." Gannett's preface successfully predicted
how *Cup of Gold* would be read in the years ahead: "And
perhaps one may find in this glowingly youthful book, in this
story of young Henry Morgan . . . a sort of key to Steinbeck
himself. . . ." As Steinbeck's oeuvre ripened with the classics
Of Mice and Men (1937) and *The Grapes of Wrath* (1939),
and as his reputation grew toward the Nobel Prize for Literature in 1962 and canonization, the practice of reading *Cup of
Gold* as a key to the writer only intensified. This interpretive
game holds special fascination because, as Jackson Benson has
noted, "After reading *The Grapes of Wrath* and *Cannery Row*,
the reader may feel that this book [*Cup of Gold*] does not even
seem to have been written by the same person."

Critics, then, have tended to search *Cup of Gold* for thematic similarities between this ambitious, swashbuckling pirate
fantasy and Steinbeck's mature realistic fiction. For example,
Joseph Fontenrose writes:

Here, too, are the Steinbeck themes of loneliness, mystic identity with the whole world (notice the great Tone at the end),
women's secret knowledge, the speed of rumor, degeneration
caused by too much security. Visible here are Steinbeck's interests in social justice, Greek and Latin literature, occult powers,

the inner life of children. And in this, his first novel, we meet the Virgin Whore, the prostitute, the competent mother, the religious bigot, the madman, the wealthy amateur scientist, and the wizard-seer—recurring character types in Steinbeck's novels.

Biographer Jay Parini adds: "Much of what a sympathetic reader finds to admire in the mature Steinbeck is present here in Ur-form: the kernel story of a voyage, or quest; the image of an idealistic young man whose dreams go sour and end in disillusion; the conception of an intimate relationship between human beings and their environment; the understanding of how power may be abused by those who have too much of it; the theme of conflict between the sexes."

Today, most critics regard *Cup of Gold* as a brilliant failure, a first novel flawed by overambition and overexuberance. Harry Thornton Moore's observations are typical: "The book is patently the work of a young man, an eager and romantic young man who is not afraid to let himself go." Young Steinbeck, writes Peter Lisca, "was an inexperienced but very ambitious writer." Acutely alive to literary possibilities and eager to try them all, he pulled from too many clashing genres and methods, sources and influences. Steinbeck sampled every technique in the writer's toolbox, and most of all, became drunk on language. In *Cup of Gold*, writes Howard Levant: "Many technical devices are evident, such as flashbacks, foreshadowing, interchapters, inserted brief narratives, internal monologue, a play on names, a dream sequence, a cluster of images and symbols, ironic confrontations and juxtapositions, parallels and oppositions, and a range of style that includes approximations of Welsh talk, the talk of the English gentry, the lingo of the New World half-breed, the formal talk of the Spanish grandee, and a precise observational, usually authorial language." For Levant, as for many other critics, the novel's very strengths, its "ambitious conception" and "richness of detail," suggest why *Cup of Gold* is a failure: "its materials and its structure are not in harmonious relationship."

If at times the novel seems to have been written by a sorcerer's apprentice, a young Merlin not in full control of his own magic or the spells and charms of his elders, *Cup of Gold* is none-theless an important early experiment in what Dennis Prindle, in the single best essay on this relatively neglected novel, calls "allegorical naturalism." According to Prindle, *Cup of Gold* combines "the turn-of-the-century tradition of high romance and quasi-Arthurian adventure" with an "aggressively modern" naturalism that proclaims "the primacy of instinct and the environment . . . over the claims of tradition and culture." Rather than criticizing *Cup of Gold* for its lack of "harmony," Prindle celebrates this first novel's deliberate dissonance. Rather than viewing *Cup of Gold* as a "false start," he sees it as an auspicious beginning, shaping "what will be an endur-ing conflict in Steinbeck between tradition and experience, framed here with Arthurian romance on one side and a slyly ironic naturalism on the other." Throughout Steinbeck's career, the author will continue to appropriate the older traditions of romance and allegory, adapting them to "the demands of an increasingly naturalistic vision."

Steinbeck would successfully locate both comedy and trag-edy in allegorical naturalism, continuing the experiments begun in *Cup of Gold*. His breakout book, the comic *Tor-tilla Flat*, transforms a group of Mexican *paisanos* into an Arthurian Round Table. His masterpiece, *The Grapes of Wrath*, treats the Dust Bowl exodus with documentary real-ism, embracing current events as *Cup of Gold* embraces his-tory, and with the same intercalary chapters of explanation. But *The Grapes of Wrath*, like its piratical precursor, is still a profound allegory—both novels are violent, all-consuming passages to a Promised Land that turns out to be a Valley of Ashes. In *The Pearl*, we have the naturalistically rendered trag-edy of a poor Mexican villager seduced by the greedy, false, ambitious dreams embodied in "the pearl of the world," a pearl that not coincidentally makes its first appearance in *Cup of Gold*. As an exercise in allegorical naturalism, *The Pearl* was so successful that even the arch-realist Ernest Heming-way fell under its spell—*The Old Man and the Sea* probably would not have been written without its example. Continu-ing within the Steinbeck canon, we find parallels between the romance and allegory of *Cup of Gold* present even in *The Log from the* Sea of Cortez—Steinbeck's nonfiction account of an expedition to study the marine biology of Baja California. Cowritten with pioneering ecologist Edward F. Ricketts, *The Log* ought to be Steinbeck's most naturalistic book. Yet the "deep, mellow pulsation of the Tone" Henry Morgan hears at the moment of his death also sounds in the final sentences of *The Log*: "The *Western Flyer* hunched into the great waves toward Cedros Island, the wind blew off the tops of the whitecaps, and the big guy wire, from bow to mast, took up its vibration like the low pipe on a tremendous organ. It sang its deep note into the wind." In *Cup of Gold*, the Tone marks the fulfillment of Gwenliana's prophecy, the moment when "a little, struggling life" enters "the sheening Purity," becoming part of a larger whole that renders the driving egotism of a Morgan meaningless. In *The Log from the* Sea of Cortez, the Tone is the keynote of Steinbeck's spiritual ecology, his belief "that all things are one thing and that one thing is all things." These are only a few examples of Steinbeck's many successful experiments in devising strategies to connect romance, allegory, and fable with naturalism, a lifelong literary enterprise that began with *Cup of Gold*.

CONCLUSION

Paradoxically, Steinbeck's own misgivings about *Cup of Gold* may hold the keys to reading this weird book with pleasure and success. On February 25, 1928, as he was putting the finishing touches on his novel, Steinbeck wrote to his friend "Dook" Sheffield:

> I shall make an elegy to Henry Morgan, who is a monument to my own lack of ability. I shall go ahead, but I wonder if that sharp agony of words will ever occur to me again. I wonder if I shall ever be drunken with rhythms any more. [. . .] I am twenty-six and I am not young any more. I shall write good novels but hereafter I ride Pegasus with a saddle and martingale, for I am

afraid Pegasus will rear and kick. I do not take joy in the unmanageable horse any more. I want a hackney of tried steadiness.

With the keenness of hindsight, we know that Steinbeck will
indeed go on to write not merely good novels, but classic novels such as *The Grapes of Wrath* and *Of Mice and Men*, that
he will produce a body of work that in 1962 will win him the
Grail of literary awards, the Nobel Prize. A special pleasure of
reading *Cup of Gold* is the portrait it affords of Steinbeck as
a young writer—alive to the "sharp agony" of words, drunk
with their rhythms, in possession of surging powers he cannot
fully control. In the pages of *Cup of Gold*, we can observe the
qualities Henry Morgan himself assigns to the young artist—"a
certain obnoxious freedom [. . .] lovable and spontaneous and
human [. . .] given to carelessness in the pursuit of passion."
We can trace the familiar Steinbeck of future books; we can
witness genius awkwardly unfolding its wings. The reader is
forewarned against complacency and set expectations of what
novels should be and do. John Steinbeck's first novel is no
"hackney of tried steadiness." *Cup of Gold* rears and kicks.
The joy of reading young Steinbeck's unbridled Pegasus is
the joy of riding an unmanageable horse—and the successful
method is to hold on tight and expect the unexpected.

SUSAN F. BEEGEL

Suggestions for Further Reading

"American Soldiers Guard Panama City; Asked by President Chiari After Rent Riots." *The New York Times* (October 13, 1925): 1.

Anderson, Maxwell, and Laurence Stallings. *The Buccaneer. Three American Plays*. New York: Harcourt, Brace, 1926. 181–263.

Benson, Jackson J. *The True Adventures of John Steinbeck, Writer*. New York: Viking, 1984.

Byrne, Donn. *Messer Marco Polo*. New York: D. Appleton-Century, 1921.

Cabell, James Branch. *Jurgen: A Comedy of Justice*. New York: Robert M. McBride, 1922.

Cordingly, David. *Under the Black Flag: The Romance and the Reality of Life Among the Pirates*. New York: Harcourt Brace, 1995.

DeMott, Robert J. *Steinbeck's Reading: A Catalogue of Books Owned and Borrowed*. New York: Garland, 1984.

Diaz Espino, Ovidio. *How Wall Street Created a Nation: J. P. Morgan, Teddy Roosevelt, and the Panama Canal*. New York: Four Walls Eight Windows, 2001.

Eddy, Darlene. "To Go A-Buccaneering and Take a Spanish Town: Some Seventeenth Century Aspects of *Cup of Gold*." *Steinbeck Quarterly* 8 (1975): 3–12.

Exquemelin, Alexander O. *The Buccaneers of America*. First published 1678. Trans. Alexis Brown. New York: Dover, 1969.

Fontenrose, Joseph. *John Steinbeck: An Introduction and Interpretation*. New York: Barnes and Noble, 1963.

French, Warren. *John Steinbeck*. Boston: Twayne, 1975.

Gannett, Lewis. "Preface." *Cup of Gold: A Life of Sir Henry Morgan, Buccaneer, with Occasional Reference to History*. New York: P. F. Collier, 1936. v–viii.

Jackson, Joseph Henry. "John Steinbeck: A Portrait." *The Saturday Review of Literature* 16.22 (September 25, 1937): 11–12.

Li, Luchen, ed. *John Steinbeck: A Documentary Volume. Dictionary of Literary Biography*. Vol. 309. Detroit: Thomson-Gale, 2005.

Lisca, Peter. *The Wide World of John Steinbeck*. New York: Gordian, 1981.

McCullough, David. *The Path Between the Seas: The Creation of the Panama Canal, 1870–1914*. New York: Simon and Schuster, 1977.

Parini, Jay. *John Steinbeck: A Biography*. New York: Henry Holt, 1995.

Pope, Dudley. *The Buccaneer King: The Biography of the Notorious Sir Henry Morgan, 1635–1688*. New York: Dodd, Mead, 1977.

Prindle, Dennis. "The Pretexts of Romance: Steinbeck's Allegorical Naturalism from *Cup of Gold* to *Tortilla Flat*." In *The Steinbeck Question: New Essays in Criticism*. Ed. Donald R. Noble. Troy, NY: Whitston, 1993. 23–36.

Sabatini, Rafael. *Captain Blood*. 1922. New York: Penguin Classics, 2003.

"Saw a Rebellion Started in Panama." *The New York Times* (October 19, 1925): 16.

Steinbeck, John. "Autobiography: Making of a New Yorker." *The New York Times* (February 1, 1953): SMA 26.

———. *Cannery Row*. 1945. New York: Penguin, 1994.

———. *The Log from the Sea of Cortez*. 1941. New York: Penguin, 1995.

———. *Steinbeck: A Life in Letters*. Ed. Elaine Steinbeck and Robert Wallsten. New York: Viking, 1975.

Stevenson, Robert Louis. *Treasure Island*. 1881. New York: Simon and Schuster, 1911.

Timmerman, John H. *John Steinbeck's Fiction: The Aesthetics of the Road Taken.* Norman: University of Oklahoma, 1986.

Valjean, Norman. *John Steinbeck, The Errant Knight: An Intimate Biography of the California Years.* San Francisco: Chronicle, 1975.

Cup of Gold

Cup of Gold

CHAPTER I

I

All afternoon the wind sifted out of the black Welsh glens, crying notice that Winter was come sliding down over the world from the Pole; and riverward there was the faint moaning of new ice. It was a sad day, a day of gray unrest, of discontent. The gently moving air seemed to be celebrating the loss of some gay thing with a soft, tender elegy. But in the pastures great work horses nervously stamped their feet, and all through the country small brown birds, in cliques of four or five, flew twittering from tree to tree and back again, seeking and calling in recruits for their southing. A few goats clambered to the tops of high lone rocks and long stared upward with their yellow eyes and sniffed the heavens.

The afternoon passed slowly, procession-like with an end of evening, and on the heels of the evening an excited wind rushed out, rustled in the dry grasses, and fled whimpering across the fields. Night drew down like a black cowl, and Holy Winter sent his nuncio to Wales.

Beside the high-road which lined the valley, ran up through a cleft in the hills, and so out into the world, there stood an ancient farm-house built of heavy stones and thatched. The Morgan who had built it played against Time and nearly won.

Inside the house a fire was burning on the hearth; an iron kettle hung over the blaze, and a black iron oven hid in the coals which fell about the edges of the flame. The brisk firelight glinted on the tips of long-handled pikes in racks upon the walls, weapons unused in the hundred years since Morgan clamored in Glendowers' ranks and trembled with rage at the flinty lines of Iolo Goch.

The wide brass bindings of a great chest, which stood in a corner, sucked in the light and glowed resplendently. Papers there were in the chest, and parchments, and stiff untanned skins, written in English and Latin and the old Cumric tongue: Morgan was born, Morgan was married, Morgan became a knight, Morgan was hanged. Here lay the history of the house, shameful and glorious. But the family was few now, and little enough likely to add records to the chest other than the simple chronicle: Morgan was born—and died.

There was Old Robert, for instance, sitting in his high-backed chair, sitting and smiling into the fire. His smile was perplexity and a strange, passive defiance. You would have said he sought to make that Fate which was responsible for his being, a little ashamed of itself by smiling at it. Often he wearily considered his existence, ringed around with little defeats which mocked it as street children torment a cripple. It was strange to Old Robert that he, who knew so much more than his neighbors, who had pondered so endlessly, should be not even a good farmer. Sometimes he imagined he understood too many things ever to do anything well.

And so Old Robert sipped the burned ale of his own experimenting and smiled into the fire. His wife would be whispering excuses for him, he knew, and the laborers in the fields removed their hats to Morgan, not to Robert.

Even his aged mother, Gwenliana, here beside him, shivering to the fire as though the very wind sounds about the house called in the cold to her, was not so judged incompetent. In the cottages there was a little fear of her and a great respect. Any day when she sat in the garden, holding her necromantic court, you might see some tall farm lad blushing and hugging his hat across his chest while he listened to Gwenliana's magic. For many years, now, she had been practicing the second sight and taking pride in it. And though the family knew her prophecies to be whole guesses whose shrewdness grew less sharp with her years, they listened to her with respect, and simulated awe, and asked of her the location of lost things. When, after one of her mystic recitations, the scissors were not discovered under the second board of the shed floor, they pretended to find them there anyway; for, had she lost the robe of augury, there would have remained only a little wrinkled old woman soon to die.

This play of claque to a simpleton was a harsh tax on the convictions of Mother Morgan. It outraged her nature, for she was one who had, apparently, come into the world to be a scourge to all foolishness. Such matters as had so obviously no connection either with the church or with the prices of things were plainly nonsense.

Old Robert had loved his wife so well and so long that he could think sharp things about her, and the thoughts could not injure his affection. When she had come home this afternoon, raging over the price of a pair of shoes she hadn't wanted anyway, he had considered: "Her life is like a book crowded with mighty events. Every day she rises to the peak of some tremendous climax which has to do with buttons or a neighbor's wedding. I think that when true tragedy comes in upon her, she will not see it over her range of ant-hills. Perhaps this is luck," he thought, and then—"I wonder, now, how she would compare the king's own death with the loss of one of the sow's red pigs."

Mother Morgan was too busy with the day itself to be bothered with the foolishness of abstractions. Some one in the family had to be practical or the thatch would blow away—and what could you expect of a pack of dreamers like Robert and Gwenliana and her son Henry? She loved her husband with a queer mixture of pity and contempt born of his failings and his goodness.

Young Henry, her son, she worshiped, though of course she could not trust him to have the least idea of what was to his benefit or conducive to his health. And all of the family loved Mother Morgan and feared her and got in her way.

She had fed them and trimmed the lamp. Breakfast was on the fire. Now she searched about for something to mend, as though she did not mend everything the moment it was torn. In the midst of her search for busyness, she paused and glanced

sharply at young Henry. It was the kind of harsh, affectionate
look which says, "I wonder, now, if he is not in the way of
catching cold there on the floor." And Henry squirmed, wondering what things he had neglected to do that afternoon. But
immediately she caught up a cloth and went to dusting, and the
boy was reassured.

He lay propped on one elbow and stared past the fire into
his thoughts. The long gray afternoon, piercing to this mysterious night, had called up strong yearnings in him, the seeds of
which were planted months before. It was a desire for a thing
he could not name. Perhaps the same force moved him which
collected the birds into exploring parties and made the animals
nervously sniff up-wind for the scent of winter.

Young Henry was conscious, this night, that he had lived
on for fifteen tedious years without accomplishing any single
thing of importance. And had his mother known his feeling,
she would have said,

"He is growing."

And his father would have repeated after her,

"Yes, the boy is growing." But neither would have understood what the other meant.

Henry, if you considered his face, drew from his parents
almost equally. His cheek bones were high and hard, his chin
firm, his upper lip short and thin like his mother's. But there,
too, were the sensual underlip, and the fine nose, and the eyes
which looked out on dreams; these were Old Robert's features,
and his was the thick, wiry hair coiled like black springs against
the head. But though there was complete indecision in Robert's
face, there was a great quantity of decision in Henry's if only he
could find something about which to decide. Here were three
before the fire, Robert and Gwenliana and young Henry, whose
eyes looked out beyond the walls and saw unbodied things—
looked into the night for the ghosts.

It was a preternatural night; a time when you might meet
corpse-candles gliding along the road, or come upon the ghost
of a Roman legion marching at double quick to reach its shel-
tering city of Caerleon before the full storm broke. And the little
misshapen beings of the hills would be searching out deserted

badger holes to cover them from the night. The wind would go crying after them through the fields.

In the house it was quiet except for the snapping fire-noises and for the swishing sound of blown thatch. A log cracked on the hearth; and out of the crevice a thin blaze leaped up and curled about the black kettle like a flower of flame. Now Mother flurried to the fireplace.

"Robert, you will never be paying attention to the fire. You should be poking at it now and again."

Such was her method. She poked a large fire to make it smaller, and, when it died, she stirred the embers violently to restore the flame.

A faint sound of footsteps came along the high-road—a sound that might have been the wind or those walking things which cannot be seen. The steps grew louder, then stopped in front of the door from whence came a timid knocking.

"Come!" Robert called. The door opened softly, and there, lighted against the black night, stood a bent, feeble man with eyes like weak flames. He paused on the threshold as though undecided, but in a moment advanced into the room, asking in a strange, creaking voice,

"Will you be knowing me, I wonder, Robert Morgan? Will you be knowing me that have been out so long?" His words were a plea.

Robert searched the shrunken face.

"Know you?" he said. "I do not think—wait!—can it be Dafydd? our little farm lad Dafydd that went away to sea years past?"

A look of complete relief came into the face of the wayfarer. He might have been applying some delicate, fearful test to Robert Morgan. Now he chuckled.

"It's Dafydd, sure; and rich—and cold." He finished with a wistfulness like a recurring pain.

Dafydd was gray-white and toughened like a dry hide. The skin of his face was stiff and thick so that he seemed to change expression with slow, conscious effort.

"I'm cold, Robert," his queer, dry voice went on. "I can't seem ever to get warm again. But anyway I'm rich,"—as though he hoped these two might balance—"rich along with him they call Pierre le Grand."

Young Henry had risen, and now he cried:

"Where have you been to, man—where?"

"Where? Why, I've been out to the Indies, that's where I've been; to Goaves and to Tortuga—that's the turtle—and to Jamaica and the thick woods of Hispaniola for the hunting of cattle. I've been all there."

"You'll be sitting down, Dafydd," Mother Morgan interrupted. She spoke as though he had never been away. "I'll go about getting something warm to drink. Will you look how Henry gobbles you with his eyes, Dafydd? Like as not he'll be wanting to go to the Indies, too." To her, the words were a pleasant idiocy.

Dafydd kept silence, though he appeared to be straining back at a desire to talk. Mother Morgan frightened him as she had when he was a tow-headed farm boy. Old Robert knew his embarrassment, and Mother, too, seemed to sense it, for when she had put a steaming cup in his hands she left the room.

Wrinkled old Gwenliana was in her seat before the fire, her mind lost in the swimming future. Her clouded eyes were veiled with to-morrow. Behind their vague blue surfaces seemed to crowd the mounting events and circumstances of the world. She was gone out of the room—gone into pure Time, and that the future.

Old Robert watched the door close behind his wife, then settled himself with turnings as a dog settles.

"Now, Dafydd," he said, and peered smiling into the fire, while Henry, kneeling on the floor, gazed with awe at this mortal who held the very distances in his palm.

"Well, Robert—it's about the green jungle I wanted to tell and the brown Indians that live in it, and about him they call Pierre le Grand. But, Robert, there's something gone out of me like a little winking light. I used to lie on the decks of ships at night and think and think how I'd talk and boast when only I came home again—but it's more like a child, I am, come home to cry. Can you understand that, Robert? Can you understand that at all?" He was leaning forward eagerly.

"I'll tell you. We took the tall plate ship they call a galleon, and we with only pistols and the long knives they have for cutting trails in the jungle. Twenty-four of us there was—only twenty-four and ragged—but, Robert, we did horrid things with those same long knives. It's no good for a man that was a farm lad to be doing such things and then thinking about them. There was a fine captain—and we hung him up by his thumbs before we killed him. I don't know why we did it; I helped and I don't know why. Some said he was a damned Papist; but then, so was Pierre le Grand, I think.

"Some we pushed into the sea with their breast plates shining and shimmering as they went down—grand Spanish soldiers and bubbles coming out of their mouths. You can see deep into the water there." Dafydd ceased and looked at the floor.

"You see, I don't want to be hurting you with these things, Robert, but it's like something alive hidden in my chest under my ribs, and it's biting and scratching to get out of me. I'm rich of the venturing sure, but most times that doesn't seem enough; I'm richer, maybe, than your own brother, Sir Edward."

Robert was smiling with tightened lips. Now and then his eyes wandered to the boy where he knelt on the hearth. Henry was taut with attention, gluttonously feeding on the words. When Robert spoke, he avoided Dafydd's eyes.

"Your soul's burdening you," he said. "You'd best have a talk with the Curate the morning—but about what I don't know."

"No, no; it's not my soul at all," Dafydd went on quickly. "That soul leaks out of a man the very first thing in the Indies, and leaves him with a dry, shrunken feeling where it was. It's not my soul at all; it's the poison that's in me, in my blood and in my brain. Robert, it's shriveling me up like an old orange. The crawling things there, and the little flying beasts that come to your fire of nights, and the great pale flowers, all poisonous. They do horrible things to a man. My blood is like cold needles sliding in my veins the moment, and the fine fire before me. All this—all—is because of the dank breathing of the jungle. You cannot sleep in it nor lie in it, nor live in it at all but it breathes on you and withers you.

"And the brown Indians—why, look!" He rolled back his

sleeve, and Robert in disgust motioned him to cover the sick white horror which festered on his arm.

"It was only a little scratch of an arrow—you could hardly see it; but it'll be killing me before years, I guess. There's other things in me, Robert. Even the humans are poisonous, and a song the sailors sing about that."

Now young Henry started up excitedly.

"But the Indians," he cried; "those Indians and their arrows. Tell me about them! Do they fight much? How do they look?"

"Fight?" said Dafydd. "Yes, they fight always; fight for a love that's in it. When they do not be fighting the men of Spain, they're at killing amongst themselves. Lithe as snakes they are, and quick and quiet and brown as ferrets; the very devil for getting out of sight before a man might get a shot at them.

"But they're a brave, strong people with the fear in them for only two things—dogs and slavery." Dafydd was immersed in his tale. "Why, boy, can you think what they would be doing to a man that might get himself taken in a skirmish? They stick him full of long jungle thorns from his head to his toes, and on the thick end of every thorn a ball of fluff like wool. Then the poor captive man stands in a circle of naked savages while they set light to the fluff. And that Indian that does not be singing while he burns there like a torch, is cursed and called a coward. Now, can you imagine any white man doing that?

"But dogs they fear, because the Spaniards hunt them with huge mastiffs when they're at slave gathering for the mines; and slavery is horrible to them. To go chained body to body into the wet earth, year on the crown of year, until they die of the damp ague—rather would they be singing under the burning thorns, and dying in a flame."

He paused and stretched his thin hands into the fireplace until they were nearly touching the blaze. The light which had come into his eyes as he talked died out again.

"Oh, I'm tired, Robert—so very tired," he sighed, "but there's one thing I want to tell you before I sleep. Maybe the telling will ease me, and maybe I can speak it out and then forget about it for the one night. I must go back to the damned place. I can never stay away from the jungle any more, because its hot

breath is on me. Here, where I was born, I shiver and freeze.
A month would find me dead. This valley where I played and
grew and worked has cast me out for a foul, hot thing. It cleans
itself of me with the cold.

"Now will you be giving me a place to sleep, with thick covers to keep my poor blood moving; and in the morning I'll be
off again." He stopped and his face flexed with pain. "I used to
love the winter so."

Old Robert helped him from the room with a hand under his
arm, then came and sat again by the fire. He looked at the boy
who lay unmoving on the floor.

"What are you thinking about now, son?" he asked very
softly after a time. And Henry drew his gaze back from the
land beyond the blaze.

"I'm thinking I'll be wanting to go soon, father."

"I know, Henry. The whole of this long year I've seen it growing in you like a strong tree—London or Guinea or Jamaica.
It comes of being fifteen and strong, with the passion for new
things on you. Once I saw the valley grow smaller and smaller,
too, until finally it smothered me a little, I think. But aren't you
afraid of the knives, son, and the poisons, and the Indians? Do
not these things put fear on you?"

"No-o-o," Henry said slowly.

"Of course not—and how could they? The words have no
meaning to you at all. But the sadness of Dafydd, and the hurt
of him, and his poor, sick body—aren't you afraid of those?
Do you want to go about the world weighed down with such
a heart?"

Young Henry considered long.

"I would not be like that," he said at last. "I would be coming back very often for my blood's sake."

His father went on smiling valiantly.

"When will you be off, Henry? It will be lonely here without you."

"Why, I'll go, now, as soon as I may," said Henry; and it
seemed that he was the older and Robert a little boy.

"Henry, will you do two things for me before you go? Will
you be thinking to-night of the long sleeplessness I'll have

because of you, and of how lost my days will be. And will you remember the hours your mother will fret about your under-clothing and the state of your religion. That's the first thing, Henry; but second, will you go up to old Merlin on the crag-top to-morrow and tell him of your going and listen to his words? He is wiser than you or I may ever be. There is a kind of magic he practices which may be a help to you. Will you do these two things, son?"

Henry had become very sad.

"I would like to stay, my father, but you know—"

"Yes, boy." Robert nodded. "It is my sorrow that I do know. I cannot be angry nor forbid your going, because I understand. I wish I might prevent it and whip you, thinking that I helped you. But go to bed, Henry, and think and think when the light is out and the dark is around you."

Old Robert sat dreaming in his chair after the boy had gone.

"Why do men like me want sons?" he wondered. "It must be because they hope in their poor beaten souls that these new men, who are their blood, will do the things they were not strong enough nor wise enough nor brave enough to do. It is rather like another chance with life; like a new bag of coins at a table of luck after your fortune is gone. Perhaps the boy is doing what I might have done had I been brave enough years past. Yes, the valley has smothered me, I think, and I am glad this boy of mine finds it in his power to vault the mountains and stride about the world. But it will be—so very lonely here without him."

II

Old Robert came in from his rose garden late the next morning and stood in the room where his wife was sweeping. She eyed the good soil on his hands with disapproval.

"He'll be wanting to go now, Mother," Robert said nervously.

"*Who* will be wanting to go, and where?" She was brusque

and busy with her sweeping; the quick, inquisitive broom
hounded dust from the corners and floor cracks and drove it in
little puffs to the open.

"Why, Henry. He'll be wanting to go to the Indies now."

She stopped her work to stare at him. "The Indies! But, Robert! Oh, nonsense!" she finished, and the broom swung more
rapidly in her hands.

"I've seen it for long and long growing in him," Robert went
on. "Then Dafydd came with his tales. Henry told me last night
that he must go."

"He's only a little boy," Mother Morgan snapped. "He can't
be going to the Indies."

"When Dafydd set out, a little time ago, there was a longing in the child's eyes that will never be satisfied at all, not
even if he does go to the Indies. Haven't you noticed, Mother,
how his eyes look away beyond the mountains at something
he wants?"

"But he may not go! He may not!"

"Ah, there is no use in it, Mother. A great gulf lies between
my son and me, but none at all between me and my son. If I
did not know the lean hunger of him so well I might forbid his
venturing, and he would run away with anger in his heart; for
he cannot understand the hunger that's in me for his staying.
It would come to the same thing, anyway." Robert gathered
conviction.

"There's a cruel difference between my son and me. I've seen
it in the years of his growing. For whereas he runs about sticking his finger into pot after pot of cold porridge, grandly confident that each one will prove the pottage of his dreaming, I
may not open any kettle, for I believe all porridge to be cold.
And so—I imagine great dishes of purple porridge, drenched
with dragon's milk, sugared with a sweetness only to be envi-
sioned. He tests his dreams, Mother, and I—God help me!—am
afraid to."

She was becoming impatient with his talking.

"Robert," she cried almost angrily, "in any time when there's
boding on us, or need, or sorrow, you hide in words. Here is a
duty to you! This boy is too young. There are horrible places

across the sea, and the winter comes in at us. He would be sure
to find his death in a cough that came to him from the winter.
You know how the dampness on his feet sets him sick. He must
not leave this farm, not even to London, I say—if these eyes
you talk about starve in his head.

"How could you possibly know what kind of people he
would be taking up with, and they telling him nonsense and
wickedness. I know the evil that's in the world. Doesn't the
Curate mention it nearly every Sabbath—'pitfalls and snares'
he calls them, do you see? And so they are, too. And here
you stand, content to talk foolishness about purple porridge
when you should be doing something or other. You must forbid it."

But Robert answered her impatiently.

"To you he is only a little boy who must be made to say his
prayers of nights and to wear a coat into the fields. You have
not felt the polished steel of him as I have. Yes, to you that
quick, hard set of his chin is only the passing stubbornness of
a headstrong child. But I do know; and I say to you, without
pleasure, that this son of ours will be a great man, because—
well—because he is not very intelligent. He can see only one
desire at a time. I said he tested his dreams; he will murder every
dream with the implacable arrows of his will. This boy will win
to every goal of his aiming; for he can realize no thought, no
reason, but his own. And I am sorry for his coming greatness
because of a thing Merlin once spoke of. You must look at the
granite jaws of him, Mother, and the trick he has of making his
cheek muscles stand out with clenching them."

"He must not go," she said firmly, and pinched her lips
tightly together.

"You see, Mother," Robert went on, "you are something
like Henry yourself, for you never admit the existence of any
idea save your own. But I will not forbid his going, because I
must not have him stealing out into the lonely dark with bread
and cheese under his coat and a hurt feeling of injustice in his
heart. I permit him to go. More, I help him to go if he wishes
it. And then, if I have misjudged my son, he will come sneak-

ing back with the fearful hope that no one may mention his cowardice."

Mother Morgan said, "Nonsense!" and went back to her work. She would dissolve this thing by disbelieving it. Oh, the thousand things she chained to Limbo with her incredulity! For many years she had beaten Robert's wild thoughts with a heavy phalanx of common sense; her troop simply charged in and overwhelmed him. Always he retired wearily and sat smiling for a time. He was sure to come back to sanity in this case as in others.

Robert was working the soil about the roots of a rose bush with his strong brown hands. His fingers lifted the black loam and then patted it gently back into place. Now and again he stroked the gray trunk of the bush with the touch of great love. It was as though he smoothed the covers over one about to sleep and touched its arm to be reassured of its safety.

The day was light, for winter had inched back a bit and returned its hostage to the world—a small, cold sun. Young Henry came and stood near an elm by the wall, a tree draggled and leafless and gaunt with nursing the winds.

"You have been thinking as I asked you?" Robert spoke quietly.

Henry started. He did not know that the man, kneeling as though in adoration of the earth, had noticed him; and yet he had come here to be noticed.

"Yes, father," he said. "How could I help be thinking?"

"And has it bound you here? Will you be staying?"

"No, father; I may not stay." He had been made sad with his father's sadness. He felt mean and shoddy to be the cause of it, but the hunger to be going still gnawed in his heart.

"Will you be walking up to speak with Merlin on the crag-top, then?" Robert pleaded. "Will you listen to his words with great care?"

"I shall go now."

"But, Henry, the day is half done with, and the track is long. Be waiting until the morrow."

"I must be away the morrow, father."

Old Robert's hands slipped away slowly to the ground and lay, half-open, on the black soil at the roots of the rose bush.

III

Young Henry turned soon from the road to climb up a broad trail which soared to Crag-top and then over the wild mountains. Its windings could be seen from below until it disappeared into the great cleft. And on the topmost point of the trail dwelt Merlin; Merlin whom the farm boys might have jeered at and stoned on his infrequent journeys down the path had they believed him harmless. But Merlin was one who collected about himself a swarm of little legends. It was established that the Tylwyth Teg obeyed him and carried his messages through the air on soundless wings. Children whispered of his acquaintance with certain mottled weasels which might carry on his vengeance had he need of such. Then, too, he kept a red-eared dog. These were terrific things, and Merlin one not to be trifled with by children who did not know all the signs for protecting themselves.

Once Merlin had been a fine poet, the old people said, and might have been a greater. They would softly sing The Sorrow of Plaith or the Spear Song, to prove it. Several times he had taken the chief prize of the Eisteddfod, and would have been chosen First Bard if an aspirant of the House of Rhys had not entered against him. Then, without known cause, and Merlin a young man, too, he had shut up his song in the stone house on Crag-top and kept it a strict prisoner there while he grew old and old—and those who had sung his songs forgot them, or died.

The Crag-top house was round like a low gray tower with windows letting sight on the valley and on the mountains. Some said that it was built by a beleaguered giant, centuries ago, to keep his virgins hidden while they were in that state; and others, that King Harold had fled there after Hastings to live out his life ever watching and peering, with his one eye, down the valley and over the mountains for the coming of Normans.

Merlin was old now; his hair and long, straight beard were white and soft as spring clouds. There was much about him of an ancient Druid priest with clear, far-seeing eyes which watched the stars.

The pathway narrowed on young Henry as he climbed. Its inward side was a stone wall cutting into the heavens knife-like, and the misshapen, vague images along the way made it seem the rock temple of some old, crude god whose worshipers were apes.

There had been grass at first, and bushes, and a few brave, twisted trees; but upward all living things died of the rock loneliness. Far below, the farmhouses huddled like feeding bugs and the valley shrank and drew into itself.

Now a mountain closed in on the other side of the trail, leaving only a broad chasm to the sky. A fierce, steady wind poured out of the blue heavens and shrilled toward the valley. Upward, the strewn rocks were larger and more black and dreadful—crouched guardian things of the path.

Henry climbed tirelessly on. What could old Merlin have to tell him, or, perhaps, to give him? A lotion to make his skin tough and proof against arrows? Some charm? Words to protect him from the Devil's many little servants? But Merlin was to talk and he to listen; and what Merlin said might cure young Henry of his yearnings, might keep him here in Cambria for always. That could not be, for there were outland forces, nameless foreign ghosts, calling to him and beckoning from across the mysterious sea.

There was no desire in him for a state or condition, no picture in his mind of the thing to be when he had followed his longing; but only a burning and a will overpowering to journey outward and outward after the earliest risen star.

The path broke on a top of solid stone, semi-spherical like the crown of a hat; and on the peak of its rise was the low, round house of Merlin, all fitted of irregular rough rocks, and a conical roof on it like a candle-snuffer.

The old man met him at the door before he could knock.

"I'm young Henry Morgan, sir, and I'm going outward from here to the Indies."

"Indeed, and are you? Will you come in and talk to me about it?" The voice was clear and low and lovely as a young wind crooning in a Spring-time orchard. There was the music of singing in it, the quiet singing of a man working with tools; and underneath, half-heard or completely imagined, there rang the seeming of harp strings lightly touched and left to thrill.

The single room was thick carpeted in black, and on the walls were hung harp and spear-head, harp and spear-head, all the way around; small Welsh harps and the great bronze leaf spears of the Britons, and these against the unfinished stone. Below these were the all-seeing windows wherefrom you might look out on three valleys and a mighty family of mountains; and lower still, a single bench circled around the room against the wall. There was a table in the center loaded with tattered books, and beside it a copper brazier, set on a Greek tripod of black iron.

The great hound nuzzled Henry as he entered so that he drew away in fright, for is there anything under the blue cup so deadly as the merest notice of a red-eared dog?

"You are going to the Indies. Sit here, boy. See! you can watch your home valley now, so that it go not flying off to Avalon." The harps caught up his tones and hummed an answering faint resonance.

"My father said I was to come here and tell you of my going and listen to your speech. My father thinks your speech may keep me here."

"Going to the Indies," Merlin repeated. "Will you be seeing Elizabeth before you go and making grand promises to flutter the heart of her and strangle the breath in her, after you're gone, from thinking of the things you will bring back to her?"

Henry blushed deeply. "Who told you I thought at all of the little rat?" he cried. "Who is it says at all that I care for her?"

"Oh, the wind whispered something," said Merlin; "and then there was some word of it in your talking cheeks and your blustering just now. I think you should be speaking to Elizabeth, not to me. Your father should have known better." His voice died away. When he spoke again it was with sad earnestness.

"Must you leave your father, boy—and he so sure alone in the valley of men who are not like him? Yes, I think that you must go. The plans of boys are serious things and unchangeable. But what can I say to you to keep you here, young Henry? Your father sends me a task difficult to fulfill.

"I went out on a tall Spanish ship a thousand years ago—it must be more than that, or perhaps I did not go at all and only dreamed it. We came at last on these green Indies, and they were lovely but unchanging. Their cycle is a green monotony. If you go there you must give up the year; must lose the pang of utter dread in the deep winter with its boding that the world has fled solar fealty to go careening into lonely space so that Spring may never come again. And you must lose that wild, excited quickening when the sun turns back, the joy of it flooding over you like the surge of a warm wave and choking you with pleasure and relief. No change there; none at all. Past and future mingle in an odious, eternal now."

"But there is no change here," young Henry interposed. "Year on top of year are the crops put in and new calves licked by their mothers; year on top of year is a pig slaughtered and the hams smoked. Spring comes, surely, but nothing happens."

"True enough, blind boy; and I see that we are talking of different things." Merlin looked out of his windows to the mountains and the valleys, and a great love for the land shone in his eyes; but when he turned back to the boy there was the look of pain in his face. His voice took on the cadence of a song.

"I will plead with you for this dear Cambria where time is piled mountain high and crumbling, ancient days about its base," he cried passionately. "Have you lost your love of wild Cambria that you would leave it when the blood of your thousand ancestors has gone soaking into the soil to keep it Cambria for always? Have you forgotten that you are of the Trojan race? Ah, but they wandered too, didn't they, when Pergamus fell in?"

Henry said, "I have lost no love, sir, but my dream is over the sea that I do not know. I know Cambria."

"But, boy, here great Arthur lived who drove his standards into Rome and sailed away undying to dear Avalon. And Avalon itself lies off our coasts, somewhere over the sunken cities; there it floats endlessly. And have you not heard them, Henry, the ghosts of all those good, brave, quarrelsome, inefficient men—Llew Llaw Giffes and Belerius and Arthur and Cadwallo and Brute? They walk like clouds through the land and guard it from the high places. There are no ghosts in the Indies, and no Tylwyth Teg.

"In these wild, black hills there are a million mysteries. Have you found out the Chair of Arthur or the meaning of the circling stones? Have you heard the voices that cry out triumph in the night, and the hunters of souls with their screaming horns and their packs of blue hounds who rush into the villages on the storm?"

"I have heard them," said Henry, shuddering. He glanced shyly at the dog asleep on the floor and spoke in a lower tone. "The Curate says these things are lies. He says the Red Book is a book for little children before the fire and a shame for men and big boys to be believing in. He told us at church school these were lying tales, and unchristian. Arthur was an unimportant chieftain, he said, and Merlin, whose name you bear, a figment of the mad brain of Geoffrey of Monmouth. He even spoke ill of the Tylwyth Teg and of the corpse-candles, and of such as his Honor, your dog, here."

"Oh, the fool!" cried Merlin in disgust. "The fool to be breaking these things! And he offers instead a story given to the world by twelve collaborators with rather slovenly convictions in some matters. Why must you go, boy? Do you not see that the enemies of Cambria fight no more with the sword, but with little pointed tongues?" The harps sang his question, then slowly ceased their throbbing, and there was silence in the round house.

Henry studied the floor with drawn brows. At last he said, "There is so much bother about me. I cannot seem to talk of this thing, Merlin. I will come back. Surely I will when this burning for new things is quenched. But don't you see that I must go, for it seems that I am cut in half and only one part of me here. The other piece is over the sea, calling and calling me to come and be whole. I love Cambria, and I will come back when I am whole again."

Merlin searched the boy's face closely. Sadly he looked up at his harps. "I think I understand," he said softly. "You are a little boy. You want the moon to drink from as a golden cup; and so, it is very likely that you will become a great man—if only you remain a little child. All the world's great have been little boys who wanted the moon; running and climbing, they sometimes caught a firefly. But if one grow to a man's mind, that mind must see that it cannot have the moon and would not want it if it could—and so, it catches no fireflies."

"But did you never want the moon?" asked Henry in a voice hushed with the room's quiet.

"I wanted it. Above all desires I wanted it. I reached for it and then—then I grew to be a man, and a failure. But there is this gift for the failure; folk know he has failed, and they are sorry and kindly and gentle. He has the whole world with him; a bridge of contact with his own people; the cloth of mediocrity. But he who shields a firefly in his hands, caught in reaching for the moon, is doubly alone; he only can realize his true failure, can realize his meanness and fears and evasions.

"You will come to your greatness, and it may be in time you will be alone in your greatness and no friend anywhere; only those who hold you in respect or fear or awe. I am sorry for you, boy with the straight, clear eyes which look upward longingly. I am sorry for you, and—Mother Heaven! how I envy you."

Dusk was stealing into the mountain creases, filling them with purple mist. The sun cut itself on a sharp hill and bled into the valleys. Long shadows of the peaks crept out into the fields like stalking gray cats. When Merlin spoke, it was with a little laugh.

"Do not think deeply of my words," he said, "for I myself am not at all sure of them. Dreams you may know by a quality we call inconsistency—but how could you classify the lightning?" Now the night was closing in quickly, and Henry jumped to his feet.

"Oh, but I must be going! The dark is in!"

"Yes, you must go, but do not think closely of my words. I may have been trying to impress you with these words. Old men need a certain silent flattery when they have come to distrust that which is spoken. Only remember that Merlin talked with you. And if you come on the Welsh folk anywhere, singing my songs that were made so long ago, tell them that you know me; tell them that I am a glorious creature with blue wings. I don't want to be forgotten, Henry. That is greater horror to an old man than death—to be forgotten."

Henry said, "I must be going now; it's really dark. And thank you, sir, for telling me these things, but you see, I must be sailing outward to the Indies."

Merlin laughed softly. "Of course you must, Henry. And catch a big firefly, won't you. Good-by, child."

Henry looked back once as the black silhouette of the house sank behind the crag's shoulder, but no light had flashed behind the windows. Old Merlin sat there pleading with his harps, and they echoed him jeeringly.

The boy quickened his steps down the path. All below was a black lake, and the farm lights stars' reflections in its deep. The wind had died, leaving a thick silence on the hills. Everywhere the sad, soundless ghosts flitted about their haunting. Henry walked carefully, his eyes on the path which glimmered pale blue before him.

IV

On the path there in the dark, Henry's mind went back to the first speech of Merlin. Should he see Elizabeth before he went sailing away? He did not like her; sometimes he thought he had discovered hatred for her, and this he nursed and warmed only to feel it grow to a desire to see her.

She was a thing of mystery. All girls and women hoarded something they never spoke of. His mother had terrific secrets about biscuits, and cried, sometimes, for no known reason.

Another life went on inside of women—some women—ran parallel to their outward lives and yet never crossed them.

A year before, Elizabeth had been a pretty child who whispered to the other girls and giggled and pulled hair when he was about; and then suddenly she had changed. It was nothing Henry could see, exactly, but rather he felt that a deep, quiet understanding had been given her. It frightened him, this wisdom which had come all at once to Elizabeth.

Then there was her body—different somehow from his, and capable, it was whispered, of strange pleasures and alchemies. Even this flowering body she kept a secret thing. A time ago they had gone together to swim in the river, and she had been unconscious of it; but now she covered herself carefully from him and appeared stricken with the thought that he might see. Her new character frightened and embarrassed Henry.

Sometimes he dreamed of her, and waked in agony lest she should ever know his dream. And sometimes it was a strange, shadowy composite of Elizabeth and his mother that came to him in the night. After such a dream, the day brought loathing of himself and her. He considered himself an unnatural monster and her a kind of succubus incarnate. And he could tell no one of these things. The people would shun him.

He thought perhaps he would like to see her before he left. There was a strange power in her this year, a drawing yet repelling power which swayed his desire like a windblown reed. Other boys might have gone to her in the night and kissed her, after they had boasted a little of their going; but then, the other boys did not dream as he did, nor did they think of her, as he sometimes did, as a loathsome being. There was surely something monstrous about him, for he could not distinguish between desire and disgust. And then, she could embarrass him so easily.

No, certainly, he would not go to her. Where had Merlin—where had any one—caught the idea that he cared a farthing for her, the daughter of a poor tenant? Not worth bothering about!

Footsteps were coming down the path behind him, loud

clashes in the quiet night, and soon a quick, thin figure came up with him.

"Might it be William?" Henry asked politely, while the road-mender stopped in the path and shifted his pick from one shoulder to the other.

"It's William right enough. And what are you doing on the path, and the dark come?"

"I've been to see Merlin and to hear him talk."

"Pest on him! That's all he ever does now. Once he made songs—good, sweet songs as I could repeat to you if I'd a mind to—but now he roosts up on that Crag-top like an old molted eagle. Once when I was going past I spoke to him about it, too, as I can prove by him. I'm not a man to be holding my tongue when I've been thinking.

" 'Why are you making no more songs?' I said to him in a tone like that. 'Why are you making no more songs?' 'I have grown to be a man,' he answered, 'and there be no songs in a man. Only children make songs—children and idiots.' Pest on him! It's an idiot himself, is the thought is on me. But what did he say to you, the old white-beard?"

"Why, you see, I'm going to the Indies and—"

"The Indies, and are you? Ah, well—I was at London once. And all the people at London are thieves, dirty thieves. There was a man with a board and little flat sticks on it. 'Try your skill, friend?' he says. 'What stick has a black mark on the underside of it?' 'That one,' says I; and so it was. But the next time—Ah, well, he was a thief, too; all of them thieves.

"People there are at London, and they do nothing but drive about and about in carriages, up one street and down another, bowing to each other, while good men sweat out their lives in the fields and the mines to keep them bowing there. What chance have I or you, say, with all the fine, soft places taken up by robbers? And can you tell me the thieving price of an egg at London?"

"I must take this road now," said Henry. "I must go home."

"Indies." The road-mender sighed with longing. Then he spat in the trail. "Ah, well—I'll stake it's all thieves there, too."

The night was very black when Henry came at last to the

poor hut where Elizabeth lived. There was a fire in the middle of the floor, he knew, and the smoke drifted up and tried to get out at a small hole in the thatch. The house had no flooring, but only rushes strewn on the packed ground, and when the family slept they wrapped themselves in sheepskins and lay in a circle with their feet to the fire.

The windows were not glazed nor curtained. Henry could see old black-browed Twym and his thin, nervous wife, moving about inside. He watched for Elizabeth to pass the window, and when at last she did, he whistled a shrill bird-call. The girl stopped and looked out, but Henry was quiet in the dark. Then Elizabeth opened the door and stood framed against the inside light. The fire was behind her. Henry could see the black outline of her figure through her dress. He saw the fine curve of her legs and the swell of her hips. A wild shame filled him, for her and for himself. Without thought and without reason he ran away into the dark, gasping and almost sobbing under his breath.

V

Old Robert looked up hopefully when the boy came into the room, and then the hope died away and he turned quickly to the fire. But Mother Morgan jumped from her seat and went angrily to Henry.

"What is this foolishness? You going to the Indies!" she demanded.

"But, Mother, I must go; truly I must—and father understands. Can't you hear how the Indies are calling to me?"

"That I cannot! It's wicked nonsense is in it. A little child you are, and not to be trusted from home at all. Besides, your own father is going to tell you it may not be."

The strong jaw of the boy set like a rock and the muscles stood out in his cheeks. Suddenly there came a flash of anger into his eyes.

"Then, Mother, if you will not understand, I tell you that I am going the morrow—in spite of all of you."

Hurt pride chased incredulity from her face, and that, too, passed, leaving only pain. She shrank from the bewildering hurt. And Henry, when he saw what his words had done, went quickly to her.

"I'm sorry, Mother—so very sorry; but why can you not let me go as my father can? I don't want to hurt you, but I must go. Won't you see that?" He put his arm about her, but she would not look at him. Her eyes stared blankly straight in front of her.

She was so sure that her view was right. Throughout her life she had insulted and browbeaten and scolded her family, and they had known her little tyranny to be the outcropping of her love for them. But now that one of them, and he the child, had used the tone she spoke with every hour, it made a grim hurt that might never be quite healed again.

"You spoke with Merlin? What did he say to you?" asked Robert from the hearth.

Henry's mind flashed quickly to Elizabeth. "He talked of things that are not in my belief," he said.

"Well—it was only a chance," murmured Robert. "You've hurt your mother badly, boy," he went on. "I've never seen her so—so quiet." Then Robert straightened himself and his voice became firm.

"I have five pounds for you, son. It's little enough; I suppose I might give you a small matter more, but not enough to help much. And here is a letter recommending you to my brother, Sir Edward. He went out before the king was murdered, and for some reason—perhaps because he was quiet—old Cromwell has let him stay. If he is there when you come to Jamaica, you may present this letter; but it's a cold, strange man who takes great pride in his rich acquaintance and might be a little annoyed with a poor relative. And so I do not know that good will come of this letter. He would dislike you unless you were able to see nothing funny in a man who looks like me, only strides about with a silver sword and plumes on his head. I laughed once, and he has not been a near brother to me since. But keep the letter; it may help you with other people if not with your uncle."

He looked at his wife sitting huddled in the shadow. "Will we not have supper, Mother?"

She made no sign that she heard him, and Robert himself poured the pot and brought the food to the table.

It is a cruel thing to lose a son for whom you have lived continuously. Somehow, she had imagined him always beside her—a little boy, and always beside her. She tried to think of the coming days, and Henry not there, but the thought was shattered on the bleak wall of a lean imagination. She attempted to consider him ungrateful so to run away from her; she recalled the harsh blow he had dealt her—but always the mind snapped back. Henry was her little boy, and, naturally, he could not be mean nor treacherous. In some way, when all this talk and pain had drifted into the thin air, he would be yet beside her, deliciously underfoot.

Her mind which had been always a scalpel of reality, her imagination which dealt purely with the present outsides of things, went fondling back to the baby who had crawled and stumbled and learned to talk. She forgot that he was going away at all, so deeply was she laved in a revery of the silver past.

He was being baptized in a long white dress. All the water of baptism collected in one big drop and rolled down his blobby nose, and she, in her passion for tidiness, wiped it off with a handkerchief and then wondered if he shouldn't be baptized again. The young Curate was perspiring and choking over his words. He was lately come to the parish and was only a local boy anyway. He was really too young, she thought, to be trusted with an affair of this importance. Perhaps it wouldn't take. He might get the words in the wrong order or something. And then—Robert had made a mess of his waistcoat again. He never could get the right button in the right hole to save him. It made him look all wracked to one side. She must go and tell Robert about his waistcoat before people in the church noticed it. Small things like that were surest to cause talk. But could she trust this foolish young curate not to let the baby fall while she went?

———

Supper was over, and aged Gwenliana rose from the table to struggle back to her seat before the fire. Quietly she was slipping back into her friendly future.

"What time will you be starting, the morning?" asked Robert.

"Why, about seven, I think, father." Henry tried to sound casual.

The ancient woman paused in her journey and looked sharply at him.

"Now where is Henry going?" she asked.

"Why, don't you know? Henry is going away from us in the morning. He is going to the Indies."

"And not coming back again?" she questioned anxiously.

"Not for a time, anyway. It's a great distance."

"Why, but—I must lay the future before him then, that's what I must do—before him like the white pages of an open book," she exclaimed in pleased excitement. "I must tell him of the future and the things in it. Let me look at you, boy."

Henry went to her and sat at her feet while she talked. There is truly a spell in the ancient Cumric tongue. It is a speech made for prophecy.

"Of course," Gwenliana said, "if I had only known of this to-day I should have got the shoulder bone of a new-killed sheep. It's a means of greater antiquity and better thought of than just snap-prophecy. And since I have grown old and rusty and lame I cannot go about any more to meet the spirits that wander the high-road. You cannot do as well if there is not the means in you to walk among the strolling dead and listen to their thoughts. But I shall give you a thorough life, grandson, and as fine a future as I ever pondered on."

She leaned back in her chair and closed her eyes, but if one had looked closely he might have seen their glint below the lids where they peered out at the set face of the boy. A long time she sat entranced, and it seemed that her old brain combed out the tangles of the past to make a straight, tellable future. At length she spoke in the low, hoarse, chanting voice that is reserved for dread things.

"This is the tale out of Abred, when earth and water battled.

And from the impact of their clash was born a little, struggling life to squirm upward through the circles toward Gwynfyd, the sheening Purity. In that first blundering flesh is written the world's history and the world's journey through the Void.

"And thou—often has Annwn set its fanged maw to entrap the little pinch of life thou carryest about, but thou hast made thy path to go around its snaring. A thousand centuries hast thou lived since earth and sea struggled in thy generation, and a thousand eons shalt thou carry about the little pinch of life that was given thee, so only thou shelterest it from Annwn, the Chaos."

Always she began her prophecies thus. It was a thing taught her by a wandering Bard, to whom it had come, from Bard to Bard, back and back to the white Druids. Gwenliana paused to let her words find footing in the boy's brain. She continued:

"This is the tale of thy present wandering. Thou shalt become a great shining for the Divine, teaching the things of God." Her secret eyes saw the boy's face fall in disappointment, and she cried:

"But wait a moment! I go too far ahead. There shall be fighting and shedding of blood, and the sword shall be thy first bride." Henry's face lighted up with pleasure. "The whisper of thy name shall be a foregathering command to the warriors of the world. Thou shalt sack the cities of the infidel and spoil him of his plunderings. The terror will precede thee like a screaming eagle over the shields of men." She knew, now, that her forecast was a success, but she hastened on to greater glories.

"The government of islands and continents shall be thine, and thou shalt bring justice and peace to them. And at last, when thou art girded with honor and repute, thou shalt marry a white-souled maiden of mighty rank—a girl of good family, and wealthy," she finished. Her eyes opened and she glanced about for their approbation.

"I could have done better with a sheep's shoulder," she said plaintively, "or if I could be walking about on the high-road now and then; but age robs you of your little pleasures and leaves you with only a cold, quiet waiting."

"Ah, well, mother, it was a good prophecy," said Old Robert; "as good as I ever heard you make. You are just coming to the peak of your occult strength, I think. And you have taken away my dread and reassured me about Henry's going. Now I am only proud of what my boy is to be. Only I wish he didn't have to kill people."

"Well, then—if you think it was really good!" said Gwenli-ana happily. "It did seem to me that the air was propitious and my eyes clear to-night. Still, I should have liked a sheep's shoulder." She closed her eyes contentedly and went to dozing.

VI

All night Old Robert tossed nervously in his bed, and his wife lay motionless beside him. At last, when the darkness was changing to silver gray in the window, she rose quietly.

"What? Have you not been sleeping, Mother? And where are you going?"

"I am going to Henry, now. I must talk with him. Perhaps he will listen to me." Only a moment she was gone, and then she returned and laid her head on Robert's arm.

"Henry is gone," she said, and her whole body stiffened a little.

"Gone? But how could he do that? Here is his first coward-ice, Mother. He was afraid to say good-by to us. But I am not sorry for his fear, because it holds the sureness of his sorrow. He could not bear to hear the thing of his feeling in words."

"Why, Mother!" He was startled at her silence and her cold-ness. "He will come back to us, Mother, in a little; perhaps when the spring grass is lifting out. Surely he will come back to us. I swear it. Can't you believe it? He is gone only for a week—a few days. Oh, believe me!

"The years are gone from us surely, dear, and now we are as we were—do you remember?—only closer—closer of all the things that have been. We are rich with all the little pictures of the past and the things he played with. They can never go from us while life is here."

She did not weep nor move nor even seem to breathe.

"Oh, my wife—Elizabeth—say that you will believe in his coming, very soon—soon—before you have missed him," he cried wildly. "Do not lie there silently and lost. He will be here when the Spring comes in. You must believe it, dear—my dear." Very softly he stroked the still cheek beside him with his great tender fingers.

VII

He had crept from the house in the false dawn, and started briskly walking on the road to Cardiff. There was a frozen, frightened thing in his heart, and a wondering whether he wanted to go at all. To his mind the fear had argued that if he waited to say good-by he would not be able to leave the stone house, not even for the Indies.

The sky was graying as he went by pastures where he had tossed and played, and by the quarry where was the cave in which he and his friends acted the delightful game of "Robbers," with Henry always the Wild Wag, Twym Shone Catti, by acclamation.

The mountains stood sharply before him, like cardboard things, and along their rims a silver fringe. A little wind of dawn blew down the slopes, fresh and sweet smelling, bearing the rich odor of moistened earth and leaves. Horses whinnied shrilly at him as he passed, then came close and gently touched him with their soft noses; and coveys of birds, feeding on belated night crawlers in the half dark, flew up at his approach with startled protests.

By sun-up there were new miles behind him. As the yellow ball slid from behind the peaks, coloring all the tattered clouds of the mountains, Henry drew a thick curtain down against the past. The pain and loneliness that had walked with him in the dark were pushed back and left behind him. Cardiff was ahead. He was coming to new country which he had never seen before, and below the morning horizon, faint and glorious, seemed to glow the green crown of the Indies.

He passed through villages whose names were unknown to

him; friendly little clusters of rude huts, and the people staring at him as at a stranger. It was a joyous thing to young Henry. Always he had stared at others who were strangers, dreaming their destinations and the delicious mystery that sent them forth. The name of Stranger made them grand beings with mighty purposes. And now he was a stranger to be thought about and stared at with a certain reverence. He wanted to shout, "I'm on my way to the Indies," to widen their dull eyes for them and raise their respect. Silly, spineless creatures, he thought them, with no dream and no will to leave their sodden, dumpy huts.

The land changed. He was coming out of the mountains to a broad, unbounded country of little rolls and flat lands. He saw large burrows like the holes of tremendous gophers, and dirty black men coming out of them with sacks of coals on their backs. The miners emptied their sacks in a pile on the ground and then walked back into the burrows. He noticed that they stooped when they walked as though the heavy bags were still bearing them down.

Mid-day came, and a long, clear afternoon, and still he trudged on. There was a new odor in the air, the sweet, compelling breath of the sea. He wanted to break into a run toward it like a thirsty horse. In the late afternoon an army of black clouds drew over the sky. A wind rushed out with snow in its breath, and the grasses bowed before it.

Still he went on into the gathering storm until it was armed with sleet which pricked his face viciously, and until the cold went piercing through his jacket. There were occasional houses to either side of the road, but Henry would seek shelter and food at none of them. He did not know the customs of this place, nor the prices of things, and his five pounds must be intact when he came at last to Cardiff.

At length, when his hands were blue and his face raw with the wild sleet, he crawled into a lonely, stone barn filled with the summer's hay. It was warm, there, and quiet after the screaming of the wind in his ears. The hay was sweet with the honey dried in its stems. Henry burrowed into the soft bed and slept.

———

It was dark night when he awakened. Half-dreaming, he remembered where he was, and at once the thoughts which he had shut from him the day before thronged back with clamoring, strident voices.

"You are a fool," said one. "Remember the big room and the pikes and the bright fire! Where are they now? Oh, you will not see them any more. They are gone out like things of dreams, and you do not even know where dreams go. You are a fool!"

"No, no; listen to me! Think of me! Why did you not wait for Elizabeth? Were you afraid? Yes, you were afraid. This boy is a coward, brothers. He is afraid of a small girl with yellow hair—a tenant's daughter."

A sad, slow voice broke in. "Think of your mother, Henry. She was sitting straight and still when you last saw her. And you did not go to her. You only looked from the doorway as you went. Perhaps she has died in her chair, with the look of hurt in her eyes. How can you tell? And Robert, your own father— Will you think of him, now—lonely, and sad, and lost. It's your doing, Henry; because you wanted to go to the Indies you did not think of any one else."

"And what do you know of the future?" asked a tiny, fearful voice. "It will be cold, and perhaps you will freeze. Or some stranger may kill you for your money, little as it is. Such things have happened. Always there has been some one to look after you and to see that you were comfortable. Oh, you will starve! you will freeze! you will die! I am sure of it!"

Then the noises of the barn edged in among his tormentors. The storm was past, but a breeze sighed around corners with infinite, ghostly sadness. Now and again it voiced a little wail of sorrow. There was a creaking in the hay as though every straw squirmed and tried to move stealthily. Bats flitted about in the dark gnashing their tiny teeth, and the mice were screaming horribly. Bats and mice seemed to be glaring at him from obscurity with small, mean eyes.

He had been alone before, but never so thoroughly alone, among new things, in a place he did not know. The terror was growing and swelling in his breast. Time had become an idling worm which crawled ahead the merest trifle, stopped and waggled its blind head, and crawled again. It seemed that hours passed over him like slow, sailing clouds while he lay shivering with fright. At last an owl flew in and circled above him, screeching maniacally. The boy's overstrung nerves snapped, and he ran whimpering from the barn and down the road toward Cardiff.

CHAPTER 2

For more than a century Britain had watched with impatience while Spain and Portugal, with the permission of the Pope, divided the New World and patrolled their property to keep out interlopers. It was a bitter thing to England there imprisoned by the sea. But finally Drake had burst the barrier and sailed the forbidden oceans in his little *Golden Hind*. The great red ships of Spain considered Drake only a tiny, stinging fly, an annoying thing to be killed for its buzzing; but when the fly had gutted their floating castles, burned a town or two, and even set a trap for the sacred treasure train across the Isthmus, they were forced to alter their conception. The fly was a hornet, a scorpion, a viper, a dragon. They named him El Draque, and a fear of the English grew up in the New World.

When the Armada fell before the English and the angry sea, Spain was terrified at this new force which emanated from such a very little island. It was sad to think of these bright carven ships lying on the bottom or torn to fragments on the Irish coast.

And Britain thrust her hand into the Caribbean; a few islands came under her power—Jamaica, Barbados. Now the products of the home island could be sold in colonies. It added prestige to a little country to have colonies, provided they were strongly populated; and England began to populate her new possessions.

Younger sons, spendthrifts, ruined gentlemen sailed out for the Indies. It was a fine way to be rid of a dangerous man. The king had only to grant him land in the Indies and then express the desire that he live on his property and cultivate the rich soil there for the good of the English crown.

The out-sailing ships were crowded with colonists; gamblers, touts, pimps, dissenters, papists—all to own the land, and none to work it. The slave ships of Portugal and the Netherlands could not move black flesh from Africa fast enough to supply the increasing demands of those who clamored for workers.

Then felons were gathered out of the prisons, and vagrants from the streets of London; beggars who stood all day before the church doors; those suspected of witchcraft or treason or leprosy or papism; and all these were sent to work the plantations under orders of indenture. It was a brilliant plan; the labor needed was supplied, and the crown actually received money for the worthless bodies of those it once fed and clothed and hanged. More could be made of this. Whole sheaves of orders of indenture, ready sealed by the government, with blank spaces for names, were sold to certain captains of ships. They were given instructions to act with extreme discretion about the names they filled in.

And rows of coffee and oranges and cane and cocoa grew and ever spread out on the islands. There was some little trouble, of course, when the terms of indenture ran out. But the slums of London bred new slaves quickly enough, God knew! and the king was never without a fine supply of enemies.

England was becoming a sea power with her governors and palaces and clerks in the New World, and ships of manufactured things were sailing out of Liverpool and Bristol in ever increasing numbers.

I

With breaking day, Henry was in the outskirts of Cardiff, all his terror gone and a new blossoming wonder in him. For it was an unbelievable thing, this city of houses, rank on rank— no two of them exactly alike—the lines of them stretching out endlessly like an army in the mud. He had never considered such magnitude when people spoke of cities.

The shops were opening their shutters, putting their goods on display, and Henry stared wide-eyed into every one as he passed. Down a long street he went until he came at last to the docks with their fields of masts like growing wheat, and their clouds and cobwebs of brown rigging in an apparent frenzy of disorder. There was loading of bundles and barrels and slaughtered animals into some of the ships, and others were sending out of their curved bellies goods in queer foreign boxes and sacks of braided straw. A tremendous bustle of excitement lived about the docks. The boy felt that holiday tingle which had come to him when men were putting up pavilions for a fair at home.

A loud song burst out of a ship just getting under weigh, and the words were clear, beautiful foreign words. The water slapping smooth hulls was a joy to him to the point of pain. He felt that he had come home again to a known, loved place, after days and nights of mad delirium. Now a great song of many voices came from the moving barque, and its brown anchor rose from the water; its sails dropped from the yards and caught the morning wind. The barque slid from its berth and moved softly down the channel.

Onward he walked to where the ships were careened, showing weeds and barnacles, gathered in many oceans, hanging to their shining sides. Here was the short, quick hammering of the calkers and the rasp of iron on wood, and brusque commands built up to roars by the speaking trumpets.

When the sun was well up, Henry began to feel hungry. He wandered slowly back to the town to find his breakfast, reluctant to leave the docks even for food. Now the crimps were coming out of their holes, and the sniffling gamblers who preyed on sailors. Here and there a disheveled, sleepy-eyed woman scurried homeward as though fearing to be caught by the sun. Seamen on shore leave rubbed their puffed eyes and looked into the sky for weather signs as they lounged against the walls. Henry wondered what these men had seen in the sailing days of their lives. He stepped aside for a line of carts and tumbrils loaded with boxes and bales for the ships, and immediately had to dodge another line coming away, loaded with goods from across the sea.

He came at last to a busy inn. "The Three Dogs" it was

called, and there they were on the sign looking very like three
startled dromedaries. Henry entered and found a large apartment crowded with people. Of a fat man in an apron he asked
whether he could get breakfast.

"Have you money?" the host asked suspiciously.

Henry let the light fall on a gold piece in his hand, and, as he
had made the sign of power, the apron was bowing and gently
pulling him by the arm. Henry ordered his breakfast and stood
looking around the inn.

There were a great many people in the room sitting at the
long tables or leaning against the walls; some, even, were seated
on the floor. A little serving girl went among them with a tray
of liquors. Some were Italians from the ships of Genoa and
Venice, come with rare woods and spices that had been carried overland on camel back from the Indian Ocean to Byzan-
tium. Frenchmen were there from the wine boats of Bordeaux
and Calais, with an occasional square-faced, blue-eyed Basque
among them. Swedes and Danes and Finns were in from the
whalers of the north ocean, dirty men who smelled of decaying
blubber; and at some of the tables were cruel Dutchmen who
made a business of carrying black slaves from Guinea to Brazil. Scattered among these foreign men were a few Cambrian
farmers, looking frightened and self-conscious and alone. They
had brought pigs and sheep from the country for victualing
the ships, and now were bolting their food so that they might
get home again before nightfall. These looked for security to
three man o' war's men wearing the King's uniform who talked
together by the door.

Young Henry lost himself in the lovely clamor of the room.
He was hearing new speech and seeing new sights: the ear-rings
of the Genoese; the short knife-like swords of the Dutch; the
colors of faces from beef red to wind-bitten brown. All day he
might have stood there with no knowledge in him of the passing of time.

A big hand took his elbow, a hand gloved in callouses; and
Henry looked down into the broad, guileless face of an Irish
seaman.

"Will you be sitting here, young man, along side of an honest

sailor out of Cork named Tim?" As he spoke he squeezed violently against his neighbor, flinging him sideways and leaving a
narrow space on the bench end for the boy. There are no men
like the Irish for being brutally gentle. And Henry, as he took
the seat, did not know that the sailor out of Cork had seen his
gold piece.

"Thank you," he said. "And where is it that you go
sailing?"

"Ah! any place that ships go I do be sailing," replied Tim.
"I'm an honest sailor out of Cork with no fault on me save
never having the shine of a coin to my pocket. And I wonder,
now, how I'm to be paying for the fine breakfast, and me with
never a shine," he said slowly and emphatically.

"Why, if you have no money, I'll buy your breakfast—so you
will be telling me of the sea and ships."

"I knew it was a gentleman you were," Tim cried. "I knew it
the minute my eyes landed on you soft like— And a small drink
to be starting with?" He shouted for his drink without waiting
for Henry's consent, and when it came, raised the brown liquor
to his eyes.

"Uisquebaugh, the Irish call it. That means water of life;
and the English call it 'Whiskey'—only water. Why! if water
had the fine body and honest glow of this, it's sailing I would
give up and take to swimming!" He laughed uproariously and
tipped the glass up.

"I'm going to the Indies," Henry observed, with thought to
bring him back to talking of the sea.

"The Indies? Why, so am I, to-morrow in the morning; out
for Barbados with knives and sickles and dress goods for the
plantations. It's a good ship—a Bristol ship—but the master's a
hard man all stiff with religion out of the colony at Plymouth.
Hell-fire he roars at you and calls it prayer and repentance, but
I'm thinking there's joy in all the burning to him. We'll all burn
a good time if he has his way. I do not understand the religion
of him; there's never an Ave Mary about it, and so how can it
be religion at all?"

"Do you think—do you think, perhaps—I could go in your
ship with you?" Henry asked chokingly.

The lids drew down over the ingenuous eyes of Tim.

"If it was ten pound you had," he said slowly, and then, seeing the sorrow on the boy's face, "five, I mean—"

"I have something over four, now," Henry broke in with sadness.

"Well, and four might do it, too. You give me your four pound, and I'll be talking with the master. It's not a bad man when you get to be knowing him, only queer and religious. No, don't be looking at me like that. You come along with me. I wouldn't run off with the four pound of a boy that bought my breakfast at all." His face bloomed with a great smile.

"Come," he said; "let's be drinking that you go with us in the *Bristol Girl*. Uisquebaugh for me and wine of Oporto for you!" Then breakfast arrived and they fell to eating. After a few mouthfuls Henry said:

"My name is Henry Morgan. What is your other name besides Tim?"

And the sailor laughed heartily.

"Why, if there was ever a name to me but Tim you might find it kicking around in a wheel rut at Cork. The father and mother of me did not wait to be telling me my name. But Tim was on me without giving. Tim is a kind of free name that you can just take and no one to mention it, like the little papers the Dissenters be leaving in the streets, and they scuttling off not to be seen with them. You can breathe Tim like the air, and no one to put hand on you."

Breakfast over, they went into the street, busy with the trade of carters and orange boys and peddling old women. The town was crying its thousand wares, and it seemed that delicate things from the far, unearthly corners of the world had been brought by the ships and dumped like clods on the dusty counters of Cardiff: lemons; cases of coffee and tea and cocoa; bright Eastern rugs; and the weird medicines of India to make you see things that are not, and to feel pleasures that fly away again. Standing in the streets were barrels and earthen jugs of wine from the banks of the Loire and the Peruvian slopes.

They came again to the docks and the beautiful ships. The smell of tar and sunburned hemp and the sweetness of the sea breathed in to them from off the water. At last, far down the row, Henry saw a great black ship, and *Bristol Girl* painted in letters of gold on her prow. And the town and all the flat hulks became ugly and squalid beside this beauty of the sea. The curved running lines of her and the sensuous sureness of her were tonic things to make you gasp in your breath with pleasure. New white sails clung to her yards like long, slender cocoons of silk worms, and there was fresh yellow paint on her decks. She lay there, lifting slightly on a slow swell, champing, impatient to be flying off to any land of your imagination. A black Sheban queen she was, among the dull brown boats of the harbor.

"Oh, it's a grand ship—a fine ship," cried Henry, wonder-struck.

Tim was proud. "But only come aboard of her, and see the fittings—all new. I'll be talking with the master about you."

Henry stood in the waist while the big seaman walked aft and pulled his cap before a lean skeleton of a man in a worn uniform.

"I have a boy," he said, though Henry could not hear; "a boy that's set his heart in the Indies, and I'm thinking you might be liking to take him, sir."

The hungry master scowled at him.

"Is he a strong boy who might be some good in the islands, Bo's'n? So many of them die within the month, and there you have trouble the next trip."

"He is there, behind me, sir. You can see him yourself, stand-ing there—and very well made and close knit he is, too."

The hungry master appraised Henry, running his eyes from the sturdy legs to the full chest. His approval grew.

"He is a strong boy, all right; and good work for you, Tim. You shall have drink money of it and a little extra ration of rum at sea. But does he know anything about the arrangement?"

"Never a bit."

"Well, then, don't tell him. Put him to working in the galley. He'll think he's working out his passage. No use of caterwaul-ing and disturbing the men off watch. Let him find out when he gets there." The master smiled and paced away from Tim.

"You can be going with us in the ship," the sailor cried, and Henry could not move for his pleasure. "But," Tim continued seriously, "the four pound is not enough for passage. You'll be working a bit in the galley and we sailing."

"Anything," Henry said, "anything I'll do, so only I can go with you."

"Then let's ourselves go ashore and have a toast to a fine, free voyage; uisquebaugh for me, and that same grand wine for you."

They sat in a dusty shop whose walls were lined with bottles of all shapes and volumes, little pudgy flasks to giant demijohns. After a time they sang together, beating out the measures with their hands and smiling foolishly at each other. But at length the warm wine of Oporto filled the boy with a pleasant sadness. He felt that there were tears coming to his eyes, and he was rather glad of it. It would show Tim that he had his sorrows—that he was not just a feather-head boy with a craving to go to the Indies. He would reveal his depths.

"Do you know, Tim," he said, "there was a girl I came away from, and she was named Elizabeth. Her hair was gold—gold like the morning. And on the night before I came away, I called to her and she came to me in the dark; the dark was all about us like a tent, and cold. She cried and cried for me to stay, even when I told her of the fine things and the trinkets and the silks I would bring back to her in a little time. She would not be comforted at all, and it's a sad thing on me to be thinking of her crying there for my leaving." The full tears came into his eyes.

"I know," said Tim softly. "I know it's a sad thing to a man to be leaving a girl and running off to sea. Haven't I left hundreds of them—and all beautiful? But here's another cup to you, boy. Wine is better to a woman than all the sweet pastes of France, and a man drinking it. Wine makes every woman lovely. Ah! if the homely ones would only put out a little font of wine in the doors of their houses like the holy water to a church, there would be more marriage in the towns. A man would never know the lack they had for looks. But have another cup of the grand wine, sad boy, and it may be a princess, and you leaving her behind you."

II

They were starting for the Indies—the fine, far Indies where boys' dreams lived. The great sun of the morning lay struggling in gray mist, and on the deck the seamen swarmed like the angry populace of a broken hive. There were short orders and sailors leaping up the shrouds to edge along the yards. Circling men were singing the song of the capstan while the anchors rose out of the sea and clung to the sides like brown, dripping moths.

Off for the Indies—the white sails knew it as they flung out and filled delicately as silken things; the black ship knew it and rode proudly on the fleeing tide before a fresh little morning wind. Carefully the *Bristol Girl* crept out of the shipping and down the long channel.

The mist was slowly mixing with the sky. Now the coast of Cambria became blue and paler blue until it faded into the straight horizon like a mad vision of the desert. The black mountains were a cloud, and then a trifle of pale smoke; then Cambria was gone, as though it had never been.

Porlock they passed on the port side, and Illfracombe, and many vague villages tucked in the folds of Devon. The fair, sweet wind carried them by Stratton and Camelford. Cornwall was slipping off behind them, league on blue league. Then Land's End, the pointed tip of Britain's chin; and, as they rounded to the southward, Winter came in at last.

The sea rose up and snarled at them, while the ship ran before the crying dogs of the wind like a strong, confident stag; ran bravely under courses and spritsail. The wind howled out of Winter's home in the north, and the *Bristol Girl* mocked it across its face to the southwest. It was cold; the freezing shrouds twanged in the wind like great harp strings plucked by a demented giant, and the yards groaned their complaint to the tugging sails.

Four wild days the persistent storm chased them out to sea with the ship in joy at the struggle. The seamen gathered in the forecastle to boast of her fleetness and the tight shape of her. And in this time Henry exulted like a young god. The wind's frenzy was his frenzy. He would stand on the deck, braced against a mast, face into the wind, cutting it with his chin as the prow cut the water, and a chanting exultation filled his chest to bursting—joy like a pain. The cold wiped off the lenses of his eyes so that he saw more clearly into the drawn distance lying in a circle around him. Here was the old desire surfeited with a new; for the winds brought longing to have sweeping wings and the whole, endless sky for scope. The ship was a rocking, quaking prison for him who would fly ahead and up. Ah! to be a god and ride on the storm! not under it. Here was the intoxication of the winds, a desire which satisfied desire while it led his yearning onward. He cried for the shoulders of omnipotence, and the elements blew into his muscles a new strength.

Then, as quickly as the devil servants of the year had rushed at them, they slunk away, leaving a clear, clean sea. The ship rode under full sail before the eternal trade wind. It is a fresh, fair wind out of heaven, breathed by the God of Navigation for the tall ships with sails. All the tension was gone from them; the sailors played about the deck like wild, strong children— for there is young happiness in the trade wind.

Sunday came, a day of sullen fear and foreboding on the *Bristol Girl*. Henry finished his work in the galley and went on deck. An aged seaman was sitting on a hatch plaiting a long splice. His fingers seemed each a nimble intelligence as they worked, for their master never looked at them. Instead, his small blue eyes, after the manner of sailors' eyes, looked out beyond the end of things.

"So you would know the secrets of the lines?" he said, without moving his gaze from the horizon. "Well, you must just watch. It's so long I've been doing it that my old head has forgotten how; only my fingers remember. If I think what I'm doing I get muddled up. Will you be a sailor and go aloft one day?"

"Why, I'd like to, if I could learn the workings," Henry said.

"It's not so hard to learn the workings. You must learn first to bear things that landsmen never heard of. That's the first thing. It's very cruel, but you may never leave it once you start. Here I've been trying to take my old hulk ashore and berth it in front of a fire for a dozen years. I want to think awhile and die. But it's no use. Every time I find myself running my legs off to get aboard some ship or other."

He was interrupted by a vicious ringing of the ship's bell.

"Come," he said; "the master will be telling us the hot tales now."

The skull-faced master stood before his crew, armed with his God. The men looked fearfully at him, as small birds gaze at an approaching snake, for his faith was in his eyes and words of fury fell from his thin lips.

"God has struck you with only the tittle of His shattering might," he shouted. "He has shown you the strength of His little finger that you may repent before you go screaming in hell-fire. Hear the name of the Lord in the frightful wind and repent you of your whorings and your blasphemies! Ah! He will punish you even for the wicked thoughts in your heads.

"There is a parable in the sea that should close about your throats like a freezing hand and choke you with the terror. But now the storm is done you have forgotten it. You are happy, and contrition is not in you. But take warning of the lesson of the Lord. Repent! Repent! or the wrath destroys you."

He swung his arms wildly and spoke of the poor lonely dead, suffering and burning for dear human faults; and at last he sent his men terrified away.

"That is not so," said the old sailor fiercely to Henry. "Do not be taking stock in his crazy talk. Who made the storm— God or devil—made it for itself and took joy of it. What being could hurl the wind so would not be bothering himself about a chip of a boat floating in immensity. I know I would not, if I were that god or devil."

The Bo's'n, Tim, had come up with his last words, and now he took Henry's arm protectingly.

"True for you," he said; "but do not let it get back to him that you say such things or even hear them with your ears, or he will be demonstrating the might of God to you with a rope's end. He and his God are a hard pair to be getting down on you, and you a boy scrubbing pots in the galley."

The trade wind blew on unceasingly, and, when his scouring and peeling were done, Henry talked with the men while he laid hand to the ropes and went aloft and learned the names and workings of the ship's gear. The sailors found him a quiet, courteous boy with a way of looking at them as though their speech were a great gift and they wise, kind men to be giving it to him; and so they taught him what they could, for very plainly this boy was born to the sea. He learned the short and long haul chanteys, the one quick and nervous and the other a slow, swinging rhythm. He sang with them the songs of death and mutiny and blood in the sea. To his lips came the peculiar, clean swearing of sailors; phrases of filth and blasphemy and horror, washed white by their utter lack of meaning in his mouth.

And in the nights he lay back quietly while the men talked of wonders seen and imagined; of mile-long serpents which coiled about ships and crushed and swallowed them, and of turtles so huge that they had trees and streams and whole villages on their backs and only sank once in five hundred years. Under the swinging lamps they told how Finns could whistle up a deadly storm for their revenge; how there were sea-rats that swam to the ships and gnawed holes through the planking until the ships sank. They spoke shudderingly of how one, sighting the dread, slimy kraken, might never see land again for the curse that was on him. Water spouts were in their speech, and mooing cows that lived in the sea and suckled their calves like land cows; and ghost ships sailing endlessly about the ocean looking for a lost port, their gear worked by seamen who were bleached skeletons. And Henry, lying there, reached breathless for their words with his avidity.

On such a night, Tim stretched himself and said, "I know nothing of your big snakes at all, nor have I seen the kraken, God save me! But I've a bit of a tale myself if you'll be listening.

" 'Twas when I was a boy like this one here, and I sailing in a free ship that tucked about the ocean picking up here and there—sometimes a few black slaves and now and then a gold ring from a Spanish craft that couldn't help itself—whatever we could get. We had a master by election and no papers at all, but there were different kinds of flags, and they on the bridge. If we did be picking out a man o' war in the glass, then we ran for it.

"Well, anyway, as I'm telling you, one morning there was a little barque to the starboard, and we wetting sail to run her down; and so we did, too. Spanish, she was, and little enough in her but salt and green hides. But when we turned out the cabin there was a tall, straight woman with black hair to her, and a long white forehead, and the slenderest fingers I ever looked on with my eyes. So we took her aboard of us and didn't take the rest. The captain was for leading the woman to the quarter deck along side of him, when the bo's'n stepped up.

" 'We're a free crew,' he says, 'and you the master by election. We want the woman, too,' he says, 'and if we don't be getting her there'll be a bit mutiny in a minute.' The captain scowled around, but there was the crew scowling back at him; so he pulled up his shoulders and laughed—a nasty kind of laugh.

" 'How will you be deciding?' he asks, thinking there would be a grand fight over the woman. But the bo's'n slipped some dice out of his pocket and threw them on the deck.

" 'We'll use these!' he says, and in a minute every man of the crew was on his knees and reaching for the dice. But I was taking a long sight of the woman there alone. I says to myself, 'That do be a hard kind of woman, and one that might be doing cruel things to hurt the man she hated. No, my boy,' I says, 'you'd best not be coming in on this game.'

"But just then the dark woman ran to the rail and picked a round shot out of the racks and jumped overside, hugging it in her arms. That was all! We ran to the rail and looked—but only a few bubbles there were to show.

"Well, it was two nights later, the afterwatch was for running into the fo'c'sle and the hair bristling up on his head. 'There's a white thing, and it swimming after us,' he says, 'and the looks on it like the woman that went overboard.'

"Of course we ran and looked over the taffrail, and I could

see nothing at all; but the others said there was a thing with long white hands reaching out for our stern post, not swimming but just dragging after us like the ship was lodestone and it a bit of iron. You can know there was little enough sleeping that night. Those that did dust off cried and moaned in their sleep; and I need not tell you what that same thing signifies.

"The next night, up comes the bo's'n out of the hold screaming like a mad one, and the hair all turned gray on his head. We did be holding him and petting him awhile, and finally he managed to whisper,

" 'I seen it! Oh, my God, I seen it! There was two long, white, soft-looking hands with slender fingers—and they came through the side and started to ripping the planks off like they were paper. Oh, my God! Save me!'

"Then we felt the ship give a list and start to settling down.

"Well, three of us came floating ashore on an extra spar, and two of them crazed—poor souls—and wild like cats. I never did be hearing whether any others were saved or not, but I'm thinking not. And that's the nearest I've ever seen with my eyes the things you do be talking of. But they say on clear nights in the Indian Ocean you can be seeing the poor murdered Hindu ghosts chasing the dead da Gama about in the sky. And I have heard that these same Hindus are a very unfruitful people to pick out, and you going in for murder."

From the first day, the cook had taken it upon himself to instruct young Henry. The man seemed to crave to give information. It was a wistful instruction, as though he feared every minute to be contradicted. He was a gray man, the cook, with sad brown eyes like a dog's eyes. There was something of a priest about him, and something of a dull lecturer, and something of a thug. His speech had the university in it, and his unclean habits the black, bitter alleys of London. He was gentle and kind and stealthily insincere. No one would ever give him a chance to prove himself trustworthy, because the whisper seemed to come from him that if it were in the least worthwhile he would be treacherous.

Now they had sailed into a warm sea, and a warm wind

drove them on. Henry and the cook would stand at the rail, watching the triangle fins of sharks cut back and forth across their wake waiting for refuse. They saw little brown clusters of weed go floating by, and the leisurely, straight-swimming pilot fish on the point of the prow. Once the cook pointed to the brown birds with long, slender wings following them; hanging, hovering, dipping, swaying, always flying, never resting.

"See these restless ones," the man said. "Like questing souls they are, indeed; and some say they are the souls of sailors drowned, souls so thick with sins that they may never rest from one year to another. Others swear that these birds lay their eggs in floating nests built on the planks of lost ships; and others, still, that they have no nests at all but are born full grown of the white lip of a wave and instantly start their life-long flight. Ay! the restless ones."

The ship started a school of fliers that skipped along the wave tops like shining silver coins.

"These are the ghosts of treasures lost at sea," the cook went on, "the murder things, emeralds and diamonds and gold; the sins of men, committed for them, stick to them and make them haunt the ocean. Ah! it's a poor thing if a sailor will not make a grand tale about it."

Henry pointed to a great tortoise asleep on the surface. "And what is the tale of the turtles?" he asked.

"Nothing; only food. It is not likely that a man will be making romances about the thing he eats. Such things are too close to him, and the romance contaminated out of them. But these same beasts have been the saving of a number of ships, and the means of making flesh on some that might otherwise be white bones on the deck of a derelict. The meat of turtles is sweet and good. Sometimes when the buccaneers are not in the way of getting wild beef, they stock their ships with these and so sail."

The sun had rushed below the water as they spoke. Far off, one black cloud whipped out tongue after tongue of dazzling lightning, but all the sky save that one spot was silken blue-black, littered with swarms of stars.

"You promised to speak with me of those same buccaneers,"

Henry begged; "they whom you call the Brethren of the Coast. Tell me, did you ever sail with them?"

The cook shifted uneasily. "There's peace between Spain and England," he said. "I would not be breaking the King's peace. No, I never sailed with them; no. But I have heard things which may be true. I have heard that the buccaneers are great fools. They plunder rich prizes and then throw their gains to the tavern hosts and brothel keepers of Tortuga and Goaves, like children throwing sand from them when they are tired of playing. Oh! great fools, I think."

"But did none of them ever take a town?" Henry asked.

"A village or so has fallen to them, but they have no leaders for such a thing."

"But a great town with a treasury?" Henry persisted.

"No, they have never done it. They are children, I tell you— strong, brave children."

"Could not a man who thought and planned carefully take a Spanish town?"

"Ho!" the cook laughed; "and are you going to be a buccaneer?"

"But if a man planned carefully?"

"Why, if there were a buccaneer who could plan at all, carefully or otherwise, it might be done; but there are no such buccaneers. They are little children who can fight like hell and die very nicely—but fools. They will sink a ship for a cup of wine, when they might sell the ship."

"If a man considered carefully and weighed his chances and the men he had, he might—"

"Yes, I suppose he might."

"There was one called Pierre le Grand who was no fool."

"Ah, but Pierre took one rich ship and then ran home to France! He was a fearful gambler, not a wise man. And he may yet come back to the Coast and lose it all and his head too."

"Still," said Henry with a grown finality, "still, I think it could be done, so only a man thought about it and considered it."

In a few days they were coming close to land. One morning the pale ghost of a mountain was sitting on the edge of the circle.

Logs and branches of trees went floating by now and again, and land birds flew out to them and rested in the rigging.

They were come to the home of Summer, whence it goes yearly to the northern places. In the day the sun was a glaring brass cymbal, the sky washed out and livid around it, and at night the big fishes swam about the ship with curving rivers of pale fire flowing behind them. From off the forepeak were hurled millions of flying diamonds by the raging prow. The sea was a round lake of quiet undulation, spread with a silken skin. Slowly, slowly, passing to rearward, the water set up a pleasant hypnosis in the brain. It was like looking into a fire. One saw nothing, yet only with infinite struggle could he move his eyes; and finally his brain dreamed off, though he was not sleeping.

There is a peace in the tropic oceans which passes a desire for understanding. Destination is no longer an end, but only to be sailing, sailing, out of the kingdom of time. For months and years they seemed to slip onward, but there was no impatience in the crew. They did their work, and lay about the deck all in a strange, happy lethargy.

One day there was a little island floating in the sea, shaped like a hay-cock and green as the first spears of barley. It was thickly covered with a tangling, fierce growth, vines and creepers and a few dark trees. Henry saw it with eyes that looked out on enchantment. They passed that island, and another and another, until, at last, in the blackness of a tropic early morning, the ship came in to Barbados. Its anchors splashed into the sea and went tugging down with the hawser flying behind them.

On the shores there was lettuce green jungle as on the little islands, and farther back, plantations with straight laid rows and white houses with red roofs; farther still, the red soil showing like wounds through the jungle of the hills; and far behind, mountains that rose sharp and hard with the appearance of strong gray teeth.

Small dug-out boats came to them, bearing rich fruits and piles of trussed up fowls. They came to sell, and to buy or steal that which the ship carried. Shining black men sang rich cadenced chants as they pulled at the oars, and Henry, close against the rail, was overjoyed with the new land. It was more than he had hoped. The sight brought happy, silly tears to his eyes.

Tim was standing near, looking crestfallen and sad. At length he came and stood in front of Henry.

"It's grieving me to be hurting a fine boy that bought my breakfast," he said. "It's grieving me so I can't sleep."

"But you have not hurt me," cried Henry. "You've brought me to the Indies where I wanted to be so badly."

"Ah!" said Tim sorrowfully, "if only I had a religion to me like the master, I might say, ' 'Tis God's will,'—and then be forgetting about it. And if I had a business or position I might be talking how a man must live. But I have no religion in me at all, save only an Ave Mary or a miserere dominie in storms; and as to position, why, I'm only a poor sailor out of Cork, and it does be grieving me to hurt a boy that bought my breakfast, and me a stranger." He was watching a long canoe that drew near to them, six strong Caribs rowing it. In the stern sat a little, nervous Englishman, whose face had not tanned with the years but had grown redder and redder until the tiny veins seemed to be running on the outside of his skin. In the little man's pale eyes there was the light of perpetual indecision and perplexity. His canoe bumped the ship's side and he climbed slowly aboard and went directly to the master.

"There it is, now," cried Tim; "and you will not be thinking too badly about me, will you, Henry—seeing the grief it does me?"

The captain was shouting, "Galley boy! Oh, galley boy! Morgan! Aft!"

Henry went back to where the Englishman and the captain were standing. He was amazed when the little colonist gingerly felt his arms and shoulders.

"I might give ten," he said to the captain.

"Twelve!" the captain snapped.

"But do you really think he is worth it? I'm not a rich man, you see, and I just thought that ten—"

"Well, you may have him for eleven, but, as God sees me, he's worth more. Look at the knit of him and the broad shoulders. He won't die like so many. No, sir, he's worth more, but you may have him for eleven."

"Well, if you really think so," the planter said hesitantly; and he began pulling money out of his pockets, money that was mixed with tangled string, and pieces of chalk, and a bit of a quill pen, and a broken key.

The master drew a paper from his pocket and showed it to the boy—an order of indenture for five years, with the name *Henry Morgan* nicely filled in, and the British seal at the bottom.

"But I don't want to be sold," cried Henry. "I didn't come to be sold. I want to make my fortune and be a sailor."

"So you shall," the master answered kindly, as though he gave permission, "after five years. Now go along with the gentleman and let us have no caterwauling. Do you think I could run this ship just bringing out boys that want to come to the Indies? You do your work and trust in God, and it may be a very good thing for you. Experience is never wasted on the sharp albeit humble soul." He pushed Henry soothingly along the deck in front of him.

At last the boy found his voice. "Tim," he cried, "Tim. They're selling me, Tim. Oh, Tim, come to me!" But there was no answer. Tim heard, and he was sobbing in his hammock like a small, whipped child.

And Henry, as he climbed over the side ahead of his new master, felt nothing at all. But for a little catching in his throat, there was no sharp feeling in him—only a heavy, sodden dullness.

III

So Henry Morgan came to be living in Barbados by authority of a white paper which forced his life and soul and body to kneel before the pleasure of one James Flower, planter.

James Flower was not a hard man, and certainly he was not a very brilliant man. His whole life had been a hunger for ideas—any ideas—the creation of them. He wanted to conceive ideas, to warm them to throbbing life, then to hurl them on an

astonished world. They would go bounding like stones started
down a long hill, awakening an avalanche of admiration. But
no ideas came to him.

His father had been a stout English curate who wrote stout
sermons which were actually published, though very few ever
bought them. His mother wrote poetry which was a kind of
summary of the sermons. Her verses were appended to the volume of rugged orthodoxy. And both his father and mother had
ideas. Both were creators in a small way.

James Flower had been reared in an atmosphere of—

"I must be walking to my publisher's now, Helen."

"But, William, a glorious thing burst upon me this morning
as I was doing my hair—such a conception! It must surely have
come from God. It will be done in couplets, I think. Oh! glorious! And it just fits in with those delightful words of yours on
humility."

"Ah, well; I must be walking to my publisher's now, to see
how the sermons are going. I sent a copy to the Archbishop,
and he may have been talking about them. Such a thing would
start a great sale, I think."

Yes, they were people with ideas, and often they shook their
heads over their dull son. He had held them in awe, had been
frightened at their greatness and ashamed of himself. And so,
early in his life, he had made a determination to have ideas.
His reading had been tremendous. King James' "Defense of
Witchcraft" came into his hands, and he set about to prove it
true. With the aid of ancient incantations and a black lotion
which contained a number of filthy ingredients together with a
large amount of hasheesh, he attempted to fly from the roof of
his house. It was while his two broken legs were healing that he
came on Scot's "Discoverie of Witchcraft."

The system of Descartes was causing a stir among learned
men, and James Flower, too, determined to reduce all philosophy to a basic postulate. He laid out paper and a number of
fine pens at his side, but he could never come on his postulate.
"I think, therefore I am," he said; "at least, I think I am." But
this led in a circle and got him nowhere. Then he joined the
new-founded school of Bacon. With persistent experiments he

burned his fingers, and tried to cross clover with barley, and pulled the legs from numberless insects, striving to discover something—almost anything; but he never did. As he had a moderate income from money left him by an uncle, his experiments were varied and extensive.

A Separatist of fanatic intensity had written a violent book in the best scientific manner—"The Effects of Alcoholic Spirits, Momentary and Perpetual." This work fell into the hands of James Flower, and he set out one evening to verify some of its more fantastic theories. In the midst of his investigation the spirit of induction left him, and, without cause or warning, he assaulted one of His Majesty's guardsmen with a potted plant. Had he only known it, this was the one spontaneous idea of his life. The matter was hushed up by an archdeacon who was related to his mother. James Flower's small fortune was invested in a plantation in Barbados, and he was sent to live there. Clearly, he did not fit in with orthodoxy and pentameters.

And so he had grown wistfully old, on the island. His library was the finest in the Indies, and, as far as information went, he was the most learned man anywhere about. But his learning formed no design of the whole. He had learned without absorbing, remembered without assimilating. His mind was a sad mass of unrelated facts and theories. In his brain, as on his shelves, Cæsar's Commentaries stood shoulder to shoulder with Democritus and a treatise on spontaneous generation. James Flower, who had cried to be a creator, became a quiet, kindly little gentleman, somewhat ineffectual and very inefficient. In his later years he had begun to mistake convictions for ideas. If a man stated any belief loudly enough he frightened James Flower, for, he said to himself, "Here is one of those divinely endowed creatures who control the fire I lack altogether."

IV

There were few white men on the great green plantation, and those who did grub there were sullen, tattered wretches, serving for some forgotten felony against the Crown. Within their bod-

ies the fever lay like a light sleeper who wakes and snarls, then
sleeps again with one malicious eye unclosed. They kneaded
the soil in the fields with their fingers, and as their years of
servitude crawled on their eyes deadened, their shoulders
slumped, and a tired, dull imbecility stretched cloying webs in
their brains. Their language was a bastard argot of London,
with a few words from the Guinea negroes and a few clattering
Carib phrases. When these men were loosed from their slavery,
they wandered listlessly about for a time, and watched the others go to work with something of longing. Then, after a little,
they either signed new papers of indenture, or went marauding
like tigers from a broken cage.

The overseer had been one of them, and now that he commanded those who had been his fellows, he inflicted suffering
in memory of his own pain.

James Flower brought Henry to the shore, and something in
the boy's silent misery touched the planter. He had never been
able to think of his slaves as men before. He had blindly followed the injunctions of the shrewd elder Cato in dealing with
his slaves. But here was one who was very obviously a human,
and possibly a gentleman. This boy had cried that he didn't
want to be a slave. The others always landed knowing their
lot, and displaying a sullen rancor which must be beaten out of
them on the cross.

"Do not be so hurt, child," the planter said. "You are very
young to be coming to the islands. In a few years you will be a
man, and strong."

"But it was on me to be a buccaneer," said Henry dully. "I
came out to the sea to make my fortune and a name. And how
can I do these things if I am a slave toiling in the fields?"

"I do not intend that you shall toil in the fields. I wanted you—
I wanted a boy to be about the house now I am growing old. I
wanted a—a kind of companion who would talk with me and
hear me talk. The other planters come to the house and drink my
wine, but when they leave I think they laugh at me and laugh at
my books—my lovely books. And so you will sit with me in the
evenings, perhaps, and we will talk of the things in books. Your
father was a gentleman, I think. You have the look.

"Now, to-day," James Flower went on mildly, "we have a hanging, and you and I must hurry to be there. I don't just know what the fellow did, but it was enough. And what says—oh! what's his name? I have read it, anyway—'The chief value of violent punishment lies with those on whom the same might fall.' Yes, I think it is well to have some one hanged every now and then. It is expensive, but very conducive to good behavior among the rest. But my overseer attends to all that. Do you know, I think he really enjoys it."

He led the boy to a square of thatched mud huts, built close together, each with its door opening out into a kind of plaza. And in the center of the square, like a horrible fetish, rose a tall gallows made of black wood and polished with oil until it shone dully in the sunlight. It was so placed that no slave could look out of his hovel without seeing the black horror that might be his end. This was the overseer's work. With his own hands he had rubbed the dark wood until it glowed. He was accustomed to stand and gaze at it, head cocked to one side, as an artist might look at his new finished work.

The planter and the boy seated themselves. The slaves were herded into the square. And Henry saw a naked black figure squirm and writhe at the end of a rope while the negroes rocked themselves back and forth on the ground and moaned; while the white slaves gritted their teeth and cursed harshly to keep from shrieking. The Caribs squatted on their hams and watched with no particular interest and no fear. Thus they might squat and watch the fire which cooked their food.

When it was all over, and the black victim hung limply by his crooked neck, the planter looked down and saw that Henry was crying nervously.

"I know it is bad the first time," he said gently. "When I first saw it, I did not sleep for a good while. But after a little, when you have seen five—ten—a dozen—go out in this way, you will come to have no feeling about it, and no more thought of it than of a chicken flopping about with a wrung neck."

Henry's breath still came in little miserable chokes.

"I can show you in the works of Holmaron on the practices of the Inquisition, a dissertation on this very thing you feel. 'The first time one sees human suffering,' he says, 'it is an unnatural thing, because, within one's experience, placid, comfortable people are the rule. But, after a number of such experiences, the sight of torture becomes a normal thing, and normal humans come to relish it to various extents.' Remind me to show you the passage sometime; though I must say I have never come to relish the matter."

In the evenings of the months that came, the two of them sat in the black depths of the veranda, and James Flower poured his unrelated facts into the ears of young Henry Morgan. The boy listened eagerly, for often the planter spoke of ancient wars and their conduct.

"And are these things in the books that line the walls?" Henry asked one night.

"All of these things, and, oh! many thousands of things more."

After a time Henry begged, "Would you be teaching me the languages of the books, sir? There must be things there I should like to read for myself."

James Flower was delighted. In teaching this boy the things he had read, he had come nearer to satisfaction than ever before. His heart was warm toward the young slave.

"The Latin and the Greek!" he cried with enthusiasm. "You shall learn them from me; and the Hebrew, too, if you wish."

"I want to read the books of war and sailing," young Henry said. "I want to read of those old wars you speak of, for one day I shall be a buccaneer and take a Spanish town."

And in the months that followed, he learned the languages very rapidly because of his wish to read the books. James Flower plunged more deeply into his volumes than ever, for his new role of teacher was very dear experience to him.

After a little while, he would say,

"Henry, will you tell the overseer to gather the molasses on the beach? A ship is in to buy it." And later still,

"Henry, is there anything I should be doing today?"

"Well, sir, there's a great ship down there, in from the Netherlands. We are in strong need of sickles. The Caribs have stolen nearly all the old ones to make swords with. We shall have trouble with those Caribs one day, sir."

"Well, see to the sickles, will you, Henry. I hate to be moving in this sun. And have the Indians punished if they steal things. Attend to that, too, will you?"

Little by little, Henry was absorbing the management of the plantation.

One evening, after Henry had been there a year, he gained the paramount respect of James Flower; rather a wistful respect, though he lost no love by it.

"Have you considered these ancient wars?" Henry asked. "I have been reading of Alexander and Xenophon and Caesar in their wars. And the thought is on me that battle and tactics— that is, successful tactics—are nothing more than a glorified trickery. The force is necessary, and the arms, of course; but the war is really won by the man who sits back, like one cheating at cards, and confounds the enemy with his trickery. Have you considered that, sir? Any one who can guess the minds of ordinary generals, as I can guess the minds of the slaves, can win battles. Such a man would have only to shun what was expected of him. Isn't that the secret of tactics, sir?"

"I had not thought of it," said James Flower just a trifle jealously. And that awe he felt for people of ideas went out to Henry. But the planter took great comfort in telling himself that, after all, he was the teacher who had awakened these ideas.

Two years after Henry had come, the overseer was released by the years from his bondage. He found his freedom too strong a drug for the mind that had been used to outside control. That mind snapped, and fury flooded in on him, so that he went shouting along the roads, striking at every passer-by. And in the night his mania became a terrible, frantic thing. He rolled on the ground under his gallows, and bloody foam frothed from his mouth while the slaves looked on in terror. At length he arose, with ragged hair and maniac, flaming eyes. He seized a torch and rushed into the fields. And Henry Morgan shot him dead as he entered the close growing rows of cane.

"Who knows the work as well as I do, and whom can you trust more, sir?" young Henry asked the planter. "I have learned things in the books and from my watching that will make this plantation a hundred times more productive."

Thus he became much more than the overseer.

Henry removed the gallows from the square, and after that the hanging was done secretly, in the night. This was not kindness. He knew, out of his own reasoning, that the unknown thing can never become the normal thing; that unseen punishments could be far more horrible to the remaining slaves than those seen under the light of the sun.

Henry had learned many things in dealing with the slaves. He knew that he must never let them see what he was thinking, for then, in some ineffable way, they had a hold on him which would be difficult to shake off. He must be cold and distant and insulting to those below him. With few exceptions, they would take insult as the sign of his superiority. Men always believed him what he seemed to be, and he could seem to be almost anything.

If one were brilliantly dressed, all men presumed him rich and powerful, and treated him accordingly. When he said things as though he meant them, nearly all acted as though he meant them. And, most important of his lessons—if he were perfectly honest and gave a strict accounting in nine consecutive dealings, then the tenth time he might steal as much as he wished, and no one would dream of suspecting him, so only he had brought the nine times forcibly enough to the attention of all men.

A growing pile of golden coins in a box under his bed gave ample proof of the validity of this last lesson. And he followed all his teachings. He never gave any man the least hold on him, nor insight into his motives and means and abilities and shortcomings. Since most men did not believe in themselves, they could not believe in one they understood to be like themselves.

These rules he gleaned gradually from his life, until he was master of the plantation, until James Flower pitifully leaned on his advice and his convictions, and until the Caribs and blacks

and felon white men hated and feared him, and yet could make
no dent in his being—could get no hold to hurt him.

James Flower was deliciously happy—happier than he had
ever been—for this boy had lifted the hideous weight of the
plantation from his shoulders. He need think no more of the
matters of tilling the soil. More and more he lay drowned in
his books. And, now he was coming to be an old man, he read
the same books over and over again without knowing it. Often
he felt a slight irritation at the careless person who had made
notes in his margins and dog-eared the pages.

And Henry Morgan had got himself a great plantation and
a great power. Under his captaincy the earth flowered and
increased. He was making the land give four times as much as
it had before. The slaves worked deliriously under the whips
which followed them to the fields, but there was nothing personal in the whips. The old overseer had delighted in punishment, but Henry Morgan was not cruel. He was merciless. He
merely speeded the wheels of his factory. One could not think
of being kind to a sprocket or a fly-wheel, and no more could
this boy think of pampering his slaves.

Henry was forcing money out of the ground, and from it was
adding to his hoard in the box under his bed—a little from the
season's sale of cane and a trifle in the buying of new cattle. It
was not stealing, but only a kind of commission for his success.
The little pile of golden coins grew and grew for the time when
Henry Morgan should go a-buccaneering and take a Spanish
town.

V

Henry had served three years, and, though he was only eighteen, he was grown and strong. His crisp black hair seemed to
curl more tightly to his head, and his mouth, from dealing with
the slaves, was more firm than ever. He gazed about him and
knew that he should be satisfied, but his eyes had never lost
the trick of looking out beyond distance and over the edge of
the present. A little hectoring wish ran through his waking and

dreaming like a thin red line. He must get back to the sea and ships. The sea was his mother and his mistress, and the goddess who might command and find him ready and alert for service. Why, his very name, in the ancient Briton tongue, signified one who lived by the sea. Yes, the ships were calling to him cruelly now. His heart sailed out, away from him with every passing merchantman.

In the big house he had studied and considered what navigation there was in books, and in the plantation's little sloop he had gone cruising in the near waters. But this was the play of a child, he thought, and it was not preparing him to be an expert sailor. It was necessary for him to learn avidly, for in the near future he must go a-buccaneering and take a Spanish town. This was the silver throne of all his desire.

And so, one evening—

"There is a thing I should like to be speaking of, sir."

James Flower raised his eyes from his book and laid his head back in the chair.

"If we had a ship to carry our produce to Jamaica," Henry continued, "we should be saving a large deal in freightage. The cost of such a ship would soon enough be eaten away by the profits. Too, we might carry the produce of the other plantations at a smaller fee than the merchantmen ask."

"But where might one come on such a ship?" James Flower inquired.

"There is one in the harbor now, one of two masts and—"

"Then buy her; buy her, and see to it. You know more about these things than I do. By the way, here is an interesting conjecture on the inhabitants of the moon. 'They may be totally unlike human beings,' he read. 'Their necks could easily be—' "

"It will be seven hundred pounds, sir."

"What will be seven hundred pounds? You seem not to pay attention as you used, Henry. Do listen to this paragraph; it is both entertaining and instructive—"

Henry careened the ship, and when he had scraped and painted her, he named her *Elizabeth* and put to sea. He had what is known as "hands" to a horseman, a warm feeling of the personality of his boat. He must learn the rules of naviga-

tion, of course; but even before that something of the spirit of
the ship crept into his soul, and part of him went back to her.
It was a steadfast love, a steady understanding of the sea. By
the thrill of her deck and the smooth touch of the wheel, he
knew instinctively how close he could bring her into the wind.
He was like a man who, laying his head on his mistress' breast,
reads the flux of her passions in her breathing.

Now he could have run away from Barbados and gone to
plundering in the staunch *Elizabeth*, but there was no need.
His hoard was not great enough and he was too young; and in
addition, he felt a curious, shame-faced love for James Flower.

Henry was content for a little while. The lust that all men
have in varying degrees—some for the flash of cards, and some
for wine, and some for the bodies of women—was, in Henry
Morgan, satisfied with the deck's lunge and pitch and the crack
of canvas. The wind, blowing out of a black, dreadful sky,
was a cup of wine to him, and a challenge, and a passionate
caress.

He sailed to Jamaica with the crops and beat about among
the islands. The returns from the plantation mounted, and
Henry's box of coins was growing heavy.

But after a few months, a dull, torturing desire came to him.
It was the yearning of the little boy, revivified and strong. The
Elizabeth had sated his old lust and left a new one. He thought
it was plunder that called him: the beautiful things of silk and
gold and the admiration of men, and on these his heart set
more zealously than ever.

Henry went to the brown women and the black in the slave
huts, striving to dull his hungering if he could not satisfy it; and
they received him, cow-eyed and passive, anxious to please.
They hoped that of his favor they might receive more food or a
jug of rum as a gift. Each time, he came away with disgust and
a little pity for their poor, hopeful prostitution.

Once, in the slave dock at Port Royal, he found Paulette
and bought her for a servant in the house. She was lithe, yet
rounded; fierce and gentle in a moment. Poor little slave of the
jumbled bloods, she was Spanish and Carib and Negro and
French. The heritage of this rag-bag ancestry was hair like a

cataract of black water, eyes as blue as the sea, set in oriental
slits, and a golden, golden skin. Hers was a sensuous, passionate beauty—limbs that twinkled like golden flames. Her lips
could writhe like slender, twisting serpents or bloom like red
flowers. She was a little child, yet old in life. She was a Christian, but she worshiped wood spirits and sang low chants in
honor of the Great Snake.

Henry thought of her as a delicate machine perfectly made
for pleasure, a sexual contraption. She was like those tall, cool
women of the night who ride with the wings of sleep—soulless
bodies—bodies of passionate dreams. He built for her a tiny,
vine-clad house roofed with banana leaves and there he played
at love.

At first Paulette was only grateful to him for bringing her to
a lazy, easy life, with comfort and days of little toil, but later
she fell frenziedly in love with him. She watched his face like a
quick terrier, waiting to jump with wild pleasure at one word
or fall fawning in the dust at another.

When Henry was serious or distraught, she was afraid; then
she would kneel before her little ebony figure of a jungle god
and pray to the Virgin for his love. Sometimes she put out cups
of milk for the winged Jun-Jo-Bee which keeps men true. With
the frantic, tender arts of her mixed bloods, she strove to hold
him surely in her sight. From her body and her hair there came
a rich orient odor, for she rubbed herself with sandalwood and
myrrh.

When he was gloomy—

"Do you love Paulette?" she would ask. "Do you love Paulette? Are you sure you love Paulette?"

"Why, certainly, I love Paulette. How could a man see Paulette,
little, dear Paulette—how touch the lips of sweet Paulette—and
not be loving her?" And his eyes would go wandering to the sea
below, seeking and seeking along the curved shore.

"But do you surely, surely love Paulette? Come, kiss the little
breasts of your own Paulette."

"Yes, surely I love Paulette. There! I have kissed them and
the charm is made. Now do be still a little. Hear the pounding
of the frogs. I wonder what startled the old bearded monkey in

the tree there; some slave, perhaps, out stealing fruit." And his eyes would go wandering restlessly to sea.

As the year went on, the soil of her love thrust up strong vines of choking fear. She knew that when he finally deserted her she would be far more than just alone. She might be forced to kneel in the field rows and dig about the plants with her fingers as the other women did. And then, one day, she would be led to the hut of a great negro with powerful muscles, and he would bruise her little golden body in his beast's clutch and make her pregnant of a black child—a strong, black child that could toil and strain in the sun when it was grown. This happened to all the other slave women of the island. The half of her mind that was very old shuddered at this thought, and that same old mind knew well that Henry would leave her one day.

Then, to her child's mind, appeared the doorway for the passage of her fright. If only he would marry her—impossible it seemed, yet stranger things had been—if only he would marry her, then she need never fear. For those strange beings, wives, were, in some curious way, by some divine intent, shielded from ugly and uncomfortable things. Ah! she had seen them in Port Royal, surrounded by their men to keep foul contact off, breathing through scented cloths to deaden the vile smells, and sometimes with little pellets of cotton in their ears to stop the cursing of the streets from entering. And Paulette knew—had she not been told?—that in their homes they lay in great, soft beds, and languidly gave orders to their slaves.

This was the blessed state she dared to hope for. And her body was not enough, she knew. Often it failed in its soft potency. If she fed him full of love, he did not come again to her bower for a time; and when she refused him to make his passion mount, either he went sullenly away or laughed and flung her roughly on the low, palm couch. She must cast about for some compelling force, some very powerful means to make him marry her.

When Henry went away with cocoa for Port Royal, she was scarcely sane. She knew his love for the ship, his passion for the sea, and she was furiously jealous of them. In her mind she saw him fondle the wheel with the strong, dear touch of lover's fingers. Ah! she could scratch and tear that wheel which robbed her.

She must make him love Paulette more than the ships, more than the sea, or anything on earth, so that he would marry her. Then she could walk haughtily among the huts and spit at the slaves; then she need never think of grubbing in the earth or bearing strong black children; then she would have red cloth to wear, and a silver chain to go about her neck. It was even possible that once in a long while her dinner might be brought to her while she lay in bed, pretending to be ill. She wriggled her toes in delight at such a thought, and made up the insulting things she would say to one fat negress with a spiteful tongue, when only she should be a wife. That old, fat wretch had called Paulette a slut before a gathering. Paulette had pulled out lots of hair before she could be held with her arms to her sides—but still, that black one should see, one day. Paulette would have her whipped on the cross.

While Henry was away a trading ship came into port, and Paulette went to the beach to see the things she brought and to watch the wind-brown sailors come ashore. And one of them, a great, broad Irishman, laden with black rum, pursued and captured her against a pile of boxes. Strong and quick, she struggled to elude him, but he held her tightly, swaying though he was.

"I've caught a fairy to mend my shoes," he laughed, and peered into her face. "Sure enough, 'tis a fairy." And then he saw that she was small and very beautiful, and he spoke tenderly and low.

"You're a lovely fairy—lovelier than the eyes of me have ever seen. Could a slim little body like you be thinking anything about a great, ugly hulk like me, I wonder? Come off and marry me, and you shall have anything 'tis in the power of a sailor to give you."

"No!" she cried. "No!" and slipped under his arm and away. The sailor sat in the sand staring dully before him.

" 'Twas a dream," he whispered; " 'twas only a dream from the spirits. There's no such thing to be happening to a poor sailor. No; for sailors there be pretty hags with sharp, hard eyes to say, 'Come! money first, sweetheart mine.' "

But now Paulette had found the way to make Henry marry her. She would contrive to get drunkenness on him, would trap him with wine, and there would be a priest nearby to come at her hushed call. Oh, surely, stranger things had been!

She laid her snare for him on his first night back from sea—a large stone flagon filled with Peruvian wine, and a priest, bribed with a stolen coin, waiting in the shadow of a tree. Henry was very tired. He had gone out short-handed and helped to work the ship himself. The little vine-clothed hut was a pleasant, restful place to him. A full white moon cast silver splashes in the sea below and strewed the ground with scarves of purple light. Sweetly there sang a little jungle breeze among the palms.

She brought the wine and filled a cup for him.

"Do you love Paulette?"

"Ah, yes! as God sees me, I love Paulette; dear, sweet Paulette." Another cup, and still, persistently—

"Are you so sure you love Paulette?"

"Paulette is a little star hanging to my breast by a silver chain."

Another cup.

"Do you love none other save only your Paulette?"

"I came longingly to find Paulette; the thought of her sailed on the sea with me." And his arms locked tightly around her little golden waist.

Another and another and another; then his arms fell away from her and his hands clenched. The girl cried fearfully,

"Oh! do you love Paulette?" for Henry had grown morose and strange and cold.

"I shall tell you of an old time," he said hoarsely. "I was a little boy, a joyous little boy, yet old enough to love. There was a girl—and she was named Elizabeth—the daughter of a wealthy squire. Ah! she was lovely as this night about us, quiet and lovely as that slender palm tree under the moon. I loved her with that love a man may exercise but once. Even our hearts seemed to go hand in hand. How I remember the brave plans we told—she and I, there, sitting on a hillside in the night. We were to live in a great house and have dear children growing up about us. You can never know such love, Paulette.

"Ah, well! It could not last. The gods slay happiness in jealousy. Nothing good can last. A gang of bastard sailors roved through the land and carried me off—a little boy to be sold for a slave in the Indies. It was a bitter thing to lose Elizabeth—a bitter thing the years cannot forget." And he was weeping softly by her side.

Paulette was bewildered by the change in him. She stroked his hair and his eyes, until his breath came more calmly. Then she began again, with almost hopeless patience, like a teacher questioning a dull child.

"But—do you love Paulette?"

He leaped up and glared at her.

"You? Love you? Why, you are just a little animal! a pretty little golden animal, for sure, but a form of flesh—no more. May one worship a god merely because he is big, or cherish a land which has no virtue save its breadth, or love a woman whose whole realm is her flesh? Ah, Paulette! you have no soul at all! Elizabeth had a white winged soul. I love you—yes—with what you have to be loved—the body. But Elizabeth—I loved Elizabeth with my soul."

Paulette was puzzled.

"What is this soul?" she asked. "And how may I get one if I have not one already? And where is this soul of yours that I have never seen it or heard it at all? And if they cannot be seen, or heard, or touched, how do you know she had this soul?"

"Hush!" he cried furiously. "Hush! or I box your mouth and have you whipped on the cross. You speak of things beyond you. What can you know of love that lies without your fleshly juggling?"

VI

Christmas came to the Hot Tropics, the fourth Christmas of Henry's servitude. And James Flower brought him a small box done up with colored string.

"It is a gift of the season," he said, and his eyes sparkled with delight while Henry untied the package. There was a little

teakwood box, and in it, lying on the scarlet silk of its lin-
ing, the torn fragments of his slavery. Henry took the shreds of
paper from the box and stared at them, and then he laughed
unsteadily and put his head down on his hands.

"Now you are no longer a servant, but my son," the planter
said. "Now you are my son, whom I have taught strange
knowledges—and I shall teach you more, far more. We will
live here always and talk together in the evenings."

Henry raised his head.

"Oh! but I cannot, cannot stay. I must be off a-buccaneering."

"You—you cannot stay? But, Henry, I have planned our life.
You would not leave me here alone."

"Sir," said Henry, "I *must* be off a-buccaneering. Why, in all
my years it has been the one aim. I must go, sir."

"But, Henry, dear Henry, you shall have half my plantation,
and all of it when I am dead—if only you will stay with me."

"That may not be," young Henry cried. "I must be off to
make me a name. It is not given that I live a planter. Sir, there
are plannings in my head that have grown perfect with ponder-
ing. And nothing may be allowed to interfere with them."

James Flower slumped forward in his chair.

"It will be very lonely here without you. I don't quite know
what I shall do without you."

Henry's mind carried him back to that old time, with Robert
smiling into the fire and saying these same words—"It will be
so lonely here without you, son." He wondered if his mother
still sat coldly upright and silent. Surely she would have got
over it. People always got over the things they feared so much.
And then he thought of small Paulette who would be crying
with terror in her hut when he told her.

"There is a little servant girl," he said; "little Paulette. I have
protected her. And if I have ever pleased you, will you do these
things for me? Always, always keep her in the house and never
let her be sent to the fields, nor whipped, nor bred with any of
the blacks. Will you do these things for me surely?"

"Of course I will," James Flower said. "Ah, but it has been
good to have you here, Henry—good to hear your voice in the
evening. What will I do in the evening now? There is none to

take your place, for you have very truly been my son. It will be lonely here without you, boy."

Said Henry, "The toiling I have done in your service has been more than repaid with the knowledge you have poured into my ears these same evenings. And I shall miss you, sir, more than I can say. But can't you understand? I must go a-buccaneering and take a Spanish town, for the thought is on me that if a man planned carefully, and considered his chances and the men he had, the thing might well be done. I have studied the ancient wars, and I must be making a name for myself and a fortune. Then, when I have the admiration of men, perhaps I shall come back to you, sir, and we may sit and talk again in the evenings. You will remember my wish about Paulette?"

"Who is Paulette?" the planter asked.

"Why, the servant girl I mentioned. Never let her go with the slaves, because I am fond of her."

"Ah, yes! I remember. And where do you go now, Henry?"

"To Jamaica. My uncle, Sir Edward, has long been Lieutenant-Governor there in Port Royal. But I have never seen him—well, because I was a bond-servant, and he is a gentleman. I have a letter to him that my father gave me years past. Perhaps he will help me to buy a ship for my plundering."

"I would help you buy a ship. You have been very good to me," the planter said hopefully.

Now Henry was dipped in a kind of shame, for in the box under his bed there glistened a pile of golden coins—over a thousand pounds.

"No," he said, "no; I have more payment in your teaching and in the father you have been to me than money could ever equal." Now he was going, Henry knew that he had grown to love this red-faced, wistful man.

Strong, glistening blacks pulled at the oars of the canoe, and it went skimming toward an anchored ship, a ship commissioned by the States-General to carry black slaves from Guinea to the islands. James Flower, sitting in the canoe's stern, was very red and very silent. But as they neared the ship's side, he lifted up his head and spoke pleadingly to Henry.

"There are books on the shelves that you have never read."

"I shall come back, one day, and read them."

"There are things in my mind I have never told you, boy."

"When I have the admiration of men, I shall come to you and you shall tell them to me."

"You swear it?"

"Well—yes, I swear."

"And how long will it take you to do these things, Henry?"

"I cannot tell; one year—or ten—or twenty. I must make a very admirable name." Henry was climbing over the ship's side.

"I shall be lonely in the evenings, son."

"And I, too, sir. Look! we cast off! Good-by, sir. You will remember Paulette?"

"Paulette?—Paulette?—Ah, yes; I remember."

VII

Henry Morgan came to the English town of Port Royal and left his baggage on the beach while he went looking for his uncle.

"Do you know where I may find the Lieutenant-Governor?" he asked in the streets.

"His palace is yonder, young man, and who knows he may be in it."

His palace—it was like a British gentleman become an official far from home. It was like the man Robert Morgan had described. His letters dated from the Palace of the Lieutenant-Governor. Henry found the Palace, a low, grubby house with walls of whitewashed mud and a roof of red tiles badly molded. There was a gaudy halberdier standing at the door, holding his great, ineffectual weapon rigidly before him, the while he maintained a tortured decorum in the face of a swarm of enemy flies.

The halberd lowered across the pathway as Henry approached.

"I am looking for Sir Edward Morgan."

"What do you wish with His Excellency?"

"Why, you see, sir, he is my uncle, and I wish to speak with him."

The soldier scowled suspiciously and stiffened his hold on the halberd. Then Henry remembered his lessons of the plantation. Perhaps this man, for all his red coat, might be something of a slave.

"Get out of my way, you damned pup," he cried. "Get out of my way or I'll see you hanged."

The man cowered and almost dropped his weapon. "Yes, sir. I'll send your word, sir." He blew a little silver call, and when a servant in green lace came to the door, he said:

"A young gentleman to see His Excellency."

Henry was led into a little room made dark with thick, gray hangings edged with dull gold. There were three dim portraits on the walls, in black frames; two cavaliers in plumed hats, holding their swords horizontally so they looked like stiff, slender tails, and a pretty lady with powdered hair and a silken gown which left her shoulders and half her breasts uncovered.

From some place beyond the curtained doorway there came the thin twanging of a harp slow struck. The servant took Henry's letter and left him alone.

And he felt very much alone. It was a house of cold, precise hair-splitting. One was aware of a polite contempt even in the pictured faces on the wall. The British arms were embroidered on the curtains of the door, the lion on one side, holding half the shield, and the unicorn, with his half, on the other. When the curtains hung straight the design was complete. In this room, Henry began to fear his uncle.

But all these thoughts of his were shocked from his brain when Sir Edward appeared. It was his father as he remembered him, and yet never his father. Old Robert would never have had a mustache like an eyelash, and nothing in Robert's life could have made him pinch his lips together until they were as thin as the mustache. These two might have been born alike as beans, but each had created his own mouth.

Robert had spoken truth; this man was his strutting counterpart. But Sir Edward was like an actor, who, though cast in a ridiculous role, yet makes his part seem the correct thing and all others absurd. His purple coat with lace at the neck and wrists, the long rapier, lean as a pencil in a scabbard of gray silk, the gray silk stockings and soft gray shoes with bowed ribbons on them, seemed to Henry the highest type of proper wear. His own good clothing was shabby by comparison.

His uncle had been looking at him steadily, waiting for Henry to speak first.

"I am Henry Morgan, sir—Robert's son," he began simply.

"I see you are. There is a resemblance—a faint likeness. And what may I do for you?"

"Why, I—I don't know. I came to call on you and inform you of my existence."

"That was kind of you—ah—very kind."

It was difficult to broach speech into this field of almost sneering courtesy. Henry asked,

"Have you heard any single thing of my parents in the long five years I have been out?"

"Five years! What have you been doing, pray?"

"I was a bond-servant, sir. But of my parents?"

"Your mother is dead."

"My mother is dead," Henry repeated in a whisper. He wondered if she had died soon after he had gone. He did not feel very badly about it, and yet the words sounded such tremendous things, such final things. This was the end of something that might never be again. "My mother is dead," he murmured. "And my father?"

"I have heard that your father does peculiar things in his rose garden. Squire Rhys wrote me of it. He plucks the full flowers and casts them into the air like one mazed. The ground is covered with petals and the neighbors stand about and laugh at him. Robert was never normal; indeed, he was never quite sane, or he might have gone far with James I. I, for one, always thought he would come to some disgrace or other. He revered nothing worthy of reverence. Why must he do this thing in the open, with the people jeering? It brings ridicule on his—ah—relatives."

"And do you think he is really insane, Uncle?"

"I do not know," Sir Edward said, and added with a touch of

impatience, "I merely quoted Squire Rhys' letter. My position does not allow me time for vain conjecture—nor much time for idle conversation," he said pointedly.

The methodic twanging of the harp had ceased, and now the curtain of the door was thrust aside and a slender girl entered the room. It was difficult to see her in this dark place. It was plain she was not beautiful, but rather proudly pretty. She was softly dressed and her face was pale. Even her hair was pale fragile gold. Altogether she seemed a wan, tired echo of Sir Edward.

The girl was startled at seeing Henry there, and he found that he was a little afraid of her in the same manner that he was growing to fear Sir Edward. She looked at Henry as though he were some distasteful food which only the strict rules of courtesy prevented her from pushing away from her place.

"Your cousin Henry," Sir Edward said shortly; and, "My motherless daughter, Elizabeth." Then, nervously, as though no good could possibly come of this contact, "Hadn't you better practice your music a little longer, my dear?"

She dropped a suggestion of a curtsey to Henry, and in a voice like her father's, greeted him.

"How d'ye do. Yes, sir, I think I had better practice. That last piece is difficult but beautiful." And she disappeared behind the curtain whence came again the slow, accurate striking of the harp.

Henry gripped his resolve, though he was afraid of this man.

"There is a thing I wish to speak of, sir. I want to go a-buccaneering, Uncle—on the sea, in a great ship with guns. And when I have taken prizes, and a cloud of men gather to my reputation, then I would be capturing a Spanish town for plunder and ransom. I am a good sailor, my uncle. I can navigate in any sea, I think; and I have it in me to plan carefully my campaign. I have read a great lot on the ancient wars. The buccaneers have never been the force I mean to make them. Why, I could form armies and navies of them, my dear uncle. In time I would lead the whole Free Brotherhood of the Coast, and it would be an armed power to reckon with.

"These things I have considered in the long years of my slavery. There is a crying in my heart to do these things. I think the end of all my dreaming is a great name and a great fortune. I know my powers. I am twenty years old; I have had several years at sea; and I have a thousand pounds. The man who helps me now—who goes with me as partner—I will make rich. I am so very sure I can do these things—so very sure.

"I ask you, my uncle, to add to my thousand pounds enough so that I may buy a fitted ship and gather the free, brave spirits about me to do my will. If you will place another thousand pounds in my hands, I swear to make you richer than you are."

The harp was no longer sounding. At the beginning of the boy's outburst, Sir Edward had held up his hand as though to stop him, but the words plunged on. And when the harp had been silenced, Sir Edward looked uneasily toward the door. Now he seemed to bring his interest back to Henry.

"I have no money to risk on unsure ventures," he said sharply. "And I have no more time for talk. The Governor is coming to consult with me in a moment. But I would say that you are a wild, careless boy who is like to come to hanging of your ventures. Your father is like you, only his is a wildness of the mind.

"And I must inform you that there is peace between Spain and England; not very good feeling, it is true, but still, peace. If you go marauding it will be my duty to see you punished, sorry for it though I may be. The Roundheads are no longer in power, and those wild things that Cromwell overlooked are carefully watched now. Remember what I say, for I would not like to hang my nephew. Now I must really bid you good day."

Tears of resentment stood in Henry's eyes.

"Thank you for coming to see me," his uncle said. "Goodby." And he went through the curtained doorway.

In the street, Henry walked moodily along. He saw his cousin a short distance ahead of him, a tall negro attendant upon her. He continued slowly that she might leave him behind, but the girl lagged on her way.

"Perhaps she wishes to speak with me," Henry thought, and

quickened his steps to come up with her. He saw, incredulously, what the darkened room had hidden. She was only a little girl, not more than fourteen at the most. Elizabeth looked up as he came beside her.

"Do you find interesting things to be doing here in the Indies?" Henry asked.

"As many as one might expect," she replied. "We have been here a good while, you know." And touching her slave's arm with her little parasol, she turned into a crossing street, and left young Henry looking after her.

He was bitter against these proud relatives who seemed to edge away from him as though he were foul. He could not call them silly, for they had impressed him too deeply. They had succeeded in making him feel alone and helpless and very young.

The narrow ways of Port Royal were deep with muddy filth, ground to thick liquid by the carts and the numberless bare feet. Port Royal bore the same resemblance to a city as the Palace of the Lieutenant-Governor did to Whitehall. The streets were only narrow alleys lined with dirty wooden houses. And each house had a balcony above the street where people sat and stared at Henry as he passed; stared not with interest, but wearily, as men in sickness watch flies crawling on the ceiling.

One street seemed to have no inhabitants save only women— black women, and white, and gray women, with fever written on their hollow cheeks. They leaned from their balconies like unclean sirens and softly called as he went by. Then, when he paid no attention to them, they shrieked like angry parrots and screamed curses and spat after him.

Near the waterfront he came to a kind of tavern with a great crowd gathered in front of it. Standing in the center of the way was a cask of wine with its head staved in, and a big, drunken man in crazy laces and a plumed hat strutted beside it. He passed out cups and basins and even hats full of wine to the reaching men. Now and then he called for a toast and a cheer, and his crowd screamed its acclaim.

Young Henry sought to pass them in his misery.

"Come drink my health, young man."

"I do not wish to drink," said Henry.

"You do not wish to drink?" The big man was overwhelmed with this new situation. Then he recovered his wrath.

"By God! you will so drink when Captain Dawes that took the supply ship 'Sangre de Cristo' this day week asks you." The lowering man came close, then suddenly drew a great pistol from his belt and pointed it waveringly at Henry's breast.

The boy eyed the pistol.

"I will drink your health," he said. And while he drank, an idea came to him. "Let me speak to you alone, Captain Dawes, sir," and he tugged the pirate into the tavern door. "About your next trip—" he began.

"My next trip and hell!" the captain roared. "I've just taken a good prize, haven't I? I've got money, haven't I? Then what is this you are squalling about a next trip? Wait till the prize is spent and the wounds healed. Wait till I've drained Port Royal dry of wine, and then come talking about the next trip." He rushed back into the street crowd. "Boys!" he yelled. "Boys, you have not drunk my health for hours. Come, shout together now, and then we will sing!"

Henry walked onward in despair. In the harbor a number of ships were lying at anchor. He approached a sailor sitting in the sand.

"That one's fast," he said, to open the acquaintance.

"Aye, good enough."

"Are there any buccaneers of note in this town?" Henry asked.

"None but that Dawes, and he's only a roaring mouse. He takes a little boat loaded with supplies for Campeche, and you'd think it was Panama he brought home for the noise he makes about it."

"But are there none others?"

"Well, there's one they call Grippo, but he takes no prizes unless they go unarmed. Afraid of his shadow, Grippo. Yes, he's in port with no prize, and drinking black rum on tick, I guess."

"Which is his ship?" Henry asked.

"Why, there she is. They call her *Ganymede*. They tell that Grippo stole her in Saint Malo when her crew was drunk. He and nine others tumbled the poor stiff wretches overside and made off with the ship for the Indies. Yes, she's a good craft, but Grippo is no master. A wonder it is that he's not wrecked her before now. Take Mansveldt; there's a master for you—a real master. But Mansveldt is in Tortuga."

"A good, swift sailer," Henry observed; "though she could carry more canvas without hurt. How about her guns?"

"They say she's over armed if anything."

And on that night, Henry found the buccaneer drinking in a hovel on the beach. The man was nearly black; two fat wrinkles cut each cheek as though a silken cord were pulled tight against the flesh until it disappeared. His eyes darted here and there like sentries before a camp of little fears.

"Are you one they call Grippo?" Henry asked.

"I took no prize," the man cried, starting back. "I take no prizes. You have nothing to fasten on me for." Once in Saint Malo he had been accosted thus, and afterwards they had whipped him on the cross until a hundred sagging mouths opened on his body and every one laughed blood. Grippo had feared all semblance of authority since then.

"Who are you?" he asked.

"I think I am going to make your fortune, Grippo," Henry said with assurance. He knew how to handle this man, for he was a counterpart of the many slaves of the plantation—fearful, and perhaps greedy. "What would you do with five hundred English pounds, Grippo?"

The black man licked his lips and glanced at the empty cup before him. "What must I do for this money?" he whispered.

"You will sell me the captaincy of the *Ganymede*."

Now Grippo was wary.

"The *Ganymede* is worth much more," he said firmly.

"But I do not want to buy the ship—only the captaincy. Look, Grippo! I'll make this compact with you. I will give you five hundred pounds for a half interest in the *Ganymede*, and all of her command. Then we will put to sea. I think I know how to win plunder if there be no interference in my company. Grippo,

I will give you a writing to this effect. If I fail in one single undertaking in the *Ganymede*, then you shall have the whole ship back, and you shall keep the five hundred pounds."

Grippo still looked into his empty cup, but suddenly he was filled with excitement.

"Give me money," he cried out. "Quick! give me the money." Then—"Oloto! Oloto! bring white wine—white wine—for the love of Christ."

CHAPTER 3

There were many glittering reputations along the coast of Darien and among the green Caribbean islands when Henry Morgan came to be a buccaneer. In the wine shops of Tortuga were tales of a thousand fortunes made and spent, of fine ships taken and sunk, of gold and plate dumped on the docks like wood.

The Free Brotherhood had grown to be a terrible thing since Pierre le Grand and a little band of hunters slipped out of the woods of Hispaniola and captured the Vice-Admiral of the plate fleet from a canoe. France and Britain and Holland had seen in these islands a good hermitage for their criminals, and for years they had unloaded worthless human freight on the Indies. There was a time in those old nations when any one who could not give a good, virtuous account of himself was crammed into a ship and sent off to be a bond-servant to any man who would pay a small sum for him. And when their time was up, these people stole guns and warred on Spain. It was not strange, for Spain was Catholic and rich, while Huguenots and Lutherans and Church of England men were poor and out at heel. They fought a holy war. Spain had locked up the treasures of the world. If poor, ruined beggars could be reaching a coin through the keyhole, who was the worse for it? Who minded except Spain? Surely England and France and Holland took little heed of it. Sometimes they provided the pirates with commissions against Aragon and Castile, so that you might come on a man who, ten years before, had been sent out in a prison ship, carrying the style of "Captain by the grace of the King."

France had the good of her wayward children at heart, for she sent out twelve hundred women to Tortuga to be the wives of buccaneers. The whole twelve hundred turned to a business more profitable than wifehood immediately they landed, but France could not help that.

They had got their name, these buccaneers, of a time when they were nothing more than cattle-hunters. There was a way of smoking meat by burning small bits of fat and flesh in the fire. This made the meat more savory than usual. It was called the boucan process, and from it the pirates were named.

But after a time these hunters came out of the woods in little, careful groups; then bands formed, and then whole fleets of eight or ten vessels. And finally thousands assembled in Tortuga, and from that spot of safety buzzed about the flanks of Spain.

And Spain could not combat them. Did she hang ten, a hundred joined their ranks; so she fortified her towns and sent her treasures on the sea under the protection of warships filled with soldiers. The numberless vessels of the Spanish colonies were nearly all driven from the sea by the fierce buccaneers. Only once in a year did the plate fleet sail out for home.

There were fine names among the Brotherhood, and exploits to make Henry Morgan squirm with jealousy if he had not been so confident of overshadowing them all one day.

Bartolomeo Portugues there was, who took a great prize. But before he could get away with it, he was captured near Campeche. The gibbet was erected on the shore for his hanging. He watched them put it up from his prison aboard ship. And in the night before his execution, he stabbed his guard and swam away, supported by a keg. Before eight days had passed, he came again with pirates in a long canoe and stole the same ship away from the harbor of Campeche. He lost her, of course, in a storm off Cuba, but the story was, nevertheless, told with glee in the taverns.

Roche Braziliano was a Hollander with a chubby face. When he was young he was driven from Brazil by the Portuguese, and from their colony he had taken his name. Curiously, he held no rancor against Portugal. His hatred turned on Spain. He was a kindly, gentle, beloved captain, so only there were no Spaniards about. His men worshiped him, and drank no other toast but to his name. Once, when his ship was wrecked in Castilla de Oro, he killed most of a troop of Spanish horse and used their beasts to ride off on. When the men of Spain were near him, Roche was a foaming beast. It was told that once he roasted prisoners on green spits over a slow fire.

As the rich shipping was driven from the sea, the buccaneers must be taking villages, and then even towns with forts. Lewis Scot pillaged Campeche and left it a black, smoking pile.

L'Ollonais had come from the Sables d'Ollone, and very rapidly he became the most feared man in the western ocean. He began with a real hatred for Spain and ended with a strong love of cruelty. He had pulled out tongues, and carved his prisoners to pieces with his sword. The Spanish men would far rather have met the devil in any form than L'Ollonais. The whisper of his name emptied the villages in his path of every living unit. It was said that the mice fled to the jungle when he came. Maracaibo he took, and New Gibraltar, and St. James de Leon. Everywhere he slaughtered men for the fierce love of it.

Once, when the blood lust was in him, he had commanded that eighty-seven prisoners be bound and laid in a row on the ground. Then he walked down the line, carrying a whetstone in one hand and a long sword in the other. That day he cut off eighty-seven heads with his own hand.

But L'Ollonais was not content with murdering the Spanish men. He went into the gentle country of Yucatan, where the people lived in ruined stone cities, and where the virgins went crowned with flowers. They were a quiet people in Yucatan, and their race was dying in an inexplicable decay. When L'Ollonais went away, the cities were heaps of stones and ashes, and there were no crowns any more.

The Indians of Darien were different; fierce, and fearless, and unrelenting. The Spaniards called them Bravos and swore that they were untamable. They had been friends of the pirates because they so hated Spain, but L'Ollonais robbed them and murdered the tribesmen. These Indians waited many years for their vengeance, and at last they caught L'Ollonais when his ship had wrecked on the shores of their country. They built a fire and danced for hours, and then they burned the Frenchman's body bit by bit before his eyes, a finger and a pinch of flesh at a time.

A lean French gentleman came into a tavern at Tortuga one night, and when they asked his name, seized a large rum keg and hurled it from him.

"Bras de Fer," he said, and no one ever questioned him farther. It was never known whether his name was hidden for a shame or a sorrow or a hatred, but all the Coast came to know of him as a great, brave captain.

These were men who made phrases to be repeated.

"No prey, no pay," the Exterminator had bawled, and now every one was saying it. When Captain Lawrence, in a small boat, was assailed by two Spanish frigates, he said to his men, "You have too much experience not to be sensible of your danger, and too much courage to fear it." This was a fine saying, and on the strength of it his followers captured the two Spanish ships and took them home to Goaves.

Not all were cruel or even violent men. Some had a curious streak of piety. There was Captain Watling who made it a point to hold divine service every Sabbath, with the whole crew standing uncovered. Daniel once shot a sailor for an irreverence. These buccaneers prayed loudly before battle, and, if they were successful, half of them trooped off to a captured cathedral to sing the Te Deum, while the other half plundered the prize.

Captains of ships maintained the strictest discipline among their men, swiftly punishing insubordination or any other wrong doing which might interfere with their success. There were no such riots at sea as were later tolerated by Kidd and Blackbeard and Lafitte.

But out of the whole history of the Brotherhood, one man towered. There was a Dutchman named Edward Mansveldt. In bravery and in soldiery he was preëminent, for he had taken Granada and St. Augustine in Florida, and St. Catherine's Isle. With a great fleet of ships he had gone cruising along the coasts of Darien and Castilla de Oro, taking what he might lay his hands on. But there was a power of dream in him. Out of his mob of ragamuffin heroes he wanted to make a strong, durable nation, a new, aggressive nation in America. As more and more of the buccaneers flocked to his command, his dream solidified. He consulted the governments of England and France. They were shocked, and forbade him to consider such a thing. A race of pirates not amenable to the gibbets of the crowns? Why, they would be plundering everybody. He must not be thinking about it at all.

But still he went on planning and planning his new govern-ment. It would be started at St. Catherine's Isle. He settled a body of his men there, and then went casting about for more to join his new nation. His ship was wrecked near the city of Havana, and Spaniards strangled Edward Mansveldt on the garotte.

These were the men Henry Morgan had set about to lead. And, confidently, he saw no barrier, so only a man planned carefully and considered his chances. These stories and these men were well enough, but they fell short in the large actions. They were improvident and vain. They might help him one day.

Mansveldt was living and Bras de Fer was an old man when Henry Morgan went sailing with black Grippo in the *Ganymede*.

I

There was excitement and curiosity in Port Royal when Mor-gan was fitting out the *Ganymede* for sea. Strange stores and unusual weapons were going into her hold. Drawn on by the quiet confidence of this young man, many sailors volunteered for his crew. The captain found five gunners of reputation in the port and signed them to go with him. When the *Ganymede* dropped her sails and slipped from the harbor, a crowd of idlers stood on the beach and watched her go.

They cruised to the coast of Darien looking for prey, but the sea appeared to be swept clean of Spanish craft. One morning, near the port of Cartagena, they sighted the tall red hull of a trading ship. Captain Morgan hid his men. No soul was allowed to show himself. Even the steersman worked in a tiny house, while a dummy wheel swung idly on the deck. Then down on the Spanish boat they bore, and the Spanish crew was overwhelmed. Here came a boat and no man working her. It smacked of witchcraft, or of one of those nameless tragedies of the sea the sailors talked about. Perhaps a plague had killed all the crew, and they could take and sell this ship. But when they were close, three masked guns spouted flame; they fired only at one spot, and when they had done, the rudder of the Spanish ship hung in splinters and she floundered about in no control. Then Captain Morgan, hanging aft, out of range of her broadside, poured shot into her hull until the flag fluttered down. It was the first prize of his planning.

A few days later he brought up with another ship and ran along side to board. The Spanish crew was massed against the bulwarks to repel the attack. And immediately the air was filled with clay powder pots which landed in the thick group and exploded. The Spanish men ran screaming to the shelter of the hold to escape this flashing death.

When Henry Morgan came at last to Tortuga, four prizes followed in his wake, and he had not lost a man. It was as easy as he had known it would be. Here were four monuments to his planning. One had only to do the unexpected thing quickly. This was the secret of successful war.

Mansveldt was in Tortuga when Henry Morgan came, and his little eyes glittered as he looked at this plunder. Soon he sent for this new leader.

"You are Captain Morgan who took the four prizes in the harbor?"

"Yes, sir, I am."

"And how did you do this thing? The Spanish ships are strongly armed and wary."

"I did it, sir, with my planning. Many nights have I considered how to do these things. I work with surprise, sir, when other men use only force."

Mansveldt regarded him with admiration.

"I am fitting out an expedition to take St. Catherine's Isle," he said. "Then I am going to form a republic of buccaneers who will fight with a patriotism. Would you like to be Vice-Admiral of this expedition? I have some reputation for picking men."

The name of Mansveldt was mighty on the seas, and Henry flushed with pleasure.

"I would like it, sir," he said quickly.

The fleet sailed out, and Captain Morgan was Vice-Admiral. There was a fine assault; the ships threw in their ragged hordes and slaughter walked on the walls. The island could not withstand the fierceness of the attack, and finally the fortress fell. Then the Dutch admiral drew up his government and left Henry Morgan in command while he went out to scour the world for recruits. He and his ship were lost and never heard from again. It was said the Spaniards strangled him in Cuba.

Captain Morgan was now the paramount leader of the Spanish Main. Ships flew from the ways to join his fleets, to sail under his command and fight with him and share in his success. He went up against Puerto Bello and sacked the town. The houses were burned and all the helpless citizens were plundered. When Captain Morgan's ships sailed off the jungle was already creeping into the ruins.

For ten years he sailed about the ocean, among the islands and along the green coasts of Tropic America, and his was the greatest name of all who had gone out for plunder. The pirates of the world came flocking to his reputation. People cheered him in Tortuga and Goaves. Numberless men volunteered for every expedition. Now all the Brotherhood waited for Captain Morgan to open a keg of liquor in the streets or to run wild through the town. He never did. Coldly he walked about, clad in a purple coat and gray silk stockings and gray shoes with bows. At his side hung a long rapier no thicker than a pencil, in a scabbard of gray silk.

At first the sailors strove to establish a comradeship with him, but he pricked them away with frigid insults. The lessons of the slaves lived on in him. He did not try to buy his popularity, and all the Free Brotherhood showered it upon him—cast their lives and their fortunes on the knees of his success.

II

Ten years of fighting and plundering and burning, and he was thirty. His graying hair seemed to coil more closely to his head. Henry Morgan was successful, the most luck-followed free-booter the world had known, and the men of his profession gave him that admiration he had craved. His enemies—and any man of Spain who had money was his enemy—shuddered at the mention of his name. They had placed him in their fears beside Drake and L'Ollonais.

He had gone out with Grippo in the *Ganymede*, assured that when his guns roared into a Spanish hull, when he stood embattled on a Spanish deck with cries and clash of iron weapons about him, there would come that flaming happiness his heart desired. These things he had experienced, and there was not even content. The nameless craving in him grew and flexed its claws against his heart. He had thought the adulation of the Brotherhood might salve the wound of his desire; that when the pirates saw the results of his planning and marveled at them, he would be pleased and flattered. And this thing happened. The men fairly fawned on him, and he found that he despised them for it and considered them fools to be taken with such simple things.

Henry had grown lonely in his glory. Old Merlin had spoken truth so long ago, for Captain Morgan had come to his success, and he was alone in his success, with no friend anywhere. The craving of his heart must lie crouched within him. All his fears and sorrows and conceits, his failures and little weaknesses, must be concealed. These, his followers, had gathered to the cry of his success; they would leave him at the first small sign of weakness.

While he was engaged in winning plunder, a little rumor had come stealthily across the isthmus, had floated among the islands and stolen aboard the ships. Men caught the whispered name and listened carefully.

"There is a woman in Panama and she is lovely as the sun. They call her the Red Saint in Panama. All men kneel to her." Thus said the whispering. The voice grew and grew until men in the taverns drank to La Santa Roja. Young seamen whispered of her in the dog watch. "There is a woman in the Cup of Gold and all men fall before her as heathen kneel before the sun." They spoke softly of her in the streets of Goaves. No one had seen her; no one could tell the tint of her cheeks or the color of her hair. Yet, in a few years, every man in the wide, wild Main had drunk to the Red Saint, had dreamed of her; many had prayed to La Santa Roja. She became to every man the quest of his heart, bearing the image of some fair young girl left on a European beach to be gloriously colored by the years. And Panama was to every man the nest of his desire. It was a curious thing. In time, no speech among gathered men could end without mention of La Santa Roja. She was become a queer delirium in the minds of the rough pirates, a new virgin for their worship. Many said she was Mary come to live on earth again, and they added her name in their prayers.

Now, when Captain Morgan had taken Puerto Bello, the Governor of Panama was filled with admiration and wonder that such a ragged band of ill-ordered men, and without uniforms, could capture such a city. He sent a messenger asking for a small sample of the weapons which had made this thing possible. Captain Morgan took the runner to a small room that had escaped the general fire.

"Have you seen the woman whom they call the Red Saint in Panama?" he asked.

"I have not seen her, no; but I have heard of her. The young men put only the Blessed Virgin before her in their worship. It is said that she is lovely as the sun."

"What is her name besides La Santa Roja?"

"I do not know. I have only heard that she is lovely as the sun. They tell in Panama that she came from Cordova and has been to Paris. It is said her family is noble. They tell how she rides great horses, sitting astride, in a meadow guarded with a thick hedge. It is said that in her hand a rapier is a living thing, and that she can fence more skillfully than any man. These things she does in secret that no one may see the crime against her modesty."

"Ah, well!" said Captain Morgan, "if she be beautiful enough what need has she of modesty. This modesty is only a kind of beauty patch which is put on when there are visitors— an enthralling gesture. I should like to see her ride. And do you know nothing more of her?"

"Only what they say in the taverns, sir—that she has stolen worship from the Blessed Saints."

Captain Morgan dreamed long in his chair while the runner waited silently. At last Henry shook his head, as though to disengage it of cloying thoughts. He drew a pistol from his belt and gave it to the messenger.

"Take this to Don Juan Perez de Guzman, and say that this is a sample of the weapons we have used in laying Puerto Bello in the dust. But my other weapons are the strong hearts of my followers. I will not send him one of these, but I will bring him a great number. And tell him to keep the pistol for a year, when I myself will come to Panama to receive it from his own hands. Do you understand?"

"I do, sir."

And in a few days the runner came again, bringing the pistol back, and a large square emerald set in a ring.

"My master begs that you accept this stone as a token of his regard. He begs that you do not give yourself the trouble to come to Panama, for then his duty would overwhelm his admiration and force him to hang you to a tree."

"It is a good message," said the captain; "a good, brave message. I should like to meet with Don Juan if only at sword's points. It has been long since any one defied me. And did you learn more of La Santa Roja?"

"Only what they tell in the streets, sir. I inquired closely for your benefit. I was told that in the streets she wears a thick veil that none may see her face. Some think she does this so that the poor men who meet her will not kill themselves for love. That is all I could learn. Have you further messages, sir?"

"Only repeat that I will go to the Cup of Gold within the year."

III

Through all his life his will had been like an iron weathervane, steadfastly pointing, always, but never long in one direction. The Indies and the sea and pillage and glory all seemed to have failed him. He had touched all things and watched them pale and shrivel at his touch. And he was lonely. His men regarded him with respect and sullen awe. They were afraid of him, and this state did not feed his vanity as once it had.

He wondered if he might not make a friend among his followers, but the time he had dwelt alone in the castle of himself had been so long that this thought filled him with a curious, boyish embarrassment. Who among his followers might be his friend? He considered them, remembering their sullen scowls, their gleaming, avaricious eyes at the division of spoil. He felt nothing but contempt for them.

But there was one whom he had noticed, a young Frenchman who was called Cœur de Gris. Captain Morgan had seen him in action, leaping about the deck like a supple animal while his rapier flicked out in lithe tongues of silver fire. He scorned a cutlass for the long thin blade. And this young man answered his orders with a smile at Captain Morgan. There was respect in his eyes, surely, but no fear, no jealousy, and no suspicion.

"I wonder if this Cœur de Gris would be my friend," mused Henry Morgan. "It is said that he has left a trail of broken hearts from Cuba to Saint Kit's, and somehow, for this, I fear him a little."

Captain Morgan sent for the young man, and when he was come, found difficulty in speaking to him.

"Ah—how are you, Cœur de Gris?"

The young man was overwhelmed by any show of warmth from this captain.

"Why, sir, I am very well. Have you orders for me?"

"Orders? No; I—I thought I would like to talk with you—that is all."

"To talk with me, sir? But to talk of what?"

"Well—How are the many little loves you are reputed to have?" the captain asked in an uneasy effort at joviality.

"Repute is kinder to me than nature, sir."

Henry Morgan plunged to his purpose.

"Listen to me, Cœur de Gris! Can you not imagine that I may need a friend? Can you not think of me as a lonely man? Consider how all my followers are afraid of me. They come for orders, but never to pass a quiet time of day. I know I made this so. It was necessary once, for I had to build up respect before I could command obedience. But now there are times when I should like to be telling my thoughts and talking of something besides war and spoil. For ten years I have ravaged the seas like a silent wolf, and I have no friend anywhere.

"I have chosen you to be my friend; first, because I like you, and second, because you have not a thing on earth you might be thinking I want to steal. Thus you may like me without fear. It is a strange thing how my men suspect me. I have given a strict accounting for every voyage, yet, if I spoke to them as friends, they would beat their brains to discover my plot. And will you be my friend, Cœur de Gris?"

"Why, certainly, I will, my Captain, and had I known of such a thing in your mind, I would have been for long. How may I serve you, sir?"

"Oh, just by talking with me now and then, and by trusting me a little. I have no motive save my loneliness. But you speak and act like a gentleman, Cœur de Gris. May I ask of your family? or do you draw this name about you like a cape, as so many do here on the Main?"

"It is very simple to tell you of my family. It is said that my father was the great Bras de Fer, and who he was no one ever knew. The people gave me my name, remembering his. My mother is one of the free women of Goaves. She was sixteen when I was born. Hers was a very ancient family, but Huguenot in worship. Their holdings were destroyed in the murders of St. Bartholomew. Thus it came about that they were penniless when my mother was born. And she was picked up by the watch in Paris streets one day and sent to Goaves with a shipload of women vagrants. Bras de Fer found her soon afterwards."

"But you say she is a free woman," said Henry Morgan, scandalized at this young man's apparent lack of shame. "Surely she has given up this—this practice, now you are successful on the sea. You are taking home enough for both of you, and more."

"I know I am, but she continues. I do not mention it, for why should I interfere with what she considers a serious work. She is proud of her position, proud that her callers are the best people in the port. And it pleases her that, although she is nearly forty, she can more than compete with the young, unseasoned squabs who come in every year. Why should I change the gentle course of her ways, even if I could? No, she is a dear, lovely woman, and she has been a good mother to me. Her only fault is that she is filled with over-many little scruples. She nags at me when I am at home, and cries so when I leave. She is dreadfully afraid that I may find some woman who may do me harm."

"That is strange, is it not?—considering her life," said Henry Morgan.

"Why is it strange? Must they have a different brain in that ancient profession? No, sir; I assure you that her life is immaculate—prayers thrice a day, and there is no finer house in all Goaves than hers. Why, sir, when last I went there, I took with me a scarf which fell to my lot in the division, a glorious thing of gossamer and gold. She would not have it. It belonged about the neck of some woman who put her faith in the Romish church, she said, and it would not be decent for a good Huguenot to wear it. Ah! she worries so about me when I am off to sea. She is terribly afraid I may be hurt, but far more afraid of the tainting of my soul. Such is all my knowledge of my family, sir."

Captain Morgan had stepped to a cupboard and brought out some queer little jugs with wine of Peru. There were two necks on each jug, and when the wine was poured out from one, a sweet, whistling sound came from the other.

"I took these from a Spanish ship," he said. "Will you drink with me, Cœur de Gris?"

"I should be very much honored, sir."

They sat a long time sipping the wine, then Captain Morgan spoke dreamily.

"I suppose, Cœur de Gris, that you will one day be stricken with the Red Saint, and then we shall have the bees of Panama buzzing out upon us. I have no doubt she is as jealously guarded as was Helen. You have heard of the Red Saint, have you not?"

The young man's eyes were glowing with the wine.

"Heard of her!" he said softly. "Sir, I have dreamed of her and called to her in my sleep. Who has not? Who in all this quarter of the world has not heard of her, and yet who knows any single thing about her? It is a strange thing, the magic of this woman's name. La Santa Roja! La Santa Roja! It conjures up desire in the heart of every man—not active, possible desire, but the 'if I were handsome, if I were a prince' kind of desire. The young men make wild plans; some to go disguised to Panama, others to blow it up with quantities of powder. They daydream of carrying the Red Saint off with them. Sir, I have heard a seaman all rotten with disease whispering to himself in the night, 'If this thing were not on me, I would go adventuring for La Santa Roja.'

"My mother frets and frets there in Goaves, lest I go mad and run to her. She is terrified by this strange woman. 'Go not near to her, my son,' she says. 'This woman is wicked; she is a devil; besides, she is without doubt a Catholic.' And no one has ever seen her that we know of. We do not know certainly that there exists such a woman as the Red Saint in the Cup of Gold. Ah! she has spread the sea with dreams—with longing dreams. I have been thinking, sir, that perhaps, sometime, the Cup of Gold may go the way of Troy town on account of her."

Henry Morgan had filled the glasses again and again. He was slumped forward in his chair, and a little crooked smile was on his mouth.

"Yes," he said rather thickly, "she is a danger to the peace of nations and to the peace of men's minds. The matter is wholly ridiculous, of course. She is probably a shrewish bitch who takes her bright features from the legend. But how might such a legend be started? Your health, Cœur de Gris. You will be a good friend to me and true?"

"I will, my Captain."

And again they sat silently, drinking the rich wine.

"But there is much suffering bound up in women," Henry Morgan began, as though he had just finished speaking. "They seem to carry pain about with them in a leaking package. You have loved often, they say, Cœur de Gris. Have you not felt the pain they carry?"

"No, sir, I do not think I have. Surely I have been assailed by regrets and little sorrows—everyone has; but mostly I have found only pleasure among women."

"Ah, you are lucky," the captain said. "You are filled with luck not to have known the pain. My own life was poisoned by love. This life I lead was forced on me by lost love."

"Why, how was that, sir? Surely, I had not thought that you—"

"I know; I know how I must have changed so that even you laugh a little at the thought of my being in love. I could not now command the affection of the daughter of an Earl."

"The daughter of an Earl, sir?"

"Yes, an Earl's daughter. We loved too perfectly—too passionately. Once she came to me in a rose garden and lay in my arms until the dark was gone. I thought to run away with her to some new, lovely country, and sink her title in the sea behind us. Perhaps even now I might be living safe in Virginia, with little joys crowding my footstool."

"It is a great pity, sir." Cœur de Gris was truly sorry for this man.

"Ah, well; her father was informed. On one dark night my arms were pinned to my sides, and she—oh, dear Elizabeth!— was torn away from me. They placed me, still bound, in a ship, and sold me in Barbados. Can you not see, Cœur de Gris, the bitterness that lies restlessly in my heart? During these years, her face has followed me in all my wanderings. Somehow I feel that I might have made some later move—but her father was a powerful lord."

"And did you never go back for her, after your imprisonment
was done?"

Henry Morgan looked down at the floor.

"No, my friend—I never did."

IV

The legend of the Red Saint grew in his brain like a powerful
vine, and a voice came out of the west to coax and mock, to
jeer and cozen Henry Morgan. He forgot the sea and his idling
ships. The buccaneers were penniless from their long inactivity.
They lay about the decks and cursed their captain for a dreaming fool. He struggled madly against the folding meshes of his
dream and argued with the voice.

"May God damn La Santa Roja for sowing the world with
an insanity. She has made cut-throats bay the moon like love-
sick dogs. She is making me crazy with this vain desire. I must
do something—anything—to lay the insistent haunting of this
woman I have never seen. I must destroy the ghost. Ah, it is a
foolish thing to dream of capturing the Cup of Gold. It would
seem that my desire is death."

And he remembered the hunger which had drawn him from
Cambria, for it was duplicated and strengthened now. His
thoughts were driving sleep away. When drowsiness crept in
on the heels of exhaustion, La Santa Roja came in, too.

"I will take Maracaibo," he cried in desperation. "I will
drown this lusting in a bowl of horror. I will pillage Maracaibo,
tear it to pieces, and leave it bleeding in the sand."

(There is a woman in the Cup of Gold, and they worship her
for unnamable beauties.)

"Make the gathering at the Isle de la Vaca! Call in true hearts
from the corners of the sea! We go to riches!"

His ships flew out to the bay of Maracaibo and the town was
frantic in defense.

"Run into this bottle harbor! Yes, under the guns!"

Cannon balls cried through the air and struck up clouds of
dirt from the walls, but the defense held ground.

"It will not fall? Then take it in assault!"

Powder pots flew over the walls, tearing and maiming the defenders in their burst.

"Who are these wolves?" they cried. "Ah, brothers! we must fight until we die! We must ask no clemency, brothers. If we fall, our dear city—"

Ladders rose against the fort, and a wave of roaring men swarmed over the walls.

"Ah, San Lorenzo! hide us! bear us away! These are no men, but devils. Hear me! Hear me! Quarter! Ah, Jesus! where art thou now?"

"Throw down the walls! Let no two stones stand together!"

(There is a woman in the Cup of Gold, and she is lovely as the sun.)

"Grant no quarter! Kill the Spanish rats! Kill all of them!"

And Maracaibo lay pleading at his feet. Doors were torn from the houses, and the rooms gutted of every movable thing. They herded the women to a church and locked them in. Then the prisoners were brought to Henry Morgan.

"Here is an old man, sir. We are sure he has riches, but he has hidden them away and we can never find any."

"Then put his feet in the fire!—why, he is a brazen fool! Break his arms!— He will not tell? Put the whip-cord about his temples!— Oh, kill him! kill him and stop his screaming— Perhaps he had no money—"

(There is a woman in Panama—)

"Have you scratched out every grain of gold? Place the city at ransom! We must have riches after pain."

A fleet of Spanish ships came sailing to the rescue.

"A Spanish squadron coming? We will fight them! No, no; we shall run from them if we can get away. Our hulls lag in the water with their weight of gold. Kill the prisoners!"

(—she is lovely as the sun.)

And Captain Morgan sailed from broken Maracaibo. Two hundred and fifty thousand pieces of eight were in his ships, and rolls of silken stuffs and plates of silver and sacks of spices. There were golden images from the Cathedral, and vestments crusted with embroidery of pearls. And the city was a fire-swept wreck.

"We are richer than we could have hoped. There will be joy in Tortuga when we come. Every man a hero! We shall have a mad riot of a time."

(La Santa Roja is in Panama.)

"Ah, God! then if I must, I must. But I fear I go to my death. It is a dreadful thing to be attempting. If this is my desire, I must, though I die." He called young Cœur de Gris to him.

"You have distinguished yourself in this fight, my friend."

"I have done what was necessary, sir."

"But you fought finely. I saw you when we engaged. Now I have made you my lieutenant in the field, my second in command. You are brave, you are sagacious, and you are my friend. I can trust you, and who among my men will bear this trust if it be worth his while to fail?"

"It is a great honor, sir. I will pay you, surely, with my fidelity. My mother will be very pleased."

"Yes," said Captain Morgan; "you are a young fool, and that is a virtue in this business as long as one has a leader. Now the men are straining to get back that they may spend their money. If it were possible they would be pushing the ships to hurry them. What will you do with your money, Cœur de Gris?"

"Why, I shall send half to my mother. The remaining sum I shall divide in two. Part I shall put away, and on the other I expect to be drunk for a few days, or perhaps a week. It is good to be drunk after fighting."

"Drunkenness has never been a pleasure to me," the captain said. "It makes me very sad. But I have a new venture turning in my brain. Cœur de Gris, what is the richest city of the western world? What place has been immune from the slightest gesture of the Brotherhood? Where might we all make millions?"

"But, sir, you do not think— Surely you cannot consider it possible to take—"

"I will take Panama—even the Cup of Gold."

"How may you do this thing? The city is strongly guarded with walls and troops, and the way across the isthmus is nigh impassable but for the burro trail. How will you do this thing?"

"I must take Panama. I must capture the Cup of Gold." The captain's jaw set fiercely.

Now Cœur de Gris was smiling quietly.

"Why do you grin at me?" demanded Captain Morgan.

"I was thinking of a chance remark I made a little time ago, that Panama was like to go the way of Troy town."

"Ah! this nameless woman is in your mind. Dismiss her! It may be there exists no such woman."

"But then, sir, we are rich enough of this last spoil."

"It would be no evil thing to grow richer. I am tired of plundering. I would rest securely."

Cœur de Gris hesitated a time, while his eyes were covered with a soft veil.

"I am thinking, sir, that when we come to Panama every man will be at his friend's throat over the Red Saint."

"Oh, you may trust me to keep order among my men—strict order—though I hang half of them to do it. A while ago I sent word to Panama that I would go there, but I did it as a joke. And I wonder, now, whether they have been fortifying themselves. Perhaps they, too, thought it a joke. Go, now, Cœur de Gris, and speak to no man of this. I make you my ambassador. Let the men throw their gold away. Encourage gambling—here—now—on the ship. Give them an example at the taverns—an expensive example. Then they will be driven to go out with me. I must have an army this time my friend, and even then we may all die. Perhaps that is the chief joy of life—to risk it. Do my work well, Cœur de Gris, and it may be one day you will be richer than you can think."

Young Cœur de Gris stood musing by the mast.

"Our captain, our cold captain, has been bitten by this great, nebulous rumoring. How strange this pattern is! It is as though the Red Saint had been stolen from my arms. My dream is violated. I wonder, when they know, if every man will carry this feeling of a bitter loss—will hate the captain for stealing his desire."

V

Sir Edward Morgan led forces against St. Eustatius, and, while the battle raged, a slim, brown Indian slipped up and drove a long knife into his stomach. The Lieutenant-Governor set his lips in a straight, hard line, and crumpled to the ground.

"My white breeches will be ruined," he thought. "Why did the devil have to do it, just when we were getting on so nicely. I should have got special thanks from his Majesty, and now I shall not be here to receive them. Heaven! he chose a painful place!" And then the full tragedy struck him.

"An ordinary knife," he muttered; "and in the stomach. I should have preferred a sword in the hand of an equal—but a knife—in the stomach! I must look disreputable with all this blood and dirt on me. And I cannot straighten up! Christ! the wretch struck a sensitive spot."

His men sadly bore him to Port Royal.

"It was unavoidable," he told the Governor; "slipped up on me with a knife and stabbed me in the stomach. Such a little devil he couldn't reach any higher, I suppose. Report the affair to the Crown, will you, sir? And please do not mention the knife—or the stomach. And now will you leave me with my daughter? I shall be dying soon."

Elizabeth stood over him in a darkened room.

"Are you hurt badly, father?"

"Yes, quite badly. I shall die presently."

"Nonsense, papa; you are only joking to excite me."

"Elizabeth, does it sound like nonsense—and have you ever heard me joke? I have several things to speak of, and the time is very short. What will you do? There is little money left. We have been living on my salary ever since the King made his last general suggestion for a loan."

"But what are you talking about, papa! You cannot die and leave me here alone and lost in the colonies. You cannot, cannot do it!"

"Whether I can or not, I shall die presently. Now let us discuss this matter while we can. Perhaps your cousin who has come to such fame through robbery will care for you, Elizabeth. I am pained at the thought, but—but—it is necessary to live—very necessary. And after all, he is your cousin."

"I will not believe it. I simply will not believe it. You cannot die!"

"You must stay with the Governor until you can meet your cousin. Tell him the exact standing of the matter; no fawning—but do not be too proud. Remember he is your own blood cousin, even though he is a robber." His heavy breathing filled the room. Elizabeth had begun to cry softly, like a child who cannot quite tell whether or not it is hurt. Finally words were forced from Sir Edward's lips.

"I have heard that you can tell a gentleman by the way he dies—but I should like to groan. Robert would have groaned if he had wished. Of course, Robert was queer—but then—he was my own brother—he would have shrieked if he had felt like it. Elizabeth, will you—please—leave the room. I am sorry—but I must groan. Never speak of it—Elizabeth—you promise—never—never to speak of it?"

And when she came again, Sir Edward Morgan was dead.

VI

Spring had come to Cambria, welling up out of the Indies and out of the hot, dry heart of Africa, and this the fifteenth Spring since Henry went away. Old Robert liked to think, and then came curiously to believe, that his son sent the Spring to Cambria out of the tropic places. There was a green fur climbing up the hills, and the trees were testing new, fragile leaves in the winds.

Old Robert's face had grown more set. Around his mouth lived less a smile and more a grimace, as though some ancient, anguished smile had frozen there. Ah! the years had been lonely, barren things, with nothing left in their arms for him. He knew the meaning, now, of Gwenliana's words—that age brought nothing with it save a cold, restless waiting; a dull expectancy of a state that might not be imagined with any assurance. Perhaps he waited for the time when Henry would come to him again. But that could scarcely be so. He was not at all sure that he wanted to see Henry any more. It would be disturbing. When one is old, one hates disturbing things.

For a long time he had wondered, "What is Henry doing now? what seeing now?" And then the boy had faded slightly, had come to be like people in old books—not quite real, yet real enough to be remembered. But Robert thought often of this abstract person, his son, of whom he heard wavering rumors now and again.

With waking on the fine morning of the Spring, Robert had said, "I will climb up to see Merlin to-day. Strange how that old man lives under the growing pressure of his years. There must be more than a hundred of them now. His body is a thin wisp—nothing more than a suggestion that here was once a body. But William says, if you can be picking thought out of William's speaking, that his voice is golden and strong as always, and that he still talks tremendous nonsense that would not be tolerated at London. It is amazing how this road-mender has his whole life curled like a kitten around four days in London. But I must be going to Merlin. It is not likely that I shall go again."

The steep, rocky path was a thing of torture to him; more a cruel thing because of his memory of lithe, powerful legs, and lungs as tireless as bellows. Once he had led all comers in the mountain race, but now he climbed a bit, then rested on a stone, and climbed again—up and up into the cleft and over the rock shoulder. It was noon when he came at last to Crag-top.

Merlin met him at the door before he had time to knock, and Merlin had no more changed than the harps and spear-heads hanging to his walls. He seemed to have discarded time like a garment. Merlin came to Robert with no surprise. It was as though he had known of this slow pilgrimage a thousand years before the day had happened.

"It is very long, Robert, since you climbed the path to me, and long since I went down it." And "down, down" sang the harps. He spoke the language of the strings, and they responded like a distant choir in high mass of the mountains.

"But it's an old man who climbs to you now, Merlin. The

trail is a beast enemy to wrestle with. You seem no older. I wonder when you will come to die. Do not your years sometimes
argue that question with you?"

"Why, to speak truthfully, Robert, I have taken it in my mind
several times—but always there were too many things to think
about. I could not take the time to die. If I did, I might not be
able to think ever again.

"For up here, Robert, that furtive hope the valley men call
faith becomes a questionable thing. Oh, without doubt, if there
were a great many about me, and they all intoning endlessly the
chant, 'There is a wise, kind God; surely we shall go on living
after death,' then I might be preparing for the coming life. But
here, alone, halfway up the sky, I am afraid that death would
interrupt my musing. The mountains are a kind of poultice for
a man's abstract pain. Among them he laughs—oh, far more
often than he cries."

"You know," said Robert, "my mother, the old Gwenliana,
made a last, curious prophecy before she died. 'This night the
world ends,' she said, 'and there will be no more earth to walk
upon.' "

"Robert, I think she spoke truth. I think her dying words
were truth, whatever may have been her other auguries. This
gnawing thought comes visiting, sometimes, and because of it
I am afraid to die—horribly afraid. If by my living I give life to
you, and fresh existence to the fields and trees and all the long
green world, it would be an unutterable deed to wipe them all
out like a chalk drawing. I must not—yet awhile.

"But enough of these foreboding things. There is no laughter
in them. You, Robert, have been too long in the valley of men.
Your lips laugh, but there is no amusement in your heart. I
think you place your lips so, like twigs over a trap, to conceal
your pain from God. Once you tried to laugh with all your soul,
but you did not make the satirist's concession—that of buying
with a little amusement at yourself the privilege of laughing a
great deal at others."

"I know that I am defeated, Merlin, and there seems to be
no help for it. Victory, or luck, or whatever you wish to call it,
appears to lie hidden in a chosen few as babies' teeth hide under

the gums. Of late years this God has played a hard, calculating game with me. There have been moments when I thought he cheated."

Merlin spoke slowly:

"Once I played against a dear young god with goat's feet, and that game was the reason for my coming here. But then, I made the great concession and signed with sad laughter. Robert, did I not hear a long time past that you were roving in your mind? Surely William stopped by and told me you had grown insane. Did you not do reprehensible things in your rose garden?"

Robert smiled bitterly. "That was one of this God's tricks," he said. "I will tell you how it was. One day, when I was pulling the dead leaves from my roses, it came upon me to make a symbol. This is no unusual thing. How often do men stand on hill tops with their arms outstretched, how often kneel in prayer and cross themselves. I pulled a bloom and threw it into the air, and the petals showered down about me. It seemed that this act gathered up and told the whole story of my life in a gesture. Then the loveliness of white petals on black earth absorbed me, and I forgot my symbol. I threw another and another, until the ground was snowed with rose leaves. Suddenly I looked up and saw a dozen men standing about laughing at me. They had come by from church. 'Hee!' they said, 'Robert has lost his mind. Hee! his sense is slipping out of him. Ho! he is a child again, throwing rose petals.' It seemed a crazed God who could allow this thing."

Merlin was shaking with a silent glee.

"Oh, Robert! Robert! why must you blame the world when it protects itself against you? I think God and the world are one to you. If there were ten people in the valley below who liked the look of rose leaves on the ground, you would only be a very queer person, interesting and something of a curiosity. They would bring strangers to your house on Sunday afternoons and exhibit you. But, since there are none, of course you are a radical who must be locked up or hanged. Judgment of insanity is truly the hanging of a man's mind. If it be whispered of him that his brain wanders, then nothing he can say will matter to any one ever again, except as a thing to laugh at.

"Can you not see, Robert? People have so often been hurt and trapped and tortured by ideas and contraptions which they did not understand, that they have come to believe all things passing their understanding are vicious and evil—things to be stamped out and destroyed by the first comer. They only protect themselves, thus, against the ghastly hurts that can come to them from little things grown up."

"I know," said Robert; "I know all that, and I do not cry out against it. My great complaint is that the only possession I carry about with me is a bag of losses. I am the owner solely of the memory of things I used to have. Perhaps it is well—for I seem to love them more now that I have them not. But I cannot understand how this fortune may be born hidden in a chosen few. My own son assaults and keeps each one of his desires, if the winds tell truth."

"You had a son, Robert; I remember now. I think I prophesied that he would rule some world or other if he did not grow up."

"And so he does. News of him comes out of the south on a light, inaccurate wind. Rumor has wings like bats. It is said that he rules a wild race of pirates; that he has captured towns and pillaged cities. The English are elated, and call him a hero and a patriotic man—and so do I, sometimes. But I fear if I were a Spaniard, he would be only a successful robber. I have heard—though I do not believe it; I do not want to believe it—that he has tortured prisoners."

"So," Merlin mused, "he has come to be the great man he thought he wanted to be. If this is true, then he is not a man. He is still a little boy and wants the moon. I suppose he is rather unhappy about it. Those who say children are happy, forget their childhood. I wonder how long he can stave off manhood.

"Robert, have you seen those great black ants which are born with wings? They fly a day or two, then drop their wings and fall upon the ground to crawl for all their lives. I wonder when your son will drop his wings. Is it not strange, Robert, how, among men, this crawling is revered—how children tear at their wings, so they may indulge in this magnificent crawling?"

"What makes boys grow to men?" Robert asked. "What circumstance rots out their wing roots?"

"Why, a great many never have wings, and some tear them off for themselves; some are sudden things and others very tedious. I do not know them all, but mine was ridicule—a kind of self-ridicule. I loved a small girl in the valley, and I suppose she was beautiful. I hope I was handsome. I made a song for her and called her the Bride of Orpheus. I rather fancied myself Orpheus, then. But she considered marriage with a deity as some manner of a crime against nature. She lectured me. Every man, so she said, owed it to something or other—his family or his community or himself, I forget just what—to make a success of himself. She was vague as to the nature of success, but she made it very plain that song was not a structure of success. And deities she abhorred, especially pagan deities. There was a man with lands and houses who was reassuringly human. Even in my old age I think spitefully that he was deplorably human. So they were married, and ridicule gnawed off my wings.

"I paraded murder and suicide and fields of glory through my mind to fight this little paining ridicule. In my shame, I thought to lock up my songs from the world, so that never again might people hear them. The world did not even know when I was gone. No little groups of people came to plead with me to return—and I had promised the ridicule they would. My bitten wings dropped; I was a man and did not want the moon. And when I tried to sing again, my voice had grown husky like a drover's voice, and my songs were thick with forethoughts and plannings."

"I wonder how I grew," Robert said. "I do not remember. Perhaps my youth went out of me sticking to coins—or perhaps it lives in those lands I used to dream of. But Henry is swimming in his dreams, and sometimes I am very jealous of him.

"Do you know, Merlin, there is a thing which has appeared strange to me. My mother, Gwenliana, thought she had the second sight, and we humored her because she took such joy of it. And on the night that Henry went away, she cast a picture of his life. Merlin, nearly all her words have come to be the truth.

Can these thoughts have come on her like a series of bright paintings? It is a strange, unlikely thing."

"Perhaps she read his desire, Robert, and sensed the strength of his desire. I taught old Gwenliana many things which had to do with magic; she was very apt at reading signs—and faces."

Old Robert rose to stretch himself. "Ah, well—I must be going now. It takes a weary time for such an aged man to be getting down the path. It will be night when I am home again. Here is William coming with his pick which was an appendage born to him. I will be going down a bit in his company and learning the way of things at London. You must love words, Merlin, to be making so many of them; and I must love pain, to be engendering it against myself.

"And, Merlin, I think you are a trickster and a fraud; every time I have gone away from you it has been with the conviction that you have said mighty things, yet, on thinking, I could never recall any of them. I think you work a subtle conjuring with the soft voice of you, and your harps."

And as he went down the path, the hanging harps crooned after him the Sorcerer's Farewell.

CHAPTER 4

Panama was a great, lovely city in 1670 when Henry Morgan determined on its destruction; a rich, strong city, and justly called the Cup of Gold. No place in all the raw New World could compare with it in beauty and in wealth.

Over a century before, Balboa had come to the shore of a new ocean. He dressed himself in scoured armor and waded into the Pacific until the gentle water washed his thighs. Then, in an oration, he firmly addressed the sea and claimed all lands it broke on for the crown of Spain. He demanded that the water be tractable and loyal, for it was to be the honored private lake of Castile and Aragon.

Behind Balboa, on the shore, huddled a small grass village of the Indians, and its name was Panama. In the native tongue this signified a place of good fishing. When the soldiers of Spain put torch to the litter of huts, and in its place built a new town, they kept the old name, Panama, which is a song. And soon the meaning justified itself, for out of this little town the nets of Spain were flung to the four directions.

Pedrarias carried the nets to the north and enmeshed the cities of the ancient Mayan race. He was enabled, of his fishing, to send strangely wrought serpents and frightful images and tiny graven insects, all of gold, to Panama. When there were no more ornaments to gather, when the temples were vacant boxes of stone, then Pedrarias threw the net of Spain over the people and drove them into the mines under his whips.

Pizarro sailed to the southward with horses and armored men, and the powerful Inca nation fell before him. He killed the rulers and ripped the life from the governmental structure.

Then diamonds, plates from the temple walls, symbols of the sun in gold, and ceremonial golden shields were shipped to Panama. And Pizarro forced the broken Inca people into the mines with whips.

A hundred captains led little bands of soldiers to the east and southeast where the fierce Indians of Darien lived in trees and caves. Here the Spanish men found nose rings and anklets and god-sticks and eagle quills filled with gold. Everything was dumped into sacks and carried on mule-back to Panama. When all the graves had been robbed of golden ornaments, even the wild Indians dug in the earth by authority of the whips.

The ships of Spain discovered little islands to the westward in whose shallow bays pearls might be found if only one dived deep enough; and in a little time the dull folk of the islands were jumping into a sea where sharks lived. And bags of pearls found their way to Panama.

All the long workings, the craftsmanship in precious things, came at last to Panama, where the melting pots received them like glowing gourmands and transformed them to thick golden logs. The warehouses were piled high with the sticks of gold, waiting for the treasure fleet to sail for Spain. At times there were bars of silver tiered up in the streets for lack of warehouse room, but they were safe from thievery in their weight.

Meanwhile the city grew to be a glorious thing. The wealth of enslaved nations was put to building thousands of fine houses with red roofs and little inset patios where rare secret flowers grew. All the colored arts and comforts of old Europe flew westward to beautify the Panamanian houses at the call of golden lumps.

The first Spaniards to invade the country had been cruel, grasping robbers; but also they were soldiers whom no bloody prospect might frighten. Small bands of them captured the New World with little force save spiritual courage. But when the peoples of Nicaragua and Peru and Darien had become gangs of whimpering slaves, when there was no danger any more, a different breed of men came to live in Panama. These were the merchants, keenly decisive when there was a farm to be wrested by law from its owner, or when the price of food was raised for outland colonists, but fearful and cowardly when steel was rattling about on steel.

The merchant class soon dominated all the isthmus. Some of the soldiers had died; others grew restless in security and marched away to new, dangerous lands, leaving the battle of foodstuffs and extravagances in the hands of the traders who doled out flour and wine, and gathered, in return, jewels and bars of gold for their coffers. The merchants combined so that all might charge the same high price for food, and with the profits they built their cedar houses roofed with rosy tiles; they dressed their women in foreign silks and were followed about in the streets by bands of retaining slaves.

A company of Genoese slave dealers came to the city and built a large warehouse for their merchandise. In it were tiers of cages where the black men sat until they were brought into the light to be felt over and bargained for.

It was a lovely city, Panama. Two thousand great cedarn houses lined its principal streets, and farther from the center were five thousand smaller dwellings for clerks and messengers and paid soldiers of the King. Clustering in the outskirts were innumerable thatched huts where the slaves were quartered. In the center of the town were six churches, two convents, and a tall cathedral, all with full gold services and vestments heavy with jewels. Already two saints had lived and died in Panama—not major saints, perhaps, but of enough importance to make their bones valuable.

One whole section of the city was crowded with the houses and stables and barracks of the King. Here, one-tenth of all the produce of the land was stored, waiting for the next plate fleet, when it would be carried on donkey-back across the isthmus to be loaded on the ship. Panama was supporting the kingdom of Spain—paying for the King's new palaces and wars. Because of the ready money in his treasury, the King gave Panama a seat of dignity. It bore a proud name: The Very Noble and Very Loyal City of Panama. Its rank was made equal with that of Cordova and Seville, for did not its officials wear golden chains of office about their necks? And the King granted to the city a resplendent coat of arms—a shield in a field of gold on the left yoke, and on the right, two caravels and a handful of gray arrows. Above all was the north star of discovery, while the Lions and Castles of the twin Spanish kingdoms circled around the shield. Truly Panama was one of the greatest cities in the world.

The center of the Cup of Gold was a broad, paved Plaza with a raised stand in the middle where music was played in the evening. While it played, the people strolled about, proving their positions by those to whom they spoke; the merchant aristocracy was very tender in its pride. A man might argue over the price of flour like a Jew in the daytime, but at night, in the Plaza, he bowed stiffly to acquaintances not so rich as he, and imperceptibly fawned on those richer.

They had grown soft in their security. The city was considered impregnable. On one side the sea protected it, and there were no foreign ships on the southern ocean anyway; to the landward side were walls and a broad morass which might be flooded in time of danger, making the city a veritable island. In addition, an attacking army must cut its way through the isthmian jungle to approach in force, must wind through narrow passes which might easily be defended by a small body of men. No one considered it possible that any sane leader could dream of the conquest of Panama. And so, when Campeche and Puerto Bello and Maracaibo fell to the buccaneers, the merchants of the Cup of Gold shrugged their shoulders and went about the usual business. It was unfortunate, of course; indeed it was sad that their own countrymen should be so used and robbed—but what could they expect? Their cities were on the wrong ocean. Panama need never think of these disturbances except with pity. God was good, and business—well, terrible; no money any more, and the farmers hanging on to their goods like thieves.

Don Juan Perez de Guzman was Governor of the Cup of Gold—a quiet nobleman whose life was devoted to being a complete gentleman and nothing else. He drilled his little army, changed his uniforms, and looked with care to the marriages of his relatives. He had been a soldier all his life—not a good campaigner, perhaps, but an extremely gallant officer.

The communications he wrote to his subordinates were magnificent. His wording of a demand for surrender by an Indian village was above reproach. The people loved their Governor. He dressed so well; he was so proud, yet condescending. They cheered him daily as he clattered down the street with a troop of horse behind him. If there were any apprehension of attack, surely the gallant figure of Don Juan would reassure the people. His were the noblest blood and the richest warehouses in the city.

Thus they lived happily in Panama, going to the green country places when the hot days were in, and returning to the balls and receptions of the town during the rainy season. And this was the Cup of Gold when Henry Morgan determined on its destruction.

One day the news crept into Panama that the terrible Morgan was coming in conquest. At first there was amused unbelief, but when more messengers came in, the city roused itself to frantic activity. The people rushed to the churches, confessed, kissed relics, and rushed home again. Hundreds of priests marched in procession bearing the Host through the streets. The dark brotherhood fiercely whipped themselves and dragged the heavy cross about for every one to see. The broken walls went unmended; the rusty cannons were not replaced. Don Juan heard mass after mass, spoke to the frenzied people, and suggested a procession of all the priests in the city.

Horrible stories began to grow up—how the buccaneers were not men at all, but animal things with heads like crocodiles and lions' claws. Grave men discussed such possibilities in the streets.

"The blessing of the day, Don Pedro."

"The Virgin's blessing, Don Guierrmo."

"What is your thought of these robbers?"

"Ah! horrible, Don Guierrmo; horrible. They are said to be demons!"

"But do you think it possible, as I have heard, that Morgan himself has three arms and wields a sword in each?"

"Who can say, my friend! The devil has even greater powers

than these, surely. Who can tell the limit of the Power of Evil? It is sacrilegious to consider it."

And later:

"You say you had it of Don Guierrmo? Surely he would not tell a questionable thing—a man of his wealth."

"I repeat only what he said—that Morgan could fire bullets from his finger-tips—that he breathed out sulphurous flames. Don Guierrmo was certain of it."

"I must tell my wife of this, Don Pedro."

So the tales grew until the people were half mad. Stories of cruelty in other cities were recalled, and the merchants who had shrugged before, turned pale on remembering. They could not believe; and yet they must believe, for the pirates were already on their way to Chagres, and their stated purpose was the conquest and pillage of the Cup of Gold. At last, under pressure, Don Juan dragged himself from church long enough to send five hundred soldiers for an ambush on the road across the isthmus. A young officer craved audience.

"Well, young man," the Governor began, "what is your wish?"

"If we had bulls, sir—if we had great numbers of wild bulls," the officer cried excitedly.

"Get them! Have the whole country scoured for bulls! Let the men gather a thousand of them! But what are we going to do with them?"

"We should stampede them on the enemy, sir."

"Marvelous plan! Genius of an officer! Ah, my dear friend— a thousand bulls? A thousand? I jested! Have them gather ten thousand of the wildest bulls."

The Governor ordered out his soldiers—two thousand of the king's troops—reviewed them, and then returned to kneel in the Cathedral. Don Juan was not afraid of fighting, but, like a prudent general, he was strengthening his secondary defense. Besides, anything that cost as much as the masses he had paid for must have some effect.

The first creeping rumor grew to a monster. Quaking citizens began to bury the plate from their houses. The churchmen threw chalices and candlesticks into the cisterns for safety, and walled up their more precious relics in passages underground.

Balboa would have strengthened the walls and flooded the approach. Pizarro's army would have been halfway across the isthmus, by this, to meet the oncoming buccaneers. But those brave times were past. The merchants of Panama thought only of their possessions, their lives, and their souls—in the order named. They never considered belting on swords or toiling at the disintegrated walls. That was for the soldiers of the King, who were paid good money to protect the citizens. The Governor must see to the defense.

Don Juan had reviewed his troops; that, to his mind, was all any general could do. The uniforms were proof against criticism, and his soldiers would have come with credit through any parade ground in Europe. Meanwhile, another mass would not hurt matters.

I

While the buccaneers were throwing away the savings of plundered Maracaibo, Henry Morgan plunged deeply into plans for his new conquest. It would require more fighting men than had ever before been assembled. The messengers of Captain Morgan went out to the four corners of the Spanish Main. His words found their way to Plymouth and Nieuw Amsterdam. Even to the wooded islands where men lived like apes, went his invitation to the great pillage.

"Every man will be rich if we succeed"; so ran the message. "This will be the most powerful blow ever struck by the Brotherhood. We will carry terror to the inmost heart of Spain. Our fleet gathers on the south side of Tortuga by October."

And soon the ships and men poured to the place of rendezvous; enormous new vessels with white sails and carven prows, ships bristling with brass cannons, old rotting hulks, their bottoms so foul with weeds that they moved through the water like logs. There came sloops and long canoes and flat-boats, forced through the water with sweeps. Even rafts drew to the meeting place, under woven palm sails.

And the men—all the blustering Brotherhood of Tortuga; the old, expert pirates of Goaves; Frenchmen, Netherlanders, English, and Portuguese—the embattled outcasts of the world. Canoe loads of slaves who had escaped the Spaniards paddled in, drawn to this expedition by a thirsting for their master's blood. The slaves were Caribs and negroes and fevered whites. Little groups of hunters appeared on the beaches of jungled islands and took ship for the south side of Tortuga.

Among the major ships were tall frigates and galleons which had been captured in old engagements. When the time came for departure, Captain Morgan had thirty-seven ships under his hand, and two thousand fighting men in addition to the mariners and boys. In the crowd of shipping lay three slim, clean sloops from New England. They had not come to fight, but to trade—powder for plunder, whiskey for gold. Powder and whiskey were the two great weapons of offense. And besides, these Plymouth men would buy old, useless ships for the iron and cordage they contained.

Captain Morgan had sent hunters into the woods to shoot cattle, and ships to the mainland to steal grain. When all returned, there was food on hand for a voyage.

No one save Cœur de Gris and Henry Morgan, of all this polyglot press of men who had come at the call of conquest, knew where that conquest was to be. No one dreamed where they would be sailing and whom fighting at the journey's end. The army of brave thieves had trooped to the name of Morgan, thirstily confident in his promise of unlimited plunder.

Henry Morgan had not dared to tell his destination. Potent though his name was, the buccaneers would have recoiled from such an impregnable objective. If they were given time to think of Panama, they would run home out of dread, for stories of the power and protection of the Cup of Gold had been told in all their islands for over half a century. Panama was a cloud city, an eerie, half-unearthly place, and armed with lightnings. Of course, there were those who believed the streets paved with golden cobbles, and certain church windows carved from single

emeralds. These legends would draw them on, if only they had
no time to think of the hazards as well.

When the ships had been careened and scraped, all the sails
mended, the cannons scoured and tested, the holds filled with
foodstuffs, then Henry Morgan called a meeting of his captains
for the purpose of signing solemn articles and dividing the fleet
into commands.

They gathered in the oaken cabin of the Admiral—thirty
captains who had brought ships to the mission. The frigate of
Captain Morgan was a fine Spanish man o' war. It had been
commanded by a Duke before it fell into the pirates' hands.
The cabin resembled a large drawing-room, paneled in dark
oak, its walls drawing slightly inward at the top. Across the
ceiling were heavy beams carved with vines and delicate, slim
leaves. On one wall had been the painted arms of Spain, but a
dagger had scraped and scratched it nearly out of sight.

Captain Morgan sat behind a broad table of which each leg
was a curious carved lion, and around him, seated on stools,
were the thirty leaders of his fleet and army. They waited impatiently for his communication.

There was the short, serious Captain Sawkins, whose eyes
burned with the fervor of Puritanism. He justified his murders
with Scripture and offered prayers of thanksgiving from a gun
carriage after a successful rape.

Black Grippo was there, an old man now, and sagging under
his unimportant infamies. He had come, finally, to regard his
God as a patient policeman whom one might possibly outwit.
Lately he had reasoned that he might flee his sins by a general
confession and reconfirmation in his mother church, and this
he intended to do when one more expedition should provide
him with a golden candlestick to bear to the confessing priest
by way of peace offering.

Holbert and Tegna, Sullivan and Meyther, sat on stools sur-
rounding Captain Morgan. In a dark corner were two whom
the whole Brotherhood knew as inseparables. They were called
simply The Burgundian and The Other Burgundian. The first
was a little fat man with a face like a red bloated sun. He was
nervous and excitable. The slightest public attention threw him

into a fit of embarrassment. When he was spoken to his face became redder, and he gave the impression of a bug frantically looking for a board under which to hide. His companion, The Other Burgundian, was his defender and guide. The Other Burgundian was taller and more powerfully made, although his left arm was gone at the elbow. These two might have been seen at any time walking together, sitting together. They seldom spoke, but always the good arm of The Other Burgundian would be about the shoulders of his dumpy friend in a gesture of protection.

Captain Morgan made his voice harsh and cold for his speech. There was a deep silence while he read the articles. A man who brought a ship might draw such and such rent; a carpenter with tools was to be paid so much; such amounts would be set aside for dependents of the slain. Then he came to the rewards to the first man to sight an enemy; the first to kill a Spaniard; the first into the city. The articles were finished.

"Now, sign," demanded Captain Morgan, and the men shuffled to the table and inscribed their names or marks.

When they were seated again, Sawkins spoke out.

"The rewards are four times as great as custom demands. Why is that?" Sawkins' training had made him abhor waste.

"The men will need bravery," Henry Morgan said calmly. "They will need urging—for we go to Panama."

"Panama!" It was almost a groan that answered him.

"Yes, Panama. You have signed articles—and I hang deserters. Look to the spirits of your men. You know something of the wealth of Panama—enough to whet their tongues; and I know the dangers well enough to be sure they are surmountable."

"But—Panama—" Sawkins began.

"I hang deserters," Captain Morgan said, and he left the cabin. Cœur de Gris remained to listen. He would report the temper of the men.

There was long silence. Every man was recalling the things he had heard about Panama.

"It is dangerous," said Sawkins, at last, "dangerous, but goodly rich. And the captain swore he knew the plan of the city and all the dangers of the fight."

These words brought sudden reassurance. If Captain Morgan knew, then they need not fear. Morgan was infallible. The room filled with nervous, quick conversation.

"Money? They walk on it. I have heard that the Cathedral—"

"But the jungle is impassable."

"They have good wine in Panama. I tasted some that came from there."

And all at once, every man seemed to think of the Red Saint.

"Why, that woman is there—La Santa Roja."

"Yes, that is right. She is there. Who do you suppose will get her?"

"The captain's not a man for women at all. I think it will be Cœur de Gris, here. He is the most favored of us."

"Well enough. Cœur de Gris is fated to die on the poniard of some man's jealousy. I would not mind killing him, because if I did not, some one else would. No, it might be my dagger."

"What would you do with a woman like that? A rope's end wouldn't be the thing, I guess."

"Well, to tell truth, I have always found those fat doubloons the most perfect instruments of rape. They glitter so."

"No, no. But see this. Nearly all women will repurchase their diamonds with their virtue. When you have the second, it is an easy thing to reacquire the first."

"What does old One-arm say about it—The Other Burgundian? Hey! will you be taking the Red Saint for your fat friend there?"

The Other Burgundian bowed.

"There would be no need," he said. "My friend is very capable. Why, I could tell a tale—" He turned to The Burgundian. "Have I your permission, Emil?"

The Burgundian seemed trying to get through the wall, but he did manage a nod.

"Then I will tell you gentlemen a story," The Other Burgundian began. "There were four friends in Burgundy; three who squeezed a little sour milk from the dugs of art, and one who had possessions. Also there was a lovely girl in Burgundy;

beautiful, accomplished, a veritable Circe, most lovely in the country. And the four friends all fell in love with this sweet exquisite.

"Each one gave her the gifts which were most dear to himself. The first folded his soul in a sonnet and laid it at her feet. The second filled a viol with her name; and I—the third, I mean—painted the rosy image of her face. Thus did we artists bid for her in all friendliness to one another. But the last of the four was the true artist. He was quiet; he was subtle. What an actor! He won her with a superb gesture. He opened his hand—so—and there, on the cushion of his palm, lay a laughing rose pearl. They were married.

"Now, soon after this marriage, Delphine gave evidence of greater virtues than any one had suspected. Not only was this paragon a perfect wife, but she was also the discreet and delightful mistress—not to one, but to all three—of the husband's friends. And Emil, the husband, did not mind. He loved his friends. Why not? They were his true friends, but poor.

"Ah, where is a force so blind, so idiotic, as public opinion! This time, two deaths and one banishment were born of it. This hydra of a Public Opinion—consider to yourselves what it did! It forced Emil to challenge his three friends. Even then, all might have ended with the kiss, the embrace—'my honor is whole again, dear friend'—if it had not been for Emil's deplorable habit of leaving his rapier point in putrefying meat. Two of the men died, and I lost my arm.

"Now, here again comes this Public Opinion, like a blundering, powerful ox. Having forced the duels, it forced the victor out of France. Here is Emil, beside me—lover, swordsman, artist, landowner. The Public Opinion— But I have strayed from the tale in my hatred of this force. What I wanted to tell you is that Emil asks no consideration, no quarter at all. I know it appears that a swarm of hungry ants has been feasting on his spirit; but let great beauty be placed before him, let the Red Saint be mirrored in those eyes, and you shall see and remember what I say. He is quiet; he is subtle; he is an artist. Where other men cry 'Virility! Force! Rape!'—Emil carries a rose pearl in his pocket as an aphrodisiac."

II

An army of flat-boats was floating on the River Chagres, each
one taxed to the limit of its buoyancy with the men of the Free
Brotherhood. Frenchmen there were, wearing striped nightcaps
and full, loose pantaloons; Frenchmen who had sailed out of
St. Malo or Calais one time, and now had no fatherland to sail
back to. Some of the barges were filled with Cockneys, dirty
men for the most part, with black teeth and the look of petty
thievery about them. There were dour, silent Zeerovers from
Holland, lumpishly sitting in their boats, gazing with the dull
eyes of gourmands along the course of Chagres.

The heavy, square barges were poled along by Caribs and
Cimarones, joyfully fierce men who loved war so well that
they could be persuaded to bend their sleek brown shoulders
to labor if the reward were blood. One section of the parade of
piracy was composed of negroes lately escaped from Spanish
servitude. They wore red bandoliers, crossing like wounds on
their naked breasts. The leader, a huge buck with a face like a
ferocious black moose, wore nothing at all save a broad yellow
belt and a cavalier hat, the plume of which hung limply down
and curled under his glistening black chin.

The boats, in a long line, edged up the stream. The English
shouted tuneless chanteys, swaying their bodies to preserve the
rhythm; the French sang softly of the little loves they might
have had; and the Cimarones and blacks chattered their endless
monologues directed at no one in particular.

And Chagres twisted on ahead in loops and tremendous horse-
shoe turns. The yellow water, like a frightened, leprous woman,
timidly caressed the hulls. On this Chagres you might pole your
boat all day, and at night make your camp not half a mile by
straight line from the starting place. It was a sluggish, apathetic
river of many shallows where the bright sand glittered in the sun.
Chagres was a dilettante in the eternal and understood business of
rivers—that of getting to the ocean with as little bother and effort
as possible. Chagres dreamed about over the country, seemingly
reluctant to lose its lazy individuality in the worried sea.

After a time the boats came to a land where the thick jungle rolled to the river's edge and stopped in a curving crest, like a frozen green wave. There were spotted tigers cruising along through the trees, watching the men with a sad curiosity. Now and then a great snake slipped from the warm log where it had been dozing in the sun, and floated in the water, rearing up its head to see this unheard of procession. Whole clans of excited monkeys dashed about among the vines, pretending to hate disturbance. They howled their indignation and hurled leaves and twigs at the boats. Fourteen hundred outlandish beings had invaded sacred Mother Jungle; the mangiest monkey on earth had, at least, his right of protest.

The day's heat had come like a breath of fever, heavy and dully bewildering. The songs from the barges thickened and died as though hot blankets had been thrown over the men. The buccaneers sat lifelessly on their benches. But the straining Indians poled on with a steady, swinging motion. The muscles slipped along their fine arms, coiled and uncoiled about their shoulders like restless serpents. Within their brooding brains was a revery of slaughter, a delightful blood dream. "On!" said their brains. "On! Ugh! the battle is two strides nearer. On! On! Ugh! Panama; the savannas of blood are two strides nearer." The long line of boats writhed up the river like a tremendous jointed snake.

The long ardent day fell back toward evening, and no human had been seen along the river banks. This was a serious matter, for there was no food in the barges. There was no room for food. Every inch was needed for men and weapons. As it was, the water washed over the low decks of the artillery rafts. It was well known that many plantations bordered the river, whereat a hungry army might refresh itself, and this knowledge had sent the pirates foodless toward Panama. All day they had watched for the plantation and had seen nothing but the green tangled jungle.

In the evening, the first boat came abreast of a landing of sticks. A languid coil of smoke rose from behind a planted row of tall trees. With loud cries of joy, the buccaneers leaped from their boats and waded to the shore. Curses and despair; the buildings were burned and deserted. This little smoke drifted from the black heap of what had been a granary, in which no single grain remained for the men to eat. Deep tracks led off into the wet jungle to show where the cattle had been driven away, but the tracks were two days old.

The hungry men went back to their boats. Ah, well; they must go hungry to-day. Hunger was a part of war, a matter to be expected and endured. To-morrow, surely, they would come on houses where wine was stored, cold and delicious; corrals where fat cows nodded stupidly, waiting to be slaughtered. A buccaneer—a true buccaneer—would sell out his life for a cup of sour wine or a bit of converse with one of the brown women of half-Spain. These were the joys of life, and a fair thing it was if the man were stabbed before he finished his drink or his conversation; but hunger— Well, to-morrow there would be food surely.

But again the sun arose, a white, fevered ulcer in the sky. There was the river of mad turnings, and along its banks deserted farms, and no food at all. News of this invasion had swept along before them like an appalling message of pestilence. No man or animal remained to greet the buccaneers.

On the third day they found a number of tough green cow hides, and they beat them between stones to soften them for eating. Some of the men had eaten half their belts. Once a little burned maize was discovered in a still burning granary, and several of the pirates died in agony from gorging on it.

The men hunted in the jungle, searched through the trees for any living thing which might be eaten. Even the cats and monkeys seemed to be leagued with Spain. The jungle was silent and creatureless now. No unit of life was left save the flying insects. Now and then a snake was caught and roasted, while its captor sullenly guarded his supper. A few mice came into the pirates' hands, but these were bolted on the spot for fear of thievery.

After four days of traveling, the river grew too shallow for the boats. The cannons were brought ashore to be dragged by man-power along a narrow path. The buccaneers straggled out in an unkempt column, while ahead of them a swarm of busy

Indians, drawing energy from their sanguinary dream, hacked and slashed out the trail through the jungle with their heavy knives. A few small groups of fleeing Spaniards were seen, and now and again small bands of Spanish Indians flushed from the thickets like coveys of frightened quail, but no enemy paused long enough to give fight. Once, beside the trail, a prepared place of ambush was discovered; a wall of earth, and the ashes of many camp-fires. It was deserted. Terror had seized the soldiers sent to fight, and they had run away.

Now the men were dragging themselves nearer and nearer to Panama. Their enthusiasm for the conquest was gone; they cursed their leader for his failure to bring food; they were drawn farther and farther by the sheer force of the example of Captain Morgan.

From the first he had led them, but now, at the head of the exhausted troops, Henry Morgan himself was beginning to doubt whether he wished very greatly to go to Panama. He tried to remember the force which had started him on his way, the magnet of unseen beauty. La Santa Roja had faded in his imagination as his hunger grew. He could not clearly remember his desire. But even though this desire should desert him utterly, he must go on. One failure, one moment of indecision, would scatter his successes like pigeons.

Cœur de Gris was beside him as he had been from the beginning, a haggard Cœur de Gris now, who lurched a little as he walked. Captain Morgan looked with pity and pride at his lieutenant. He saw the eyes like shallow crystal, and a wild light in them as of approaching madness. Captain Morgan felt less lonely with the young man by his side. He knew that Cœur de Gris was grown to be a part of him.

The sun's heat was falling from the heavens like a burning rain. It struck the ground and then slowly rose again, burdened with dampness and the nauseous odor of rotting leaves and roots. Once Cœur de Gris was driven to his knees by the heat, but immediately he rose to trudge onward. Henry Morgan saw his staggering walk, and glanced at the trail ahead with indecision.

"Perhaps we should be resting here," he said. "The men are exhausted."

"But no. We must go on and go on," Cœur de Gris replied. "If we stop here, the men will only be weaker when we start again."

Henry Morgan mused: "I wonder why you are so avid in my mission. You move forward when even I begin to doubt myself. What is it that you expect to find in Panama, Cœur de Gris?"

"I expect to find nothing," the young man said. "Are you try- ing to trap me into a statement of disloyalty? I know the prize is yours before we arrive. I admit it, sir. But, you see, I am like a great, round stone set in motion down a hill, so much reason have I for going to Panama. You, sir, set me in motion."

"It is strange that I should so want Panama," Henry said.

The flushed face of the lieutenant turned on him in anger.

"You do not want Panama. It is the woman you want, not Panama." His voice was as bitter as his words, and now he was pressing his palms against his temples.

"It is true," the captain murmured. "It is true that I want the woman; but that is still more strange."

"Strange?" Wild resentment broke out in Cœur de Gris. He shouted, "Strange? Why is it strange to be lusting after a woman who is known to be beautiful? Would you call each one of these men strange, or every male thing on earth strange? Or are you endowed with a god-like lust? Do you bear the body of a Titan? Strange! Yes, surely, my Captain; copulation and its contemplation are things completely unique among men!"

Henry Morgan was bewildered, but there was a little terror in him also. He seemed to have witnessed the walking of a loathsome, unbelievable ghost. Could it be that these men felt as he did?

"But I think there is more than lust," he said. "You can- not understand my yearning. It is as though I strove for some undreamed peace. This woman is the harbor of all my questing. I do not think of her as a female thing with arms and breasts, but as a moment of peace after turmoil, a perfume after rancid filth. Yes, it is strange to me. When I consider the years that are gone away, I am bewildered at my activity. I went to mighty trouble for silly, golden things. I did not know the secret which makes the earth a huge chameleon. My little wars seem the

scrambling of a person strange to me, a person who did not
know the ways of making the world change color. I mourned,
in the old time, when each satisfaction died in my arms. Is it
any wonder they all died? I did not know the secret. No, you
cannot understand my yearning."

Cœur de Gris was grasping his aching temples between his
hands. "I do not understand!" he cried scornfully. "Do you
think I do not understand? I know; to your mind your feelings
are new things, discoveries of fresh importance. Your failures
are unprecedented. This gigantic conceit will not allow you to
believe that this Cockney behind you—yes, he who sometimes
rolls on the ground in fits—might have the same hopes and
despairs as yourself. You cannot believe that these men feel
as deeply as you do. I suppose it would surpass your wildest
thought if I should say I want the woman as much as you do,
or that I could be telling sweet sentences to La Santa Roja, perhaps, better than you could."

Captain Morgan had flushed under the lash of words. He
did not believe it. It was monstrous to think that these men
could feel as he did. Such a comparison made him, somehow,
unworthy.

"You wonder why I say these things?" Cœur de Gris continued. "I will tell you. The pain has made me mad, and I am
going to die." He walked on silently for a little distance, then
suddenly he screamed and fell heavily to the ground.

For a full minute Captain Morgan looked at him. Then a
great, harsh wave seemed to break forth in his chest. He knew
that minute how much he had come to love the young lieutenant, knew that he could not bear to lose young Cœur de Gris.
Now he had dropped to his knees beside the silent figure.

"Water!" he cried to the nearest buccaneer, and when the
fellow only stared at him: "Water! bring water—water!"
His hand was hysterically jerking at a pistol in his belt. They
brought him water in a hat. All the pirates saw their cold captain kneeling on the ground, stroking the damp, shining hair of
Cœur de Gris.

The young man's eyes opened slowly and he tried to rise.

"I am sorry, sir. The pain in my head, you know— The sun

sucked out my wits. But you must get up, sir! The men will lose respect for you if they see you kneeling here."

"Lie still, boy! Lie quietly! You must not move yet. I am afraid. In a moment I thought you were dead, and all the world shriveled. Lie quietly! Now I am glad. You must not move. Now we will take the Cup of Gold together, and it shall be a chalice of two handles." He lifted Cœur de Gris and carried him to the shade of a huge tree. The buccaneers rested on the ground while their lieutenant regained his strength.

Cœur de Gris was leaning back against the tree. He was smiling at the captain with a queer womanish affection.

"Am I like the Cockney?" Henry Morgan asked a little wistfully; "like the Cockney with fits?"

Cœur de Gris laughed.

"You know nothing at all about the man. You might be proud to resemble him. I will tell you, for I know that to you he is only a figure of wood to take orders. The man's name is Jones. All his life he has wanted to be a preacher of the Gospel. He thought his fits were visitations of the Holy Ghost, testing him for some divine mission. Once he stood on a corner and spoke to the people of London, and the watch came upon him as he talked. The law took him as a vagrant and shipped him to the islands.

"This Jones, after his term was done, became a pirate to keep from starving. There was a division of spoil from a raid, and to his share fell a woman slave, a Spaniard with negro blood. He married her to save her reputation. He did not know how little was left to save. You see, sir, his wife is a Catholic. She will not let him read the Bible when he is at home. And do you know, sir, he truly believes that thievish circumstance has robbed him of success; not success as you and I know it, but the success that comes of God's especial favor. He imagines he might have been a Protestant Savonarola."

"But his fits—" said Henry Morgan. "His horrible fits— I have seen them."

Again the young man laughed.

"The fits? Ah, the fits are a gift—an heirloom."

"And you think he feels?"

"Yes, perhaps he does. Remember, he married her to save her name, and kept her with him when he found what that name was. And you will see him bashfully claim a crucifix at the division of spoil. He will take her a crucifix from Panama. Think, man! He is a Separatist from the church. He abhors crucifixes!"

III

Onward the buccaneers drove themselves toward Panama. They had eaten leather and bitter jungle roots, rodents and snakes and monkeys. Their cheeks were shallow cups under their cheek bones; their eyes glittered with fever. Now that their enthusiasm was gone, they were dragged onward by the knowledge of their captain's infallibility. Morgan could not fail because he never had failed. Surely he had a plan which would put the gold of the New World in their pockets. And the word gold, though it had lost its meaning of reality, was more important than the word hunger.

On the eighth morning a scout came to Captain Morgan.

"The way is blocked, sir. They have thrown up a little earthwork in front of us and mounted cannons."

At a command, the head of the wriggling column swung to the left and began to gnaw its way through thicker underbrush. In the evening they came to the top of a small, round hill, and there below them was Panama laved in the golden light of the western sun. Each man searched his neighbors' face to be assured that this was not his own personal hallucination.

One pirate moved to the hill's edge. He stopped still and shouted crazily, and then his companions saw him running down the hill, dragging at his sword as he ran. A herd of cattle was feeding in the hollow below them, left there by some blundering Spaniard. In a moment the whole fourteen hundred men were stampeding down the hill. They killed the cows with their swords; they lunged and slashed at the frightened animals. Soon, very soon, the blood was dripping down the beards of the famished men, the red drops falling on their shirts. During that night they gorged themselves into unconsciousness.

While the dark was down, the pirate scouts were ranging over the plain like were-wolves; they slipped to the walls and counted the soldiers before the town.

And early in the morning, Captain Morgan aroused his men and called them together to give them the orders for the day's fight. Henry Morgan had come to know the buccaneering soul. He lifted out the brains of his men and molded them for battle. He spoke to their fears.

"It is nine days' journey back to the river mouth where the ships lie—nine days, and no food at all. You could not get to the ships even if you wanted to run away. And here is Panama. While you were sleeping like hogs, the scouts were busy. Before this city, four thousand soldiers are drawn up, with wings of cavalry. These are not countrymen with guns and knives, but drilled soldiers in red coats. This is not all. There are bulls to be loosed against you—against you cattle hunters." A laugh followed his last words. Many of these men had lived in the jungle and had made their livelihood with hunting wild cattle.

The captain rubbed their avarice:

"Gold and jewels past hope of counting are in the city. Every man of you will be rich if we succeed."

Their hunger:

"Think of the roasted meats, the barrels of wine in the cellars, the spiced puddings. Imagine them!"

Their lust:

"Women slaves there are in the city, and thousands of other women, God knows! Your difficulty will be only in judging which to choose from the multitude that will fall to us. These are not grubby field women, but great ladies who lie in silken beds. How will your skins feel in beds like those, do you suppose?"

And last, because he knew them very well, he raised the standard of their vanity.

"The names of those who take part in this fight will climb the stairs of history. This is no pillage, but glorious war. Imagine to yourselves the people of Tortuga pointing to you and saying, 'That man was in the fight at Panama. That man is a hero, and rich.' Think how the women of Goaves will run after you when

you go home again. There is the Cup of Gold before you. Will
you run away? Many will die in the field to-day, but those who
remain will carry golden Panama home in their pockets."

A hoarse cheer arose. The French kissed their hands to Henry
Morgan; the Caribs chattered and rolled their eyes. The gour-
mand Zeerovers looked dully at the white city.

"One thing more," said the captain. "The troops will be
drawn up in a line, if I know these Spanish captains. They like
to make as great a show as possible. Your orders are to fire at
their center, all of you; and when that center is weakened, then
charge and split them."

They mowed out on the plain, a dense cloud of men. Two
hundred marksmen walked in advance, while the rest were
grouped behind.

Now Don Juan, the Governor of Panama, stood with his
neat army, a long line of foot soldiers in companies of two files.
He looked at the rough formation of the enemy with contempt.
Almost gayly he signaled for the first advance.

The Spanish cavalry swung out, wheeling and whirling across
the plain. Now they formed a V, and now a hollow square.
Moving at a fast trot, they went through all the intricate evolu-
tions of a review; they made triangles, T's. In one moment every
sword glanced in the sunlight, then was made to disappear by
twisting wrists, and then to flash again. Don Juan groaned with
admiration.

"Look at them, my friends; look at Rodriguez, my beloved
captain. Ah, Rodriguez! is it really I who have taught you these
things? Can it be that this is the Rodriguez I held in my arms a
little time ago? He was a baby then, but now he is a man and
a hero. See the line, the sureness, the precision. See Rodriguez
with his troop, my friends. How may these beasts of buccaneers overcome horsemen like mine?"

Rodriguez, at the head of his troop, seemed to hear the Governor's praise. His shoulders stiffened. He rose in his stirrups
and gave the signal for the charge. The bugles sang excitedly.
The hooves roared with a hollow rolling sound over the turf.
Their coming was like a red wave with a silver crest. Rodriguez turned in his saddle and looked proudly at the hurtling

troop behind him, following his orders as though they were the multimembers of one great body governed by his brain. Every saber was lined along a horse's neck. Rodriguez turned again to look once more at his lovely Panama before the shock. And then the whole troop rode headlong into a marsh. They knew it was there, but in the enthusiasm of the moment, in the excitement of their figures, they had forgotten about it. In a second the horse of Panama was a broken jumble of men and fallen beasts. They were flies caught in a green flypaper.

Don Juan looked dazedly at the pile of writhing, mangled bodies out on the plain, and then he burst into sobs like a child who has seen his bright toy broken in the road. The Governor did not know what to do. His brain was heavy with a red sorrow. He turned about and started plodding homeward. He would go and hear a mass in the Cathedral, he thought.

The Spanish staff had grown frantic. Red and gold uniforms were rushing about in every direction. Every officer shouted commands at the top of his voice. The young lieutenant who had brought up the cattle finally made himself heard.

"Turn loose the bulls—the bulls," he cried, over and over, until the others were shouting it also. The Indians who held the bulls tore out the nose rings and began prodding the great beasts forward with their goads. Slowly the herd moved out across the plain. Then a red monster broke into a slow run, and immediately the whole band was running.

"They will trample these robbers into the grass," said a Spanish officer wisely. "Where they pass, we shall find buttons, pieces of weapons—nothing more—on the bloody ground."

The bulls galloped slowly toward the rough line of the buccaneers. Suddenly the two hundred marksmen knelt and fired—fired quickly, like men hunting game. A kicking, bellowing wall seemed to rise up in the path of the running animals. Those of the herd that were not crippled halted in their tracks, sniffed the blood, milled, and then stampeded in terror back on the Spanish ranks. The officer was right. Where they passed, nothing remained except buttons and broken weapons and bloody turf.

In the horror of the stampede the buccaneers had charged.

Now they dashed into the hole the bulls had made, and drove the split defenders left and right. There were a few war cries, but these were continental soldiers. They could not understand this kind of fighting. These terrible vagrants laughed and killed men with both of their hands. The men of Spain held ground for a little while, but then their hearts broke under their fine red coats, and they ran away to hide in the jungle. Little knots of buccaneers pursued them, spitting those who fell exhausted. Soon the defending troops were scattered. Some of them climbed into the trees and hid themselves among the leaves; some lost themselves in the mountains and were never found. The Cup of Gold lay helpless before Henry Morgan.

A crowd of shouting men poured through the undefended gate and up the broad street. At crossing alleys, part of the line changed its course, like a river flowing backwards into its tributaries. Now and then a party would detach itself from the main body and move on one of the imposing houses. There would be kicks on the door, a rush, and the door would fold inward like the cover of an enormous book. The men would crowd through the entrance—cries and a scream or two. An old woman leaned from a window and looked with curiosity at the invaders. Then disappointment showed in her face.

"Hi!" she screamed to a window across the way. "Look at this, will you! These thieves look very much like our own Spaniards. They are not devils at all, but only men." She seemed to resent their humanity. She withdrew her head as though she renounced them for being only men.

In the afternoon a fire broke out. Tall flames lanced into the sky. A section caught, a street; half the city was burning.

Henry Morgan went to the Palace of the Governor to establish his quarters, and there, in the doorway, stood Don Juan Perez de Guzman, with a naked rapier in his hand.

"I am the Governor," he said brokenly. "My people looked to me to defend them against this scourge. I have failed—but perhaps I can manage to kill you."

Henry Morgan looked at the ground. Something about this hysterical man unnerved him. "I did not set the fire," he said. "Some of your own slaves did that out of revenge, I think."

Don Juan moved forward with his drawn rapier. "Defend yourself!" he cried.

Captain Morgan did not change his position.

The sword dropped from the Governor's hand. "I am a coward—a coward," he cried. "Why did I not strike without speaking? Why did you not oppose me? Ah, I am a coward! I waited too long. I should never have spoken at all, but driven my point into your throat. I wanted to die a moment ago—to die as a kind of atonement for my failure—and to take you with me as a peace offering to my conscience. Panama is gone—and I should be gone, too. It is as though a finger continued to live after the body has died. But I cannot die now. I haven't the courage. And I cannot kill you. I realize how I pretended. Ah! if I had only acted quickly! If I had not spoken—" He walked away toward the gate and the open country. Henry Morgan watched him drunkenly lurching out of the city.

The black night came. Nearly all of the city was in flame, a garden of red fire. The tower of the Cathedral crashed down and threw a heaven of sparks into the air. Panama was dying in a bed of flame, and the buccaneers were murdering the people in the streets.

All night the captain sat in the audience chamber while his men brought in the gathered plunder. They piled golden bars on the floor like cord-wood, bars so heavy that two men carried each of them with difficulty. There were little stacks of jewels like glittering haycocks, and in a corner the precious vestments of the church were heaped, the stock of a heavenly old clothes market.

Henry Morgan sat in a tall chair carved in the likeness of many serpents.

"Have you found La Santa Roja?"

"No, sir. The women of the town are more like devils."

Prisoners were brought in to be put to the torture with a thumbscrew taken from the Spanish prison.

"Kneel! Your wealth? [Silence] Turn, Joe!"

"Mercy! Mercy! I will lead you; I swear it. A cistern near my house."

Another—

"Kneel! Your wealth? Turn, Joe!"

"I will lead you."

As regular, ruthless, and unfeeling they were as master slaughterers in a cow pen.

"Have you found La Santa Roja? I will hang all of you if she is harmed."

"No one has seen her, sir. The men, except a few, are drunk."

All through the night— With each confession of wealth concealed, the victim was led out by a party of searchers, and soon they would return, bearing cups and silver plates, jewels, and clothing of colored silk. The glowing treasure in the Hall of Audience was becoming one enormous heap.

And Captain Morgan, wearily:

"Have you found the Red Saint?"

"We have not found her, sir, but we are seeking and inquiring over the whole city. Perhaps in the daylight, sir—"

"Where is Cœur de Gris?"

"I think he is drunk, sir, but—" He looked away from Henry Morgan.

"But what? What do you mean?" the captain cried.

"Nothing; I mean nothing at all, sir. It is almost certain that he is drunk. Only it takes such gallons of wine to make him drunk, and perhaps he has found a friend in the meantime."

"Did you see him with any one?"

"Yes, sir; I saw him with a woman, and she was drunk. I could swear that Cœur de Gris was drunk, too."

"Did you think the woman might have been La Santa Roja?"

"Oh, no, sir; I am sure it was not she. Only one of the women of the town, sir."

There was a clash of golden service thrown on the pile.

IV

A yellow dawn crept out of the little painted hills of Panama and grew bolder as it edged across the plain. The sun flashed up from behind a peak, and its golden rays sought for their city. But Panama had died, had felt the quick decay of fire in one red night. But then, as the sun is a fickle sphere, the seeking beams found joy in the new thing. They lighted on the poor ruins, peered into upturned dead faces, raced along the cluttered streets, fell headlong into broken patios. They came to the white Palace of the Governor, leaped through the windows of the audience chamber, and fingered the golden heap on the floor.

Henry Morgan was asleep in the serpent chair. His purple coat was draggled with the mud of the plain. The gray-clad rapier lay on the floor beside him. He was alone in this room, for all the men who had helped to pick the city's bones during the night had gone away to drink and to sleep.

It was a high, long room, walled with panels of polished cedar. The beams of the ceiling were as black and heavy as old iron. It had been a court of justice, a place of wedding feasts, the hall where ambassadors were toasted or murdered. One door opened on the street; the other, a broad, arched opening, let into a lovely garden about which the Palace lay curled. In the middle of the garden a little marble whale spouted its steady stream into a pool. There were giant plants in red glazed pots, plants with purple leaves and flowers whose petals bore arrow heads or hearts or squares in cardinal. There were shrubs, lined with harsh tracery in the mad colors of the jungle. A monkey no larger than a rabbit picked over the gravel of the path, looking for seeds.

On one of the stone seats of the garden a woman was sitting. She pulled a yellow flower to bits while she sang fragments of a tender, silly song—"I would pluck the flower of the day for you, my love, where it grows in the dawning." Her eyes were black, but opaque. They were the rich, sheening, shallow black of a dead fly's wings, and under the lids there were sharp little lines. She could draw up the under lids of her eyes so that they shone with laughter, though her mouth remained harsh and placid. Her skin was very pale, her hair straight and black as obsidian.

Now she looked at the sun's inquisitive light, and now

at the arched doorway of the Hall of Audience. Her singing stopped. She listened intently a moment, then started the gentle song again. There was no other sound save the distant cracklings of the fire which still burned among the palm slave huts on the outskirts of the city. The little monkey came at a funny, crooked gallop along the path. He stopped in front of the woman and raised his black paws above his head as though in prayer.

The woman spoke softly to him. "You have learned your lesson well, Chico. Your teacher was a Castilian with a fearful mustache. I am well acquainted with him. Do you know, Chico, he wants what he considers my honor. He will not be satisfied until he has added my honor to his own, and then he will be almost boastful. You have no idea of the size and weight of his honor even as it is. But you would be satisfied with a nut, wouldn't you, Chico?" She dropped a piece of her flower to the tiny beast, whereupon he seized it, put it in his mouth, and spat in disgust.

"Chico! Chico! you forget your teacher! That is all wrong. You will get no woman's honor by it. Place the flower over your heart, kiss my hand with a loud snapping sound, and then stride off like a fierce sheep out searching for wolves." She laughed and glanced again toward the doorway. Although there was no sound, she rose and walked quickly toward the Hall of Audience.

Henry Morgan had turned slightly in his chair, and his turning allowed the sunlight to beat upon his eyelids. Suddenly he sat up and stared about him. He looked with satisfaction at the heap of treasure on the floor, then gazed full in the eyes of the woman standing under the broad arch.

"And have you ruined our poor city enough for your satisfaction?" she asked.

"I did not burn the city," Henry said quickly. "Some of your Spanish slaves set the torch." The words had been forced from him. He remembered that he was surprised. "Who are you?" he demanded.

She moved a step into the hall. "My name is Ysobel. It was said that you sought me."

"Sought you?"

"Yes. I have been called La Santa Roja by certain young idiots," she said.

"You—the Red Saint?"

He had prepared a picture in his mind, a picture of a young girl with blue, seraphic eyes that would fall before the steady stare of a mouse. These eyes did not fall. Under their soft black surfaces they seemed to be laughing at him, making light of him. This woman's face was sharp, almost hawk-like. She was beautiful, truly, but hers was the harsh, dangerous beauty of lightning. And her skin was white—not pink at all.

"You are the Red Saint?"

He was not prepared for this change of idea. He was staggered at such a revolt against his preconceptions. But, said his mind, twelve hundred men and more had broken their way through the jungle, had dashed on the city like a brutal wave. Hundreds of humans had died in the agony of wounds, hundreds were crippled, the Cup of Gold was a ruin; and all these things had been done that Henry Morgan might take La Santa Roja. With all this preparation, it must be certain that he loved her. He would not have come if he had not loved her. Whatever the shock of her appearance, he could not circumvent the logic that he loved her. It must be so. Always he had thought of the "Saint" in her name; and now he perceived the reason for the adjective. But a queer feeling was seeping in on him—no logical feeling at all. He remembered such sensations from a time long gone; he was drawn, yet repelled by this woman, and he felt her power to embarrass him. Morgan closed his eyes, and the figure of a slender little girl with golden hair stood in the darkness of his brain.

"You are like Elizabeth," he said, in the dull monotone of one dreaming. "You are like, and yet there is no likeness. Perhaps you master the power she was just learning to handle. I think I love you, but I do not know. I am not sure."

His eyes had been half closed, and when he opened them there was a real woman before him, not the wraithlike Elizabeth. And she was gazing at him with curiosity, and perhaps, he thought, with some affection. It was queer that she had come to him when no one had forced her to come. She must be fascinated. He reached into his memory for the speeches he had built on his way across the isthmus.

"You must marry me, Elizabeth—Ysobel. I think I love you, Ysobel. You must come away with me and live with me and be my wife, under the protection of my name and of my hand."

"But I am already married," she interposed; "quite satisfactorily married."

He had even foreseen this. During the nights of the march he had planned this campaign as carefully as he might have planned a battle.

"But is it right that two, meeting and flaming white fire, should go apart for stark eternity, should trudge off into bleak infinity; that each of these two should bear black embers of a flame that has not burned itself to death? Is there anything under heaven to forbid us this burning? Heaven has given the deathless oil; each of us carries a little torch for the other. Ah, Ysobel—deny it, or shrink from the intruding knowledge if you will. You would vibrate to my touch like the fine body of an old violin.

"You are afraid, I think. There is in your mind a burrowing apprehension of the world; the prying world, the spiteful world. But do you not be fearsome, for I say to you that this world is a blind, doddering worm, knowing three passions only—jealousy, curiosity, and hate. It is easy to defeat the worm, so only you make the heart a universe to itself. The worm, having no heart, cannot conceive the workings of a heart. He lies confounded by the stars of this new system.

"Why do I tell you these things, Ysobel—knowing you will understand them? You must understand them. Perhaps I know by the dark, sweet music of your eyes. Perhaps I can read the throbbing heart-beats on your lips. Your beating heart is a little drum urging me to battle with your fears. Your lips are like twin petals of a red hibiscus.

"And if I find you lovely, am I to be put in fear by a dull circumstance? May I not speak my thought to you whom it most concerns next to myself? Do not let us go apart bearing black embers of a flame that has not burned itself to death."

When he had started to speak she listened carefully to his words, and then a little pain had flitted across her face; but when he had done there was only amusement in her eyes—that and the lurking ridicule under their surfaces. Ysobel laughed softly.

"You forget only one thing, sir," she said. "I do not burn. I wonder if I shall ever burn again. You do not carry a torch for me—and I hoped you did. I came this morning to see if you did. And I have heard your words so often and so often in Paris and Cordova. I am tired of these words that never change. Is there some book with which aspiring lovers instruct themselves? The Spanish men say the same things, but their gestures are more practiced, and so a little more convincing. You have much to learn."

She was silent. Henry looked at the floor. His amazement had raised a fog of dullness in his brain.

"I took Panama for you," he said plaintively.

"Ah—yesterday I hoped you did. Yesterday I dreamed you had, but to-day—I am sorry." She spoke softly and very sadly.

"When I heard of you and your blustering up and down the ocean, I thought of you, somehow, as the one realist on an earth of vacillation. I dreamed that you would come to me one day, armed with a transcendent, silent lust, and force my body with brutality. I craved a wordless, reasonless brutality. The long thought of it bore me up when I was paraded by my husband. He did not love me. He was flattered with the thought that I loved him. It gave him importance and charm in his own eyes, neither of which were his. He would take me through the streets and his eyes would say, 'See what I have married! No ordinary man could marry such a woman; but then, I am not an ordinary man.' He was afraid of me—a little man, and afraid of me. He would say, 'With your permission, my dear, I shall exercise the prerogative of a husband.' Ah, the contempt I have for him!

"I wanted force—blind, unreasoning force—and love not for my soul or for some imagined beauty of my mind, but for the white fetish of my body. I do not want softness. I am soft. My husband uses scented lotions on his hands before he touches

me, and his fingers are like thick, damp snails. I want the crush
of hard muscles, the delicious pain of little hurts."

She searched his face closely, as though looking once more
for a quality which had been lost.

"I thought richly of you once; you grew to be a brazen figure of the night. And now—I find you a babbler, a speaker of
sweet, considered words, and rather clumsy about it. I find you
are no realist at all, but only a bungling romancer. You want
to marry me—to protect me. All men, save one, have wanted
to protect me. In every way I am more able to protect myself
than you are. From the morning of my first memory I have
been made sick with phrases. I have been dressed in epithets
and fed endearments. These other men, like you, would not
say what they wanted. They, like you, felt it necessary to justify
their passion in their own eyes. They, like you, must convince
themselves, as well as me, that they loved me."

Henry Morgan had sunk his head, seemingly in shame. Now
he started toward her.

"But I will force you then," he cried.

"It is too late—I would perforce think of you standing there,
declaiming your considered words. While you wrenched at my
clothing, I would picture you fawning before me, blurting out
your words. And I should laugh, I'm afraid. I might even protect myself—and you, who should be somewhat an authority
on rape, must know the consequence of that. No, you have
failed—and I am sorry of your failure."

"I love you," he said miserably.

"You speak as though it were some new, tremendous thing.
Many men have loved me; hundreds have said they did. But
what are you going to do with me, Captain Morgan? My husband is in Peru, and my inheritance is there also."

"I—I do not know."

"But am I to be a slave—a prisoner?"

"Yes; I must take you away with me. The men would laugh
at me, else. It would ruin discipline."

"If I must be a slave," she said, "if I must go away from
my own country, I hope I shall be your slave—yours or the
property of a charming young buccaneer I met last night. But I

do not think you will take me, Captain Morgan. No; I do not think you will force me to go, for I will, perhaps, twist the knife I have already in your breast."

Henry Morgan was aroused.

"Who was this young buccaneer?" he asked crossly.

"Ah, you perceive the knife," said Ysobel. "And how do I know the fellow? But he was charming, and I should like to see him again."

The captain's eyes were flaming with rage.

"You will be locked up," he said harshly. "You will remain in a cell until the time when we go again to Chagres. And we shall see whether this knife you speak of is sharp enough to keep you here in Panama."

As she followed him across the garden to her jail, her clear laughter rang out. "Captain Morgan, it has just occurred to me—I have begun to see that a great many different kinds of men make the same kind of husband."

"Get to your cell," he ordered her.

"Oh—and Captain Morgan, you will find an old woman on the steps of the Palace. My duenna, she is. Send her to me, please. And now, good-by for the time, sir; I must get to my devotions. The sin to be dissolved, Captain Morgan, is truthfulness. It is a bad thing for the soul, truthfulness."

He went slowly back to his chair in the Hall of Audience. He was filled with a kind of shame for his manhood. It was as though she had plucked his rapier from its scabbard and scratched his face with it while he stood helpless before her. She had beaten him without apparent effort. Now he quailed before the knowledge of his men's laughter when they discovered his embarrassment. There would be snickering when his back was turned. Groups of pirates would be silent as he passed, and when he had gone they would break into sharp laughter. This hidden ridicule was terrifying to Henry Morgan. His hates began to raise their heads; hatreds not for Ysobel, but for his own men who would laugh at him; for the people of Tortuga who would tell the story in the taverns; for the whole Indian Coast.

Now from the little prison across the garden came a shrill

voice praying to the Virgin. The penetrating sound charged the whole Palace with a fervent cacophony. Henry Morgan listened with shame-sharpened ears for mockery in the words or in the tone, but there was no mockery. Over and over, a shrill Ave Maria; the tone of a fearful, pleading sinner—Ora pro nobis. A shattered world, and the black skeleton of a golden city—Ora pro nobis. No mockery at all, but broken-hearted repentance reading its poor testimony on the dropping beads. A shrill woman's voice, piercing, insistent—it seemed to be digging at a tremendous, hopeless sin. She had said it was the sin of truthfulness. "I have been honest in my being, and that is a black lie on the soul. Forgive my body its humanity. Forgive my mind which knows its limitations. Pardon my soul for being anchored this little time to both. Ora pro nobis."

The mad, endless rosary cankered in Henry's brain. At last he seized his rapier and his hat and ran from the hall into the street. Behind him the treasure lay smiling under the slanting sun.

The streets about the Governor's Palace had not been touched by the fire. Captain Morgan walked along the paved way until he came to the ways of ruin. Here blackened walls had spilled their stones into the road. Those houses which had been made of cedar were vanished into the frames of smoking ashes which marked their places. Here and there lay murdered citizens grinning their last agony into the sky.

"Their faces will be black before the night," Henry thought. "I must have them removed or the sickness will come."

Dallying clouds of smoke still arose from the city, filling the air with the sickly odor of damp things burning. The green hills beyond the plain seemed incredible to Henry Morgan. He regarded them closely and then looked back at the city. This destruction which had seemed so complete, so awful, during the night, was, after all, a pitifully small and circumscribed destruction. Henry had not thought of the hills remaining green and standing. This conquest, then, was more or less unimportant. Yes, the city was in ruins. He had destroyed the city, but the woman who had drawn him to the Cup of Gold eluded him. She escaped while she still lay in his power. Henry winced at his impotence, and shuddered that other people should know it.

A few buccaneers were poking about in the ashes, looking for melted plate which might have escaped the search of the night before. Turning a corner, Henry came upon the little Cockney Jones, and saw him quickly thrust something into his pocket. A flame of rage arose in Captain Morgan. Cœur de Gris had said that there was no difference between this epileptic dwarf and Henry Morgan. No difference, indeed! This man was a thief. The rage changed to a fearful lust to hurt the little man, to outrage him, to hold him up to scorn as Henry Morgan had been scorned. The cruel desire made the captain's lips grow thin and white.

"What have you in your pocket?"

"Nothing—nothing, sir."

"Let me see what you have in your pocket." The captain was pointing a heavy pistol.

"It's nothing, sir—only a little crucifix! I found it." He drew out a golden cross studded with diamonds, and on it a Christ of ivory. "You see, it's for my wife," the Cockney explained.

"Ah! for your Spanish wife!"

"She's half negro, sir."

"You know the penalty for concealing spoil?"

Jones looked at the pistol and his face grayed. "You would not— Oh, sir, you would not—" he began chokingly. Then he seemed to be clutched by invisible, huge fingers. His arms dropped stiffly to his sides, his lips sagged open, and a dull, imbecilic light came into his eyes. There was a little foam on his lips. His whole body twitched like a wooden dancing figure on a string.

Captain Morgan fired.

For a moment the Cockney seemed to grow smaller. His shoulders drew in until they nearly covered his chest, like short wings. His hands clenched, and then the whole contracted mass fell to the ground, convulsing like a thick, animate jelly. His lips drew back from his teeth in a last idiot snarl.

Henry Morgan stirred the body with his foot, and a change stirred in his mind. He had killed this man. It was his right to kill, to burn, to plunder—not because he was ethical nor even because he was clever, but because he was strong. Henry Mor-

gan was the master of Panama and all its people. There was no
will in Panama save Henry Morgan's will. He could slaughter
every human in the country if he so chose. All this was true. No
one would deny it. But in the Palace back there was a woman
who held his power and his will in contempt, and her contempt
was a stronger weapon than his will. She fenced at his embarrassment and touched him at her convenience. But how could
that be? he argued. No one was master in Panama but himself,
and he had just killed a man to prove it. Under the battering
of his arguments the power of Ysobel waned and slowly disappeared. He would go back to the Palace. He would force her as
he had promised. This woman had been treated with too much
consideration. She did not realize the significance of slavery,
nor did she know the iron of Henry Morgan.

He turned about and walked back toward the Palace. In the
Hall of Audience he threw off his pistols, but the gray rapier
remained at his side.

Ysobel was kneeling before a holy picture in her little whitewashed cell when Henry Morgan burst upon her. The dried
duenna shrank into a corner at the sight of him, but Ysobel
regarded him intently, noted his flushed face, his half-closed,
fierce eyes. She heard his heavy breathing, and with a smile of
comprehension rose to her feet. Her laughter rang banteringly
as she drew a pin from her bodice and assumed the position
of a fencer, one foot forward, her left arm held behind her for
balance, the pin pointed before her like a foil.

"En garde!" she cried. Then the captain rushed at her. His
arms encircled her shoulders and his hands were tearing at
her clothing. Ysobel stood quite still, but one hand darted
about with its pin—striking, striking—like a small white serpent. Little spots of blood appeared on Henry's cheeks, on his
throat.

"Your eyes next, captain," she said quietly, and stabbed
him thrice on the cheekbone. Henry released her and stepped
away, wiping his bloody face with the back of his hand. Ysobel laughed at him. A man may beat—may subject to every
violation—a woman who cries and runs away, but he is helpless before one who stands her ground and only laughs.

"I heard a shot," she said. "I thought perhaps you had killed some one to justify your manhood. But your manhood will suffer now, will it not? Word of this encounter will get about somehow; you know how such things travel. It will be told that you were beaten with a pin in the hands of a woman." Her tone was gloating and cruel.

Henry's hand slipped to his side, and the lean rapier crept from its sheath like a frozen serpent. The light licked viciously along its lank blade. At last the needle point came out, and the steel turned and pointed at the woman's breast.

Ysobel grew sick with terror. "I am a sinner," she said. Then a dawning relief came into her face. She motioned the aged duenna to her and spoke in rapid, clattering Spanish.

"It is true," said the old woman. "It is true."

At the end of her speaking, Ysobel thriftily drew aside the webby lace of her mantilla that it might not be spotted with blood. The duenna began interpreting.

"Sir, my mistress says that a true Catholic who dies at the hand of an infidel goes to heaven. This is true. Further, she says that a Catholic woman who dies protecting her holy marriage vow goes straightway to heaven. This also is true. Lastly, she thinks that such a woman might, in course of time, be canonized. Such things have happened. Ah, sir! Captain, be kind! Permit me to kiss her hand, now, before you strike. What grace to have kissed the hand of a living saint! It may do much for my own sinful soul."

Ysobel spoke to her again.

"My mistress bids you strike; more, she urges it, pleads for the blow. The angels are hovering about her head. She sees the great light, and the holy music is sounding in her ears."

The rapier point lowered. Henry Morgan turned away and gazed out into the sunlit garden. Little Chico came galloping along the path and sat down in the open doorway. The little beast clasped his paws and raised them above his head as though in prayer. The lean rapier made a sharp swishing sound as it drove into its scabbard. And Captain Morgan stooped to pick up the tiny monkey. He walked away stroking Chico's head with his forefinger.

V

Henry Morgan lifted a golden cup from the heap of loot. It was
a lovely, slender chalice with long curved handles and a rim of
silver. Around its outer edge four grotesque lambs chased each
other, and inside, on the bottom, a naked girl lifted her arms in
sensual ecstasy. The captain turned the cup in his hands. Then,
suddenly, he hurled it at a little fiery pyramid of diamonds. The
stones scattered from their neat pile with a dry, rustling sound.
Henry Morgan turned and went back to his serpent chair. He
was thinking of the little Cockney, Jones; thinking of the cold
hand of epilepsy which had seized him in his last moment of
life. The hand had been always behind him, a giant hand to
wring the man's body until the white drops of agony oozed
from his lips. Henry wondered, now, why he had wanted to
hurt the little man, to torture him, and finally to kill him. Jones
had been shadowed through all his life by a sleepless tormen-
tor. Of course, this murder had been caused by the words of
Cœur de Gris who had said that Jones was like Henry Morgan.
Yes, he knew it now, and he knew, also, a red shame for his
trumped charge of thievery. Why could he not have killed the
man without explanation?

And Cœur de Gris—where was he now? He had seen
Ysobel—that was fairly sure—and she had noticed him. Perhaps she loved Cœur de Gris, with his bright hair and his curious way with women. And how could he keep this young man
from knowing his defeat, from hearing the adventure of the
pin and all the ignominy of Henry Morgan's dealings with La
Santa Roja? The pistol which had killed Jones was lying on the
floor. Henry picked it up and methodically went to loading it.
He did not fear ridicule from Cœur de Gris, but rather sym-
pathy and understanding. Henry did not want understanding
now. His lieutenant would look at him with compassion and
some pity; and there would be something superior about the
pity, something faintly ironic. It would be the pity of a young,
handsome man who condones the amorous failure of one not
so handsome. And then, Cœur de Gris was something like a

woman for knowing things—something like Ysobel. He gathered information with a mysterious hidden eye.

And the Red Saint. Henry must take her away with him, of course. He could do nothing else. Perhaps, after a long time, she would fall in love with him, but not, surely, because of merits in himself. Her contempt had convinced him that he had no merits; that he was a monstrous being, set apart from other men by unmentionable ugliness. She had not said so much, but she had intimated it. No, he had not the qualities like to draw a woman to his side when there were other men about. But perhaps, if she saw no other men, she might ignore the qualities so lacking in him. She might come, at last, to build on something he possessed.

He thought of the last scene with her. Now that he was calm, his wild action seemed the showing off of a thick-legged little boy. But how could any man have done otherwise? She had beaten assault with laughter—sharp, cruel laughter which took his motives out and made sport of them. He might have killed her; but what man could kill a woman who wanted to be killed, who begged to be killed? The thing was impossible. He rammed a bullet into the muzzle of his pistol.

A draggled, unkempt figure came through the doorway. It was Cœur de Gris, a red-eyed, mud-spattered Cœur de Gris with the blood of the battle still on his face. He looked at the heap of treasure.

"We are rich," he said without enthusiasm.

"Where have you been, Cœur de Gris?"

"Been? Why, I have been drunk. It is good to be drunk after fighting." He smiled wryly and licked his lips. "It is not so good to stop being drunk. That is like child-birth—necessary, but unpleasant and unornamental."

"I wanted you by my side," said Henry Morgan.

"You wanted me? I was informed that you wanted no one—that you were quite complete and happy in yourself—and so I got a little drunker. You see, sir, I did not want to remember your reason for being alone." He paused. "It was told me, sir, that the Red Saint is here." Cœur de Gris laughed at his own ill-concealed emotion. He changed his manner with an effort of will. His tone became jocular.

"Tell me the truth, sir. It is a small gift to a man to know what he has missed. Many people have no other gift during their whole lives. Tell me, sir, has the sweet enemy fallen? Has the castle of flesh capitulated? Does the standard of Morgan float over the pink tower?"

Henry's face had flushed. The pistol in his hand rose quietly, steadied by an inexorable madness. There was a sharp crash and a white billow of smoke.

Cœur de Gris stood as he was. He seemed to be intently listening to some distant, throbbing sound. Then a grimace of terror spread on his face. His fingers frantically explored his breast and followed a trickle of blood to its source, a small hole in his lung. The little finger edged into the hole. Cœur de Gris smiled again. He was not afraid of certain things. Now that he knew, he was not frightened any more.

Captain Morgan stared stupidly at the pistol in his hand. He seemed surprised to discover it there, startled at its presence.

Cœur de Gris laughed hysterically.

"My mother will hate you," he cried ruefully. "She will practice all her ancient curses upon you. My mother—" he choked over his breath. "Do not tell her. Make some gleaming lie. Build my poor life up to a golden minaret. Do not let it stop like a half-finished tower. But, no—you need build only a foundation. If you give her that, she will continue the structure of heroic memory. She will make for me a tomb of white, inaccurate thoughts." His throat filled with blood. "Why did you do it, sir?"

The captain looked up from his pistol.

"Do it?" He saw the bloody lips, the torn breast; he started up from his chair and then fell back again. Misery was writing lines about his eyes. "I do not know," he said. "I must have known, but I have forgotten."

Cœur de Gris went slowly to his knees. He steadied himself with his knuckles on the floor. "It is my knees, sir; they will not bear me any more," he apologized. He seemed to be listening for the throbbing sound again. Suddenly his voice rose in bitter complaint.

"It is a legend that dying men think of their deeds done.

No— No— I think of what I have not done—of what I might have done in the years that are dying with me. I think of the lips of women I have never seen—of the wine that is sleeping in a grape seed—of the quick, warm caress of my mother in Goaves. But mostly I think that I shall never walk about again—never, never stroll in the sunshine nor smell the rich essences the full moon conjures up out of the earth— Sir, why did you do it?"

Henry Morgan was staring at the pistol again. "I do not know," he muttered sullenly. "I must have known, but I have forgotten. I killed a dog once—and I have just killed Jones. I do not know why."

"You are a great man, captain," Cœur de Gris said bitterly. "Great men may leave their reasons for the creative hands of their apologists. But I—why, sir, I am nothing any more— nothing. A moment ago I was an excellent swordsman; but now, my being—that which fought, and cursed, and loved—it may never have been, for all I know." His wrists weakened and he fell to his side and lay there coughing at the obstruction in his throat. Then, for a time, there was no sound in the room save his uneven gasping for breath. But suddenly he raised himself on one elbow and laughed; laughed at some cosmic joke, some jest of the great rolling spheres; laughed triumphantly, as though he had solved a puzzle and found how simple it was. A wave of blood rode to his lips on the laughter, and filled up his throat. The laugh became a gushing sigh, and Cœur de Gris sank slowly to his side and was still, because his lungs would no longer force breath.

Henry still stared at the pistol in his hand. Slowly he raised his eyes to the open window. The streaming rays of the sun made the treasure on the floor glow like a mass of hot metal. His eyes wandered to the body in front of him. He shuddered. And then he went to Cœur de Gris, picked him up, and sat him in a chair. The limp body fell over to one side. Henry straightened it and braced it in an upright position. Then he went back to his serpent chair.

"I raised my hand like this—" he said, pointing the pistol at Cœur de Gris. "I raised my hand like this. I must have. Cœur de Gris is dead. Like this, I raised it—like this—and pointed—

How did I do it?" He bowed his head, then raised it with a chuckle.

"Cœur de Gris!" he said; "Cœur de Gris! I wanted to tell you about La Santa Roja. She rides horses, you know. She has no womanly modesty at all—none at all—and her looks are only moderate." He peered at the propped figure before him. The eyes of Cœur de Gris had been only half closed, but now the lids slipped down and the eyes began to sink back in his head. On his face was the frozen distortion of his last bitter laughter.

"Cœur de Gris!" the captain shouted. He went quickly to the body and laid his hand on its forehead.

"This is a dead thing," he said musingly. "This is only a dead thing. It will bring flies and sickness. I must have it taken away at once. It will bring the flies into this room. Cœur de Gris! we have been fooled. The woman fences like a man, and she rides horses astride. So much labor lost for us! That's what we get for believing everything we hear—eh, Cœur de Gris?—But this is only a dead thing, and the flies will come to it."

He was interrupted by a tramp of feet on the stair. A band of his men entered, driving in their midst a poor frightened Spaniard—a mud-draggled, terrified Spaniard. The lace had been torn from his neck, and a little stream of blood ran from one sleeve.

"Here is a Spaniard, sir," the leader said. "He came to the city bearing a white flag. Shall we respect the white flag, sir? He has silver on his saddle. Shall we kill him, sir? Perhaps he is a spy."

Henry Morgan ignored the speech. Instead he pointed to the body in the chair.

"That is only a dead thing," he announced. "That is not Cœur de Gris. I sent Cœur de Gris away. He will be back soon. But that is— I raised my hand like this—do you see?—like this. I know exactly how I did it; I have tried it again and again. But that is a dead thing. It will bring the flies to us." He cried, "Oh, take it away and bury it in the earth!"

A buccaneer moved to lift the body.

"Don't touch him! Don't dare to touch him! Leave him where

he is. He is smiling. Do you see him smile? But the flies— No, leave him. I will care for him myself."

"This Spaniard, sir; what shall we do with him? Shall we kill him?"

"What Spaniard?"

"Why, this one before you, sir." He shoved the man forward. Henry seemed to awaken from a deep dream.

"What do you want?" he asked harshly.

The Spaniard struggled with his fright.

"It—it is my wish and the wish of my padrone to have speech with one Captain Morgan if he will have the goodness. I am a messenger, Señor—not a spy, as these—these gentlemen suggest."

"What is your message?" Henry's voice had become weary.

The messenger took reassurance from his changed tone.

"I come from one man very rich, Señor. You have his wife."

"I have his wife?"

"She was taken in the city, Señor."

"Her name?"

"She is the Doña Ysobel Espinoza, Valdez y los Gabilanes, Señor. The simple people of the city have called her La Santa Roja."

Henry Morgan regarded him for a long time. "Yes, I have her," he said finally. "She is in a cell. What does her husband wish?"

"He offers ransom, Señor. He has reason to wish his wife with him again."

"What ransom does he offer?"

"What would Your Excellency suggest?"

"Twenty thousand pieces of eight," Henry said quickly.

The messenger was staggered. "Twenty thous—viente mil—" He translated fully to comprehend the enormity of the amount. "I perceive that Your Excellency also wants the woman."

Henry Morgan looked at the body of Cœur de Gris. "No," he said; "I want the money."

Now the messenger was relieved. He had been prepared to think this great man a great idiot. "I will do what may be done, Señor. I will come back to you in four days."

"In three!"

"But if I do not arrive, Señor?"

"If you do not arrive, I shall take the Red Saint away with me and sell her in the slave docks."

"I shall strive, Señor."

"Give him courtesy!" the captain commanded. "Do not mistreat him in any way. He is to bring us gold."

As they were leaving, one man turned back and let his eyes lovingly caress the treasure.

"When is the division to be, sir?"

"In Chagres, fool! Do you think I would divide it now?"

"But, sir, we would like to be having a bit of it in our hands— for the feel of it, sir. We have fought hard, sir."

"Get out! You'll have none of it in your hands until we come to the ships again. Do you think I want to have you throwing it to the women here? Let the Goaves women get it from you."

The men went out of the Hall of Audience grumbling a little.

VI

The buccaneers were rioting in Panama. Barrels of wine had been rolled to a large warehouse. The floor had been cleared of its clutter of merchandise, and now a wild dance was in progress. Numbers of women were there, women who had gone over to the pirates. They danced and flung about to the shrieking of flutes as though their feet did not sound on the grave of Panama at all. They, dear economists, were gaining back some of the lost treasure, using a weapon more slow, but no less sure, than the sword.

In a corner of the warehouse sat The Burgundian and his one-armed protector.

"See, Emil! That one there— Consider to yourself her hips now!"

"I see her, 'Toine, and it is good of you. Do not think I do not appreciate your trouble for my pleasure. But I am silly enough to have an ideal, even in copulation. This proves to me that I am still an artist, if not a gentleman."

"But see, Emil. Notice for a moment the fullness of her bosom."

"No, 'Toine; I see nothing that endangers my rose pearl. I will keep it by me a while yet."

"But, really, my friend, I think you lose your sense of beauty. Where is that careful eye we used to fear so on our canvases?"

"The eye is here, 'Toine. It is still here. It is your own little eye which makes nymphs of brown mares."

"Then— Then, Emil, since you persist in your blindness, perhaps you would condescend to loan me your rose pearl. There— I thank you. I shall return it presently."

Grippo was seated in the middle of the floor, sullenly counting the buttons on his sleeve.

"—eight, nine— There were ten. Some bastard has stolen my button. Ah, this world of thieves! It is too much. I would kill for that button. It was my favorite button. One, two, three— Why there are ten. One, two, three, four—" About him the dancers rocked and the air was reeking with the shrill cries of the flutes.

Captain Sawkins glowered at the dancers. He firmly believed that to dance was to go to hell by a short route. Beside him, Captain Zeigler sadly watched the flow of liquor. This Ziegler was called the Tavern Keeper of the Sea. It was his practice, after a raid, to keep the men at sea until they had spent their plunder buying the rum which he supplied. Once he had a mutiny, it is said, because for three months he sailed around and around one island. He could not help it. The men still had money and he still had rum. This night he was saddened by these barrels of liquor which were being drunk without any obbligato of coins ringing on the counter. It was unnatural to him and mischievous.

Henry Morgan was sitting alone in the Hall of Audience. He could barely hear the crying music of the dance. Throughout the day little bands of men had come in, bearing bits of belated treasure dug from the earth or drawn with iron hooks from the cisterns. One old woman had swallowed a diamond to save it, but the searchers dug for that, too, and found it.

Now a gray twilight was in the Hall of Audience. All through the day Henry Morgan had been sitting in his tall chair, and the day had changed him. His eyes, those peering eyes which had looked out over a living horizon, were turned inward. He had been looking at himself, looking perplexedly at Henry Morgan. In the years of his life and of his adventuring, he had believed so completely in his purpose, whatever it may have been at the moment, that he had given the matter little thought. But to-day he had considered himself, and, in the gray twilight, he was bewildered at the sight of Henry Morgan. Henry Morgan did not seem worthy, or even important. Those desires and ambitions toward which he had bayed across the world like a scenting hound, were shabby things now he looked inward at himself. And wonderment like the twilight was about him in the Hall of Audience.

As he sat in the half dark, the wrinkled duenna crept in and stood before him. Her voice was like the crumpling of paper.

"My lady wishes to speak with you," she said.

Henry rose and walked heavily after her toward the cell.

A candle was burning before the holy picture on the wall. The madonna represented was a fat, Spanish peasant, holding a flabby child at which she looked with sad astonishment. The priest who painted it meant to put reverence on her face, but he had so little experience with reverence. He had been successful, however, in making it a good portrait of his dull mistress and his child. Four *reales*, the picture brought him.

Ysobel sat under the picture. When Henry entered she went quickly to him.

"It is said I am to be ransomed."

"Your husband sent a messenger."

"My husband! I am to go back to him? to his scented hands?"

"Yes."

She pointed to a chair and forced Henry to seat himself.

"You did not understand me," she said. "You could not understand me. You must know something of the life I have traveled. I must tell you this thing, and then you will understand me, and then—"

She awaited his interest. Henry was silent.

"Don't you wish to hear this thing?" she asked.

"Yes."

"Well, it is short. My life has been short. But I want you to understand me, and then—"

She looked sharply into his face. Henry's mouth was pinched as though in pain. His eyes contemplated bewilderment. He made no reply to her pause.

"It was this way, you see," she began. "I was born here in Panama, but my parents sent me to Spain when I was a small child. I lived in a convent in Cordova. I wore gray dresses and lay in watch before the Virgin on my nights given to adoration. Sometimes I went to sleep when I should have been praying. I have suffered for that laxness. When I had been there a number of years, the bravos raided my father's plantation here in Panama and killed all of my family. I was left with no relative save one old grandfather. I was alone, and I was sad. I did not sleep on the floor before the Virgin for a time.

"I had grown handsome, that I knew, for once a Cardinal who was visiting the school looked at me, and his lips trembled, and the great veins stood out on his hands when I kissed his ring. He said, 'Peace be with you, my daughter. Have you anything you would like to confess to me privately?'

"I heard the cry of the water sellers over the wall, and I heard the scuffle of a quarrel. Once two men fought with swords in sight of me, where I stood on a stick and looked over the wall. And one night a young man brought a girl to the shadow of the gate and lay with her there within two paces of me. I heard them whisper together, she protesting her fears, and he reassuring her. I fingered my gray gown and wondered whether this boy would plead with me if he knew me. When I spoke to one of the sisters about this night she said, 'It is wicked to hear such things, and more wicked to think of them. You must do penance for your curious ears. What gate did you say?'

"The fishmonger would cry, 'Come, little gray angels, and look on my basket of catch. Come out of your holy prison, little gray angels.'

"One night I climbed over the wall and went away from the city. I do not mean to tell you of my journeying, but only of the day when I came to Paris. The King was riding through the streets, and his equipage was glittering and gold. I stood high on my toes in the crowd of people and watched the courtiers go riding by. Then, suddenly, a dark face was thrust before me, and a strong hand took my arm. I was led to a doorway apart from the people.

"See, Captain; he whipped me with a thong of hard leather he had only for that purpose. His face had something of a beast's snarl hiding very near the surface. But he was free—a bold, free, thief. He killed before he stole—always he killed. And we lived in entryways, and on the floors of churches, and under the land arch of a bridge, and we were free—free from thoughts and free from fears and worries. But once he went away from me, and I found him hanging by the neck on a gallows—oh, a great gallows festooned with men hanging by their necks.

"Can you understand that, Captain? Do you see that as I saw it? And does it mean anything at all to you?" Her eyes were on fire.

"I walked back to Cordova, and my feet were torn. I did penance until my body was torn, but I could not drive out all the evil. I was exorcised, but the devil was deep in me. Can you understand that, Captain?" She looked into Henry's face and saw that he had not been listening. She stood beside him and moved her fingers in his graying hair.

"You are changed," she said. "Some light is gone out of you. What fear has fallen on you?"

He stirred from his revery.

"I do not know."

"I was told that you killed your friend. Is it that which burdens you?"

"I killed him."

"And do you mourn for him?"

"Perhaps. I do not know. I think I mourn for some other thing which is dead. He might have been a vital half of me, which, dying, leaves me half a man. To-day I have been like a bound slave on a white slab of marble with the gathered vivisectors about me. I was supposed to be a healthy slave, but the scalpels found me sick with a disease called mediocrity."

"I am sorry," she said.

"You are sorry? Why are you sorry?"

"I think I am sorry because of your lost light; because the brave, brutal child in you is dead—the boastful child who mocked and thought his mockery shook the throne of God; the confident child who graciously permitted the world to accompany him through space. This child is dead, and I am sorry. I would go with you, now, if I thought it possible to warm the child to life again."

Henry said, "It is strange. Two days ago I planned to tear a continent out of the set order and crown it with a capital of gold for you. In my mind, I built up an empire for you, and planned the diadem you should wear. And now I dimly remember the person who thought these things. He is an enigmatic stranger on a staggering globe.

"And you—I feel only a slight uneasiness with you. I am not afraid of you any more. I do not want you any more. I am filled with a nostalgia for my own black mountains and for the speech of my own people. I am drawn to sit in a deep veranda and to hear the talk of an old man I used to know. I find I am tired of all this bloodshed and struggle for things that will not lie still, for articles that will not retain their value in my hands. It is horrible," he cried. "I do not want anything any more. I have no lusts, and my desires are dry and rattling. I have only a vague wish for peace and the time to ponder imponderable matters."

"You will take no more cups of gold," she said. "You will turn no more vain dreams into unsatisfactory conquests. I am sorry for you, Captain Morgan. And you were not right about the slave. Ill he was, indeed, but not with the illness you have mentioned. But I suppose your sins are great. All men who break the bars of mediocrity commit frightful sins. I shall pray for you to the Holy Virgin, and She will intercede for you at the throne of Heaven. But what am I to do?"

"You will go back to your husband, I suppose."

"Yes, I will go back. You have made me old, Señor. You have pricked the dream on which my heavy spirit floated. And I wonder whether, in the years to come, you will blame me for the death of your friend."

Henry flushed quickly.

"I am trying to do something of that sort now," he said. "It does not seem worth the while to lie any more, and that is only one more proof of dead youth. But now, good-by, Ysobel. I wish I loved you now as I thought I did yesterday. Go back to your husband's scented hands."

She smiled and raised her eyes to the holy picture on the wall. "Peace go with you, dear fool," she murmured. "Ah, I too have lost my youth. I am old—old—for I cannot console myself with the thought of what you have missed."

VII

Henry Morgan stood in the doorway of the Hall of Audience and watched a little troupe of Spaniards ride through the streets toward the Palace. The troupe was surrounded on all sides by a mob of buccaneers. First in the line came the messenger, but a changed messenger. Now he was dressed in scarlet silk. The plume of his hat and his sword's scabbard were white in token of peace. Behind him rode six soldiers in silver breast-plates and the Spanish helmets which looked like half mustard seeds. The last soldier led a riderless white mare with crimson trappings and a line of golden bells on its brow band. The white saddle cloth nearly touched the ground. Following the mare were six mules bearing heavy leathern bags, and the group was rear-guarded by six more soldiers.

The cavalcade drew up before the Palace. The messenger leaped from his horse and bowed to Henry Morgan.

"I have here the ransom," he said. He looked worried and tired. The weight of his mission was riding heavily on his spirit. At his command the soldiers carried the leather bags into the Hall of Audience, and only when they were all deposited with the rest of the treasure did the anxiety leave his face.

"Ah," he said, "it is good. It is the treasure. Twenty thousand pieces of eight—not one lost by the wayside. I invite you to count them, Señor." He whipped a little dust from his foot. "If my men could have refreshments, Señor; wine—" he suggested.

"Yes. Yes." Henry motioned to one of his followers. "See that these men have food and drink. Be courteous, as you love life."

Then he went to the bags to count the ransom. He made little towers of shining coins and moved the towers about on the floor. Money was bright, he thought. It could have been cut in no more charming shape, either. A square would not answer, nor an elipse. And money was really worth more than money. He tumbled a tower and built it up again. It was so extremely certain—money. One knew beforehand what it would do if set in motion; at least, he knew up to a certain point. Beyond that point it did not matter what it accomplished. One might buy wine with money. One had the wine. And if the merchant's clerk should kill his master for the same coins, it was unfortunate; it was, perhaps, Fate or something like that, but one had his wine just the same.

And all this pile of golden vessels, these crosses and candlesticks and pearl vestments, would be money like this. These bars of gold and silver would be cut into round flakes and each flake stamped with a picture. The picture would be more than a picture. Like the kiss of a saint, it would endow the flake with power; the picture would give it a character and a curious, compelling soul. He flung the coins into a heap and patiently set about to rebuild them. Enough towers for Jerusalem!

Now Ysobel came from the patio and stood beside him.

"What an amount of money," she said. "Is that my ransom?"

"Yes; it is the gold which purchases you."

"But what a very great deal! Am I worth that much, do you think?"

"To your husband you are. He paid it for you." He moved ten towers into a line.

"And to you—how much? How many of these golden chips?"

"You must have been worth that much to me. I stated the price."

"Wouldn't they skip well on the water!" she said. "How they would skip! Do you know, I can throw like a boy, with my arm bent."

"It was said you were capable," he announced.

"But am I really worth that much?"

"The money is here, and you are to go. It has bought you. A thing must be worth what is paid for it, or there could be no trade."

"It is good," she said. "It is comforting to know one's value to a *real*. Have you any idea of your worth, Captain?"

Henry Morgan said, "If I were ever captured and a ransom demanded for me, I would not be worth a copper penny. These dogs of mine would laugh and shrug. A new captain would rise to lead them, and I—well, I would be subject to the pleasure of my captors, and I think I could foretell their pleasure. You see, I have been at revaluing myself in the last few days. I may have some value to historians because I have destroyed a few things. The builder of your Cathedral is forgotten even now, but I, who burned it, may be remembered for a hundred years or so. And that may mean something or other about mankind."

"But what is there about me that is worth all this gold?" she insisted. "Is it my arms, do you suppose? My hair? Or is it that I am the embodiment of my husband's vanity?"

"I do not know," said Henry. "With the revaluation of myself, the whole economic system of emotions and persons has changed. To-day, were I to demand a ransom, perhaps you would not be flattered."

"Do you so hate me, Captain Morgan?"

"No, I do not hate you; but you are one of the stars of my firmament which has proven to be a meteor."

"That is not gallant, sir. That is quite different from your speech of a few days past," she observed spitefully.

"No. It is not gallant. I think that hereafter I shall be gallant for two reasons only—money and advancement. I tried to be gallant for the pure, joyous looks of things. You see, I was honest with myself before and I am honest with myself now. These two honesties are antithetical."

"You are bitter."

"No; I am not even bitter. The food that bitterness feeds on is gone out of me."

"I am going now," she said softly and wistfully. "Have you

nothing more to say to me about myself? Nothing more to ask of me?"

"Nothing," he answered, and immediately went to piling the coins again.

The messenger entered from the street. He had drunk deeply, for the removed burden of his mission had made him joyous. He bowed to Ysobel and to Henry Morgan; bowed warily, with an eye to his balance.

"We must go, Señor," he announced loudly. "The way is long." He led Ysobel to the white mare and helped her into the saddle. Then, at his signal, the column moved off down the street. Ysobel looked back once as they started, and it seemed that she had taken a mood from Henry Morgan, for there was a puzzled smile on her lips. But then she bent her head over the mare's neck; she was intently studying the mare's white mane.

The messenger had remained standing at Henry's side in the doorway. Together they watched the fluid line of riders swing away while the sunlight glinted on the soldiers' armor. In the center of the troupe, the white mare seemed a pearl in a setting of silver.

The messenger put his hand on Henry's shoulder.

"We know how to understand each other, we men of responsibilities," he said drunkenly. "It is not as though we were children to have secrets. We are men, brave men and strong. We may confide in each other. You may tell me the thing nearest your heart if you wish, Señor."

Henry shook the hand from his shoulder. "I have nothing to tell you," he said brusquely.

"Ah; but then I will tell you something. Perhaps you wondered why the husband of this woman was willing to pay such a vast sum for her. She is only a woman, you say. There are many women to be had more cheaply—some for a *real* or two. Her husband is a fool, you say. But I would not have you think that of my master. He is no fool. I will tell you how it is. Her grandfather still lives, and he is the owner of ten silver mines and fifty leagues of fertile land in Peru. Doña Ysobel is the heiress. Now if she were killed or carried off— But you understand, Señor— Poof! The fortune into the King's arms!" He laughed at the cleverness of his reasoning. "We understand each other, Señor. We have tough skulls—not the soft heads of chickens. Twenty thousand—it is nothing to be reckoned against ten silver mines. Ah, yes; we understand each other, we men of responsibilities."

He clambered into his saddle and rode away still laughing. Henry Morgan saw him join the undulating cavalcade and now there was a ruby with the pearl in the silver setting.

Captain Morgan went back to the treasure. He sat on the floor and took the coins into his hands. "The most human of all human traits is inconsistency," he thought. "It is a shock to learn this thing, almost as great a shock to a man as the realization of his humanity. And why must we learn that last? In all the mad incongruity, the turgid stultiloquy of life, I felt, at least, securely anchored to myself. Whatever the vacillations of other people, I thought myself terrifically constant. But now, here I am, dragging a frayed line, and my anchor gone. I do not know whether the rope was cut or merely worn away, but my anchor is gone. And I am sailing around and around an island in which there is no iron." He let the gold pieces slip through his fingers. "But perhaps here is my iron for the making of a new anchor," he thought. "This is hard and heavy. Its value may fluctuate somewhat in the economic currents, but at least it has a purpose, and only one purpose. It is an absolute assurance of security. Yes, perhaps this is the one true anchor; the one thing a man may be utterly sure of. Its claws hook tightly to comfort and security. Strangely, I have a craving for them both."

"But other men have a share in this gold," part of his brain argued.

"No, my dear conscience; we have an end of acting now. I have put on new glasses; rather they have been locked about my head, and I must order my life in accordance with the world I see through these new lenses. I see that honesty—public honesty—may be a ladder to a higher, more valuable crime; veracity a means to more subtle dissimulation. No; these men have no rights they can enforce. These men were too free with the rights of others to deserve consideration." He stumbled happily on the thought. "They steal, and so shall their plunder be stolen.

"But I said I was finished with evasions and conscience drugging. What have I to do with right, now—or reason, or logic, or conscience? I want this money. I want security and comfort, and I have the power between my hands to take both. It may not be the ideal of youth, but I think it has been the world's practice from the beginning. Luckily, perhaps, the world is not operated by youth. And besides," he said, "these fools of men do not deserve any of it. They would be throwing it away in the brothels when we came home again."

VIII

The buccaneers went out of ruined Panama. They carried all of the treasure with them across the isthmus on the backs of mules. When at last Chagres was reached, they were exhausted; nevertheless, the following day was set for the division of spoils. In order that this might be facilitated, the whole of the treasure was stored in one ship, the great galleon which had been commanded by a Duke before the pirates captured it. From this center the plunder was to be divided. Captain Morgan was in good spirits. The journey was over, he told the men, and it was time for pleasure. He rolled out forty kegs of rum onto the beach.

Early in the morning, a sleepy pirate opened his red eyes and looked toward the sea. He saw the water where the galleon had been. He called his comrades, and in a moment the shore was lined with disappointed men who wistfully searched the horizon. The galleon had put to sea during the night, and all the wealth of Panama had gone with her.

There was rage among the buccaneers. They would give chase; they would run down the fugitive and torture Captain Morgan. But they could not pursue. The other ships were worthless. Some lay on the sandy bottom with great holes punched in their sides; of others, the masts were sawed nearly through.

Then there was cursing and violence on the beach. They swore brotherhood in the name of revenge. They planned the horror of the retribution. And they scattered. Some starved; some were tortured by the Indians. The Spaniards caught and strangled some of them, and England virtuously hanged a few.

CHAPTER 5

I

A multifarious population was crowded on the beach at Port Royal. They had come to see the Captain Morgan who had plundered Panama. Great ladies, dressed in the silken stuffs of China, were there because, after all, Henry Morgan came of a good family—the nephew of the poor dear Lieutenant-Governor who was killed. Sailors were there because he was a sailor; little boys because he was a pirate; young girls because he was a hero; business men because he was rich; gangs of slaves because they had a holiday. There were prostitutes with berry juice squeezed on their lips, and with restless eyes searching the faces of unaccompanied men; and there were girl children whose hearts mothered the scared little hope that the great man might just possibly look in their direction and find the understanding he must crave.

In the crowd were sailors whose pride lay in the fact that they had heard Captain Morgan curse; tailors who had fitted breeches to his legs. Each man who had seen Henry Morgan and had heard him speak, collected a group of admirers. These lucky ones had taken a bit of greatness from the contact.

The negro slaves, freed from their field work on this day of interest and rejoicing, gazed with huge, vacuous eyes at the galleon riding in the harbor. Plantation owners strode about among the people, talking loudly of what they would say to Henry Morgan when they had him out to dinner, and what they would advise him. They spoke lightly and carelessly of him, as though it were their constant practice to entertain plunderers of Panama.

Certain tavern keepers had broached casks of wine on the beach from which they gave freely to all who asked. Their gain would come later, with the thirst they only whetted.

On a small pier waited the party of the Governor; handsome young men in laces and silver buckles, with a squad of pikemen to give them an official appearance. The sea fanned delicate, unbreaking waves on the beach. It was late morning, and the sun a glaring crucible in the sky, but no one felt the heat; the people had eyes and feelings for nothing but the tall galleon riding in the harbor.

Noon had come when Henry Morgan, who had been watching the beach through a glass, decided to enter the city. His stagecraft was not merely vanity. In the night a small boat had come alongside with the news that he might be arrested for fighting the enemies of the King. Henry thought the approval of the people would weigh in his favor. All morning he had watched the approval grow as the crowd became more and more excited.

But now his long boat was lowered and the sailors took their places. As it approached the shore, the gathered mob broke into yells, and then a concerted roaring cheer. The people threw their hats, leaped, danced, grimaced, tried to shriek conversation at one another. At the pier, hands were extended to grasp Henry's before he was out of the boat. And immediately he had stepped up, the pikemen formed about the official party and with weapons lowered forced a rough passage among the fighting, craning spectators.

Henry glanced with apprehension at the soldiers who surrounded him. "Am I under arrest?" he asked of the cavalier who walked beside him.

"Under arrest!" The man laughed. "No! We couldn't arrest you if we would. The mob would tear us to pieces. And if we did succeed in the arrest, they would rip out the stones of the jail with their fingers to free you. You do not realize what you are to these people, sir. For days they have talked of nothing save your coming. But the Governor wants to see you immediately, sir. He couldn't come here himself for obvious reasons."

They arrived at the mansion of the Governor.

"Captain Morgan," said Governor Moddyford, when they were alone, "I don't know whether my news is good or bad. Word of your conquest has come to the ears of the King. Both of us are ordered to England."

"But I had a commission—" Henry began.

The fat head and shoulders of the Governor shook a sad negative. "Now I wouldn't mention the commission, Captain, if I were you, even though I myself did issue it. There are clauses in your commission which might get us both criticized. As it is, we may be hanged; but I don't know—I don't know. Of course, there is peace between Spain and England—but no good feeling, none at all. The King is angry with us, but I think a few thousand pounds distributed in the right quarters might placate him were he mad with rage. The English people is filled with joy over the conquest. Don't worry about it, Captain; certainly I do not." He looked keenly into Henry's eyes. "I hope, sir, that you can spare those few thousands when the time comes."

Said Henry, officially, "I have tried to serve the spirit of my sovereign's wish, not the outward play of his politics." And then, "Surely, Sir Charles; I have enough to buy the King's favor though it cost half a million. They say the King is a good man and a judge of fine women, and I never knew one such not to need money."

"There is another thing, Captain," said the Governor uneasily. "Your uncle was killed some time ago. His daughter is here in my house. Sir Edward was nearly penniless when he died. Of course, you understand, we would like to have her stay here with us always, but I do not think she is quite happy. I think she chafes under what she thinks is charity. You will look to her welfare, of course. Sir Edward died nobly and was commended by the King, but after all the commendation of the Crown cannot be spent."

Henry smiled. "My uncle would have died nobly. I am sure this uncle of mine made every move in his life—yes, even to the paring of his nails—as though the complete peerage were looking on, ready to make critical comments. How did he die? Making a short, fitting oration? Or with the damned thin lips of him pressed together as though he disapproved of death for social reasons? Ah, that man! His life was a fine, simple part, and he was very true to it." Henry spoke laughingly. "I hated my uncle. I think he frightened me. He was one of the few people I feared. But tell me how he died."

"It is whispered that he groaned once. I traced the rumor and found that some servant had been hiding behind a curtain. He doubtless told of it."

"Too bad! Too bad! What a cruel shame it is to ruin a perfect life with an exhalation. But now I am not afraid of him any more. If he groaned, there was humanity in him, and weakness. I despise him, but I love him for it. As to my cousin, I shall take her off your hands, you may be sure. I dimly remember her as a tall little girl with yellow hair—a little girl who played abominably on the harp; at least it sounded abominable to me, though it may have been quite good."

Moddyford came to a subject he had been wanting to broach.

"I have heard that you met the Red Saint in Panama and released her for a ransom. How did that happen? She was said to be the pearl of the earth."

Henry reddened.

"Oh, well," he said, "it seemed to me that the legend flattered her. She was nice looking, surely; and I don't say some men would not have been struck with her. But she was not the kind of woman I admire for myself. She was rather free in her speech, you know—spoke of things unfeminine, in my opinion. Besides, she rode horses astride, and fenced. In short, she was without that modesty we have come to look for in well-bred women."

"But as a mistress— Surely, as a mistress?"

"Well, you see, I received seventy-five thousand pieces of eight for her. To my mind that is worth more than any woman who was ever born."

"That much ransom? How did she happen to bring so much?"

"Why, on investigation, I found that she was an heiress. And as I say, she was nice looking, but still—the legend flattered her."

Meanwhile, in another room, Lady Moddyford was earnestly talking to Elizabeth.

"I find I must speak to you as a mother, my dear, a mother who is looking to your future. There is absolutely no doubt that your cousin will look out for you; but would you be happy that way?—just hanging to his purse-strings, I mean? Look at him in another light. He is rich, well-favored. You understand, my dear, that it is impossible to be delicate about this, and I do not know that it would be desirable even if it were possible. Why don't you marry your cousin? If nothing else came of it, you would be the one woman on earth who could not criticize her husband's relatives."

"But what are you suggesting, Lady Moddyford?" Elizabeth put in meekly. "Isn't it some kind of crime to marry one's cousin?"

"Not a bit of it, my dear. There is nothing in church or state to forbid it, and I, myself, would favor such a marriage. Sir Charles and your cousin have been ordered to England. Sir Charles thinks a knighthood might be arranged. Then you would be Lady Morgan, and you would be rich."

Elizabeth mused: "I only saw him once, for a moment, and then I don't think I quite liked him. He was excited and red. But he was very respectful and gentle. I think he wanted to be friends with me, but my father—you know how Papa was. Perhaps he would make a good husband," she said.

"My dear, any man makes a good husband if he is properly looked after."

"Yes, it might be the best way out. I am tired of being pitied for my poverty. But with this new popularity, do you think he would notice me? He might be too proud to marry a penniless cousin."

"Dear Elizabeth," Lady Moddyford said firmly, "don't you know by now that almost any woman can marry almost any man as long as some other woman doesn't interfere? And I shall arrange matters so that no one will get in your way. You may trust me for that."

Elizabeth had made up her mind. "I know; I shall play for

him. I have heard how music affects these fierce men. I shall
play him my new pieces—The Elves' Concourse, and God
Bears the Weary Soul to Rest."

"No," broke in Lady Moddyford. "No, I wouldn't do that
if I were you. He might not like fine music. There are better
ways."

"But you said those pieces were very pretty; you said it yourself. And haven't I read how music soothes men until they can
hardly bear it?"

"Very well, my dear; play for him, then, if you will. Perhaps
he— But play for him. Such things may run in the family—the
love of music, I mean. Of course, you know, you must admire
him and at the same time be a little afraid of him. Make him
feel that you are a poor, helpless little creature completely
hemmed in with tigers. But you must arrange it in your own
way. You have a good start, for you may appeal to him for
protection from the beginning." She sighed, "I don't know
what we should do without protection. I don't know when Sir
Charles would have proposed to me. The dear was frightened
out of his life to begin. One afternoon we sat on a bench and I
positively searched the landscape for something to frighten me.
We must have been there three hours before a little water-snake
ambled along the path and terrified me into his arms. No, I
can't think what we should do without protection. Sir Charles
has a man in the garden all the time looking for snakes. And do
you know, I have always liked snakes. I had three of them for
pets when I was a little girl."

The next morning Lady Moddyford brought them together,
and, as soon as she gracefully could, left them alone.

Elizabeth looked fearfully at her cousin.

"You have done great, terrible things on the ocean, Captain
Morgan—enough to freeze one thinking about them," she said
falteringly.

"The deeds were not great, nor very dreadful. Nothing is as
good or as bad as the telling of it."

And he thought, "I was wrong about her—very wrong. She is
not supercilious at all. It must have been her father—the devil—
who gave me a wrong impression of her. She is quite nice."

"I am sure yours were great, if your modesty would let you admit it," she was saying demurely. "Do you know, I used to tremble at the tales they told of you, and hope that you were not in need or trouble."

"Did you? Why did you? I didn't think you ever noticed me."

Her eyes had filled with tears. "I have had trouble, too."

"I know. They told me about your trouble, and I was sorry for you, little cousin Elizabeth. I hope you will let me help you in your trouble. Won't you sit here beside me, Elizabeth?"

She looked shyly at him. "I'll play for you, if you like," she said.

"Ye-es—yes, do."

"Now this is the Elves' Concourse. Listen! You can hear their little feet pattering on the grass. Everybody says it is very sweet and pretty." Her fingers methodically worked at the strings.

Henry thought her hands lovely as they flew about. He forgot about the music in watching her hands. They were like little white moths, so delicate and restless. One would hesitate in touching them because handling might ruin them, and yet one wanted to stroke them. The piece was ending with loud bass notes. Now it was finished. When the last string had ceased its vibration, he observed:

"You play very—precisely, Elizabeth."

"Oh, I play the notes as they come," she said. "I always think the composer knew his business better than I do."

"I know, and it is a comfort to hear you. It is nice to know that everything is to be in its place—even notes. You have eradicated a certain obnoxious freedom I have noticed in the playing of some young women. That kind is very lovable and spontaneous and human, of course, but given to carelessness in the interest of passion. Yes, as I become older, I grow to be taking satisfaction in seeing the thing I expected come about. Unsure things are distracting. Chance has not the tug on me it once had. I was a fool, Elizabeth. I went sailing and sailing looking for something—well, something that did not exist, perhaps. And now that I have lost my unnamable desires, I may not be happier, but there is more content on me."

"That sounds wise and worldly, and a little bit cynical," she observed.

"But if it is wisdom, then wisdom is experience beating about in an orderly brain, kicking over the files. And how could I be otherwise than worldly. And cynicism is the moss which collects on a rolling stone."

"That is clever, anyway," she agreed. "I suppose you have known a great many of those young women you spoke of."

"What young women, Elizabeth?"

"The ones who played badly."

"Oh! Yes, I have met a few."

"And did you—did you—like them?"

"I tolerated them because they were friends of my friends."

"Did any of them fall in love with you? I know I am not delicate, but you are my cousin, and almost my—my brother."

"Oh, some said they did—but I suspect they wanted my money."

"Surely not! But I shall play for you again. This will be a sad piece—God Bears the Weary Soul to Rest. I always think it is better to have seriousness with the lighter musics."

"Yes," he said. "Yes; so it is."

Again her fingers worked over the strings.

"It is very beautiful, and sad," said Henry, when it was finished. "I liked it wonderfully well, but don't you think, Elizabeth—don't you think that sixth string from the end might be a little—tighter?"

"Oh, I wouldn't have it touched for the world!" she cried. "Before we came out from England, Papa had a man—a harp man—go over the whole thing thoroughly. I wouldn't feel just right with Papa if it were tampered with. He hated people who fiddled with things."

They sat silently after her outburst, but at length she looked pleadingly into his eyes. "You aren't angry with me about the string, are you, Cousin Henry? I just have deep feelings like that. I can't help it."

"No, of course I am not angry." She was so little and so helpless, he thought.

"Where will you be going, now that you are rich and famous and covered with honors?"

"I don't know. I want to live in an atmosphere of sure things."

"Why, that's just the way I think," she exclaimed. "We must be somewhat alike. Things come to you if you do not go looking for them, I say. And nearly always I know what is going to happen to me, because I hope for it and then sit still."

"Yes," said Henry.

"Papa's death was a great shock," she said, and again the tears were in her eyes. "It's a terrible thing to be left alone and nearly no—no relatives or friends. Of course, the Moddyfords have been lovely to me, but they couldn't be like my own people. Oh, dear! I have been so lonely. I was glad when you came, Cousin Henry, if only because we are of one blood." Her eyes were glistening with tears, and her underlip trembled violently.

"But you must not cry," Henry said soothingly. "You will not need to worry any more, Elizabeth. I am here to take your trouble from your shoulders. I will help you and care for you, Elizabeth. I wonder how you bore the grief that fell on you. You have been brave to hold your head so high when misery was tugging at your spirit."

"I had my music," she said. "I could retire into my music when the grief was too bitter."

"But now, Elizabeth, you need not even do that. You will come with me to England when I go, and you will be comfortable and safe with me for always."

She had sprung away from him.

"But what are you suggesting? What is this thing you are proposing to me?" she cried. "Isn't it some sin—some crime— for cousins to marry?"

"Marry?"

"Oh!" She blushed, and her eyes glittered again with her quick tears. "Oh! I am ashamed. You did mean marry, didn't you? I am ashamed." Her agitation was pitiful.

"After all, why not?" thought Henry. "She is pretty; I am

sure of her family; and besides, she is rather a symbol of this security I have been preaching. I could be sure of never doing anything very radical if she were my wife. I really think I do want security. And besides," his thought finished, "I really cannot let her suffer so."

"Oh, surely I meant marry. What else could you have thought I meant? I am only clumsy and crude about it. I have startled you and hurt you. But, dear Elizabeth, there is no crime or sin about it. Many cousins marry. And we know all about each other, and our family is one. You must marry me, Elizabeth. Truly I love you, Elizabeth."

"Oh!" she stammered. "O-oh! I cannot think of it. I mean, I am—ill; I mean—my head whirls. You act so suddenly, Henry—so unexpectedly. Oh, please let me go. I must talk about it to Lady Moddyford. She will know what to say."

II

King Charles the Second and John Evelyn were sitting in a tiny library. A bright fire crackled on the hearth, throwing its flickerings on the books which lined the walls. On a table beside the two men were bottles and glasses.

"I knighted him this afternoon," the King was saying. "He got pardon and a knighthood for two thousand pounds."

"Well, two thousand pounds—" murmured John Evelyn. "Certain tradesmen will, perhaps, bless his knighthood."

"But that's not it, John. I could have got twenty. He took about a million out of Panama."

"Ah, well; two thousand pounds—"

"I ordered him to come in here to-night," said the King. "These sailors and pirates sometimes have a tale or two worth repeating. You'll be disappointed in him. He is—lumpish, I think is the word. You get the impression that a great mass is planted before you; and he moves as though he pushed his own invisible cage ahead of him."

"You might create a title," John Evelyn suggested. "It seems wasteful to let a million get away without even trying."

Sir Henry Morgan was announced.

"Step in, Sir. Step in!" The King saw that he had a glass of wine in his hands. Henry seemed frightened. He gulped the wine.

"Good job of yours in Panama," the King observed. "It was better to burn it now than later, and I have no doubt we should have had to do it later."

"I thought of that when I set the torch, Sire. These hoggish Spaniards want to over-run the world."

"You know, Captain, piracy—or, to be delicate, freebooting—has been a good thing for us, and a bad thing for Spain. But the institution grows to be a nuisance. I spend half of my time making excuses to the Spanish Ambassador. I am going to commission you Lieutenant-Governor of Jamaica."

"Sire!"

"No thanks! I am acting on the advice of an adage. Piracy must be stopped now. These men have played at little wars long enough."

"But, Sire, I myself was a buccaneer. Do you want me to hang my own men?"

"That is what I inferred, Sir. Who can track them down better than you who know all their haunts?"

"They fought with me, Sire."

"Ah; conscience? I had heard that you were able to do about as you pleased with your conscience."

"Not conscience, Sire, but pity."

"Pity is misplaced in a public servant or a robber. A man may do what it is profitable to do. You yourself have demonstrated two of these premises. Let us see you labor with the third," the King said acidly.

"I wonder if I can."

"If you wonder, then you can," John Evelyn put in.

The King's manner changed.

"Come! drink!" he said. "We must have life, and perhaps later, song. Tell us a tale, Captain, and drink while you tell it. Wine adds capitals and asterisks to a good tale—a true story."

"A tale, Sire?"

"Surely. Some story of the colonial wenches; some little interlude in piracy—for I am sure you did not steal only gold." He motioned a servant to keep Henry's glass filled. "I have heard of a certain woman in Panama. Tell us about her."

Henry drained his glass. His face was becoming flushed.

"There is a tale about her," he said. "She was pretty, but also she was an heiress. I confess, I favored her. She would inherit silver mines. Her husband offered one hundred thousand pieces of eight for her. He wanted to get his hands on the mines. Here was the question, Sire, and I wonder how many men have been confronted with one like it? Should I get the woman or the hundred thousand?"

The King leaned forward in his chair. "Which did you take? Tell me quickly."

"I remained in Panama for a while," said Henry. "What would Your Majesty have done in my place? I got both. Perhaps I got even more than that. Who knows but my son will inherit the silver mines eventually."

"I would have done that," cried the King. "You are right. I would have done just that. It was clever, sir. A toast, Captain— to foresight. Your generalship, sir, runs to other matters than warfare, I see. You have never been defeated in battle, they say; but tell me, Captain, were you ever defeated in love? It is a good scene—an unusual scene—when a man admits himself bested in love. The admission is so utterly contrary to every masculine instinct. Another glass, Sir, and tell us about your defeat."

"Not by a woman, Sire— But once I was defeated by Death. There are things which so sear the soul that the pain of it follows through life. You asked for the story. Your health, Sire.

"I was born in Wales, among the mountains. My father was a gentleman. One summer, while I was a lad, a little princess of France came to our mountains for the air. She had a small retinue, and being lively and restless and clever, she achieved some freedom. One morning I came upon her where she bathed alone in the river. She was naked and unashamed. In an hour— such is the passionate blood of her race—she was lying in my arms. Sire, in all my wanderings, in the lovely women I have seen and the towns I have taken, there has been no pleasure like the days of that joyous summer. When she could escape, we played together in the hills like little gods. But this was not enough. We wanted to be married. She would give up her rank and we would go to live somewhere in America.

"Then the Autumn came. One day she said, 'They are ready to take me away, but I will not go.' The next day she did not come to me. In the night I went to her window and she threw a little note to me, 'I am imprisoned. They have whipped me.'

"I went home. What else could I do? I could not fight them, the stout soldiers who guarded her. Very late that night there was a pounding on the door and cries, 'Where is a doctor to be had? Quick! The little princess has poisoned herself.' "

Henry lifted his eyes. The King was smiling ironically. John Evelyn drummed the table with his fingers.

"Yes?" said the King. "Yes?" He chuckled.

"Ah, I am old—old," Henry moaned. "It is a lie. She was a peasant child, the daughter of a cottager."

He staggered to his feet and moved toward the door. Shame was burning in his face.

"Captain Morgan, you forget yourself."

"I—forget—myself?"

"There are certain little courtesies. Custom demands that you render them to our person."

"I plead pardon, Sire. I plead your permission to leave. I—I am ill." He bowed himself from the room.

The King was smiling through his wine.

"How is it, John, that such a great soldier can be such a great fool?"

Said John Evelyn, "How could it be otherwise? If great men were not fools, the world would have been destroyed long ago. How could it be otherwise? Folly and distorted vision are the foundations of greatness."

"You mean that my vision is distorted?"

"No, I do not mean that."

"Then you imply—"

"I wish to go on with Henry Morgan. He has a knack for piracy which makes him great. Immediately you imagine him as a great ruler. You make him Lieutenant-Governor. In this you are like the multitude. You believe that if a man do one thing magnificently, he should be able to do all things equally well. If a man be eminently successful in creating an endless line of mechanical dew-dads of some excellence, you conceive him capable of leading armies or maintaining governments. You think that because you are a good king you should be as good a lover—or vice-versa."

"Vice-versa?"

"That is a humorous alternative, Sire. It is a conversational trick to gain a smile—no more."

"I see. But Morgan and his folly—"

"Of course he is a fool, Sire, else he would be turning soil in Wales or burrowing in the mines. He wanted something, and he was idiot enough to think he could get it. Because of his idiocy he did get it—part of it. You remember the princess."

The King was smiling again.

"I have never known any man to tell the truth to or about a woman. Why is that, John?"

"Perhaps, Sire, if you would explain the tiny scratch I see under your right eye, you could understand. Now the scratch was not there last night, and it has the distinct look of—"

"Yes—yes—a clumsy servant. Let us speak of Morgan. You have a way, John, of being secretly insulting. Sometimes you are not even conscious of your insults. It is a thing to put down if you are to be around courts for any length of time."

III

Sir Henry Morgan sat on the Judge's Bench at Port Royal. Before him, on the floor, lay a slab of white sunlight like a blinding tomb. Throughout the room an orchestra of flies sang their symphony of boredom. The droning voices of counsel were only louder instruments against the humming obbligato. Court officials went about sleepily, and the cases moved on.

"It was the fifteenth of the month, my lord. Williamson went to the Cartwright property for the purpose of determining— determining to his own satisfaction, my lord, whether the tree stood as described. It was while he was there—"

The case sang to its monotonous conclusion. Sir Henry, behind his broad table, stirred sleepily. Now the guards brought in a sullen vagrant, clothed in rags of old sail.

"Charged with stealing four biscuits and a mirror from So-and-So, my lord."

"The proof?"

"He was detected, my lord."

"Did you, or did you not, steal four biscuits and a mirror?" The prisoner's face became even more sullen.

"I told 'em."

"My lord," the guard prompted.

"My lord."

"Why did you steal these articles?"

"I wan'ed 'em."

"Say my lord."

"My lord."

"What did you want with them?"

"I wan'ed the biscuits for to eat."

"My lord."

"My lord."

"And the mirror?"

"I wan'ed the mirror for to look at myself in."

"My lord."

"My lord."

They led the man to his imprisonment.

Now the guards brought in a thin, pasty woman.

"Charged with harlotry and incontinence, my lord."

"Incontinence is illegal," said Sir Henry irritatedly, "but since when have we been punishing people for harlotry?"

"My lord, the nature of this woman— The public health demands— We thought the case would be understood."

"Ah! I see. She must be locked up. Take her away quickly."

The woman began to cry sulkily.

Sir Henry rested his forehead on his hands. He did not look up at the next prisoners.

"Charged with piracy on the high seas, my lord; with disturbing the King's peace; with an act of war against a friendly nation."

Sir Henry glanced quickly at the prisoners. One was a rotund little man with eyes of terror, and the other a lean, grizzled fellow whose one arm was gone.

"What is the proof against the prisoners?"

"Five witnesses, my lord."

"So? Make your plea!"

The tall man had put his good arm about the shoulders of his companion.

"We plead guilty, my lord."

"You plead guilty?" Sir Henry cried in amazement. "But no pirate pleads guilty. It is a case unprecedented."

"We plead guilty, my lord."

"But why?"

"Fifty people saw us in action, my lord. Why should we take up your time in denying what fifty people will swear to? No, we are resigned, my lord. We are content, both with the recent action and with our lives." The wiry arm squeezed about the small round tub of a buccaneer.

Henry sat very silently for a time. But finally he raised his tired eyes. "I sentence you to be hanged."

"Hanged, my lord?"

"Hanged by the neck until you are dead."

"You are changed, Sir."

Sir Henry started forward and closely scrutinized the prisoners. Then his lips smiled. "Yes," he said quietly, "I am changed. The Henry Morgan you knew is not the Sir Henry Morgan who sentences you to death. I do not kill ferociously any more, but coldly, and because I have to." Sir Henry raised his voice. "Let the court be cleared, but guard the doors! I wish to speak privately with the prisoners."

When they were alone he began:

"I know well that I am changed, but tell me what is the change you see."

The Burgundians looked at each other. "You speak, Emil."

"You are changed, Sir, in this way. Once you knew what you were doing. You were sure of yourself."

"That is so," broke in the other. "You do not know—you are not sure of yourself any more. Once you were one man. It is possible to trust one man. But now you are several men. If we should trust one of you, we should be in fear of the others."

Sir Henry laughed. "That is more or less true. It is not my fault, but it is true. Civilization will split up a character, and he who refuses to split goes under."

"We have forgotten about civilization, thanks to our Mother," Antoine muttered fiercely.

"What a pity to hang you."

"But is it so necessary to hang us, sir? Could we not escape or be pardoned?"

"No, you must be hanged. I am sorry, but it must be so. Such is my duty."

"But duty to your friends, sir—to the men who bore arms with you, who mixed their blood with yours—"

"Listen, Other Burgundian; there are two kinds of duty, and you would know that if you remembered your France. You mentioned one species, and it is the weaker kind. The other, the giant duty—that which will not be overlooked—might be called the duty of appearances. I do not hang you because you are pirates, but because I am expected to hang pirates. I am sorry for you. I would like to send you to your cells with saws in your pockets, but I cannot. As long as I do what is expected of me, I shall remain the Judge. When I change, for whatever motive, I may myself be hanged."

"That is so, Sir. I remember." He turned to his friend who stood shaking in the grip of horror. "You see, such is the case, Emil. He does not like to tell us this thing because it hurts him. Perhaps he punishes himself in this manner for something he had done or failed to do. Perhaps he remembers Chagres, Emil."

"Chagres!" Sir Henry bent forward with excitement. "What happened after I sailed away? Tell me!"

"You were cursed, sir, as it is given to few men to be cursed. You were tortured in men's minds. They feasted on your heart and sent your soul to hell. I enjoyed the scene rarely, because I knew that every man there envied you while he reviled you. I was proud of you, sir."

"And they scattered?"

"They scattered and died, poor little children."

"Anyway, I should have hated to fall in with those poor little children! Tell me," Sir Henry's voice had become wistful, "tell me about Panama. We did go there, didn't we? We really captured Panama, didn't we, and looted it? It was I who led you, wasn't it?"

"It was so. It was a grand fight and an ocean of plunder—but, after all, you know more about that last than we do."

"Sometimes I doubt whether this body ever went to Panama. I am sure this brain did not. I would like to stay and talk to you of that old time, but my wife expects me. She is apt to fuss if I am late for luncheon." He spoke jocosely. "When would you like to be hanged?"

The Burgundians were whispering together.

"Ah, there is that 'hanged' again. When would we like to be hanged? Any time, sir. We do not wish to put you to the trouble, but if you insist—any time there is a man and a rope idle." Antoine approached the table. "Emil wishes to offer one last compliment. It is a gift for your wife—a gift the history of which alone would make it valuable. Emil has treasured this gift to the end, and of this talisman he has reaped a harvest—for talismanic it is, in truth, sir. But Emil thinks its period of duty should end, sir. He believes that by taking this means he can stop the series of events which has flowed out from his treasure. And Emil, unfortunately, will have no farther use for it. Emil kisses the hand of Lady Morgan—presents his respects and dignified compliments." He dropped a rose pearl on the table and turned quickly away.

After they had been led out, Sir Henry sat at his bench and stared at the pearl. Then he put it in his pocket and walked into the street.

He came to the squat, white Palace of the Lieutenant-Governor. It was exactly as Sir Edward had left it. Lady Morgan would not have felt right if a detail had been changed. She met Henry at the door.

"We are to have dinner with the Vaughns. And what am I to do about the coachman? He's drunk. I've told you and told you to lock your closet, but you will not pay attention to me.

He sneaked into the house and got a bottle off your shelf. He must have done that."

"Open your hand, my dear. I have a gift for you."

He dropped the rose pearl into her palm.

For a moment she looked at the rosy sphere and her face flushed with pleasure, but then she searched his face suspiciously.

"What have you been up to?"

"Up to? Why, I have been holding court."

"I suppose you got this in court!" Her face lighted up. "I know! You suspected my displeasure at your actions last night. You were practically intoxicated, if you must know the truth; and all the people were staring at you and whispering. Don't say a word. I saw them and I saw you. And now you want to bribe my feeling—my decency."

"Suspected your displeasure! My dear, I suspected it all the way home with you, and nearly all night after I got here. You are right. I strongly suspected your displeasure. In fact, I was certain of it. But I will tell you the truth about the pearl."

"You will tell the truth only because you know you cannot deceive me, Henry. When will you give up the idea that I don't know every little thought you possess?"

"But I didn't try to deceive you. You didn't give me time."

"It takes no more time to tell the truth than—"

"Listen to me, Elizabeth, please. I tried two pirates this morning and they gave it to me."

She smiled a superior smile. "They gave it to you? Why? Did you release them? It would be like you to release them. Sometimes I think you would still be one of them if it weren't for me. You never seem to realize, Henry, that it is really I who have made you what you are—a knight and a gentleman. You made yourself a buccaneer. But tell me, did you release these pirates?"

"No; I sentenced them to death."

"Ah! Then why did they give you the pearl?"

"My dear, they gave it to me because they had nothing else to do with it. They might have presented it to the hangman, but one would feel a trifle diffident about giving pearls to the man

who put a rope about one's neck. Friendship isn't possible with
one's hangman, I should imagine. Thus, they gave it to me, and
I—" he smiled broadly and innocently, "I am giving it to you
because I love you."

"Well, I can easily find out about the pirates, and as to your
affection—you love me as long as I have my eye on you, and no
longer. I know you thoroughly. But I am glad they are hanged.
Lord Vaughn says they are a positive danger even to ourselves.
He says they may stop fighting Spain at any moment and start
on us. He says they are like vicious dogs, to be exterminated as
soon as possible. I feel a little safer every time one of them is
out of the way."

"But, my dear, Lord Vaughn knows nothing about buccaneers, while I—"

"Henry, why do you keep me here with your talking, when
you know I have a thousand things to attend to. You think,
because you have all the time in the world, that I can afford to
help you idle. Now do see to the coachman, because I should
be terribly embarrassed if he were not fit. His livery will not
suit Jacob by any pinching. Did I tell you he is drunk? Get him
sober for to-night if you must drown him to do it. Now hurry
along. I won't feel right until I know he can sit up straight."
She turned to reënter the house, then came back and kissed him
on the cheek.

"It's really a nice pearl. Thank you, dear," she said. "Of
course, I am going to have Monsieur Banzet value it. After
what Lord Vaughn said, I have very little faith in pirates. They
might have been trying to bribe you with paste, and you would
never know the difference."

Sir Henry walked toward the stables. Now, as on other occa-
sions, he was gently moved by uneasiness. Now and then there
came a vagrant feeling that, in spite of all Elizabeth's declama-
tion to the effect that she knew him thoroughly, perhaps she
really did. It was disquieting.

IV

Sir Henry Morgan lay in an enormous bed; a bed so wide that his body, under the coverlid, seemed a snow-covered mountain range dividing two great plains. From the walls about the room the shiny eyes of his ancestors regarded him. On their faces were smirks which said, "Ah, yes! A knight, to be sure—but we know how you bought your knighthood." The air in the room was heavy and thick and hot. So always the air seems in a room where a man is about to die.

Sir Henry was staring at the ceiling. For an hour he had been puzzled with this mysterious ceiling. Nothing supported it in the middle. Why did it not fall? It was late. Every one about him was silent; they went sneaking about pretending to be ghosts, he thought. They were trying to convince him that he was dead already. He closed his eyes. He was too tired or too indifferent to keep them open. He heard the doctor come in, and felt him reading the pulse. Then the big, confident voice boomed:

"I am sorry, Lady Morgan. There is nothing to do now. I do not even know what is the matter with him. Some old jungle fever, perhaps. I could bleed him again, I suppose, but we have taken a great deal of blood already, and it seems to do no good. However, if he begins to sink, I shall try it again."

"Then he will die?" Lady Morgan asked. Henry thought she showed more curiosity than sorrow.

"Yes, he will die unless God intervenes. Only God can be sure of his patients."

And then the room was cleared of people. Henry knew that his wife was sitting near the bed. He could hear her crying softly beside him. "What a pity it is," he thought, "that I cannot go to death in a ship so she might pack my bag for me. It would give her so much satisfaction to know that I was entering heaven with a decent supply of clean linen."

"Oh, my husband— Oh, Henry, my husband."

He turned his head and looked at her curiously, and his gaze went deep into her eyes. Suddenly he was seized with despair.

"This woman loves me," he said to himself. "This woman

loves me, and I have never known it. I cannot know this kind of love. Her eyes—her eyes—this is something far beyond my comprehension. Can she have loved me always?" He looked again. "She is very near to God. I think women are nearer to God than men. They cannot talk about it, but, Christ! how it shines in their eyes. And she loves me. During all her hectoring and badgering and brow-beating, she has loved me—and I have never known it. But what would I have done if I had known it?" He turned away. This sorrow was too great, too burning and awful to regard. It is terrifying to see a woman's soul shining through her eyes.

So he was to die. It was rather pleasant if death was like this. He was warm and very tired. Presently he would fall asleep, and that would be death—Brother Death.

He knew that some other person had come into the room. His wife leaned over until she came within his upstaring vision. She would be annoyed if she knew he could turn his head if he wished.

"The Vicar, dear," his wife said. "Do be nice to him. Oh, do listen to him! It may help you—afterwards." Ah, she was practical! She was going to see that some compact was made with the Almighty if she could. Her affection was an efficient thing, but her love—that which glittered in her wet eyes—was frightful.

Henry felt a warm, soft hand take his. A soothing voice was talking to him. But it was difficult to listen. The ceiling was swaying dangerously.

"God is Love," the voice was saying. "You must put your faith in God."

"God is Love," Henry repeated mechanically.

"Let us pray," said the voice.

Suddenly Henry remembered a moment of his childhood. He was being tortured with an ear-ache, and his mother was holding him in her arms. She stroked his wrist with her fingertips. "This is all nonsense," she was saying. He remembered how she said it. "This is all nonsense. God is Love. He will not let little boys suffer. Now repeat after me—'The Lord is my shepherd. I shall not want.' " It was as though she administered a medicine. In the same tone she would have commanded, "Come, take this oil!"

Henry felt the warm fingers of the Vicar creep to his wrist and begin a stroking movement.

"The Lord is my shepherd. I shall not want," Henry droned sleepily. "He maketh me to lie down in green pastures—" The stroking continued, but more harshly. The Vicar's voice became more loud and authoritative. It was as though, after years of patient waiting, the Church had at last got Henry Morgan within its power. There was something almost gloating about the voice.

"Have you repented your sins, Sir Henry?"

"My sins? No, I had not thought of them. Shall I repent Panama?"

The Vicar was embarrassed. "Well, Panama was a patriotic conquest. The King approved. Besides, the people were Papists."

"But what are my sins, then?" Henry went on. "I remember only the most pleasant and the most painful among them. Somehow I do not wish to repent the pleasant ones. It would be like breaking faith with them; they were charming. And the painful sins carried atonement with them like concealed knives. How may I repent, sir? I might go over my whole life, naming and repenting every act from the shattering of my first teething ring to my last visit to a brothel. I might repent everything I could remember, but if I forgot one single sin, the whole process would be wasted."

"Have you repented your sins, Sir Henry?"

He realized, then, that he had not been talking at all. It was difficult to talk. His tongue had become lazy and sluggish. "No," he said. "I can't remember them very well."

"You must search in your heart for greed and lust and spite. You must drive wickedness from your heart."

"But, sir, I don't remember ever having been consciously wicked. I have done things which seemed wicked afterwards, but while I was doing them I always had some rather good end in view." Again he was conscious that he wasn't really speaking.

"Let us pray," the voice said.

Henry made a violent effort with his tongue. "No!" he cried.

"But you prayed before."

"Yes, I prayed before—because my mother would have liked it. She would have wanted me to pray at least once, more as a proof of her training than for any other reason, a reassurance to her that she had done her duty by me."

"Would you die heretic, Sir Henry? Aren't you afraid of death?"

"I am too tired, sir, or too lazy, to consider problems of heresy. And I am not afraid of death. I have seen much violence, and no man whom I have admired was afraid of death, but only of dying. You see, sir, death is an intellectual matter, but dying is pure pain. And this death of mine is very pleasant so far. No, sir; I am not afraid even of dying. It is comfortable, and it would be quiet if I could only be left alone. It is as though I were about to sleep after a great effort."

He heard the Vicar's voice again; but, though the warm hand still stroked his wrist, the voice came from a mighty distance.

"He will not answer me," the Vicar was saying. "I am perplexed for his soul."

Then he heard his wife speaking to him. "You must pray, dear. Every one does. How can you get to heaven if you do not pray?"

There she was again, intent on making a contract with God. But Henry did not want to look at her. Naïve though her philosophy was, her eyes were as deep and as sad as the limitless sky. He wanted to say, "I won't want to get to heaven once I am dead. I won't want them to disturb me." They made such a commotion about this death.

The doctor had come back into the room. "He is unconscious," the booming voice proclaimed. "I think I *will* bleed him again."

Henry felt the scalpel cut into his arm. It was pleasant. He hoped they would cut him again and again. But the illusion was contradictory. Rather than feeling the blood leaving him, he sensed a curious warmth slipping through his body. His breast and arms tingled as though some robust, ancient wine were singing in his veins.

Now a queer change began to take place. He found that he could see through his eyelids, could see all about him without moving his head. The doctor and his wife and the Vicar and even the room were sliding away from him.

"They are moving," he thought. "I am not moving. I am fixed. I am the center of all things and cannot move. I am as heavy as the universe. Perhaps I am the universe."

A low, sweet tone was flowing into his consciousness; a vibrant, rich organ tone, which filled him, seemed to emanate from his brain, to flood his body, and from it to surge out over the world. He saw with a little surprise that the room had gone. He was lying in an immeasurable dark grotto along the sides of which were rows of thick, squat columns made of some green, glittering crystal. He was still in a reclining position, and the long grotto was sliding past him. Of a sudden, the movement stopped. He was surrounded by strange beings, having the bodies of children, and bulbous, heavy heads, but no faces. The flesh where their faces should have been was solid and unbroken. These beings were talking and chattering in dry, raucous voices. Henry was puzzled that they could talk without mouths.

Slowly the knowledge grew in him that these were his deeds and his thoughts which were living with Brother Death. Each one had gone immediately to live with Brother Death as soon as it was born. When he knew their identity, the faceless little creatures turned on him and clustered thickly about his couch.

"Why did you do me?" one cried.

"I do not know; I do not remember you."

"Why did you think me?"

"I do not know. I must have known, but I have forgotten. My memory is slipping away from me here in this grotto."

Still insistently they questioned him, and their voices were becoming more and more strident and harsh, so that they overwhelmed the great Tone.

"Me! answer me!"

"No; me!"

"Oh, leave me! Let me rest," Henry said wearily. "I am tired, and I cannot tell you anything anyway."

Then he saw that the little beings were crouching before an approaching form. They turned toward the form and cowered, and at length fell on their knees before it and raised trembling arms in gestures of supplication.

Henry strained his attention toward the figure. Why, it was Elizabeth coming toward him—little Elizabeth, with golden hair and a wise young look on her face. She was girdled with cornflowers, and her eyes were strangely puzzled and bright. With a little start of surprise she noticed Henry.

"I am Elizabeth," she said. "You did not come to see me before you went away."

"I know. I think I was afraid to talk with you. But I stood in the darkness before your window, and I whistled."

"Did you?" She smiled at him gladly. "That was nice of you. I cannot see, though, why you should have been afraid of me—of such a little girl. It was silly of you."

"I do not know why," he said. "I ran away. I was motivated by a power that is slipping out of all the worlds. My memories are leaving me one by one like a colony of aged swans flying off to some lonely island in the sea to die. But you became a princess, did you not?" he questioned anxiously.

"Yes, perhaps I did. I hope I did. I, too, forget. Tell me, did you really stand there in the dark?"

Henry had noticed a peculiar thing. If he looked steadily at one of the crouched, faceless beings, it disappeared. He amused himself by staring first at one and then at another until all of them were gone.

"Did you really stand there in the dark?"

"I do not know. Perhaps I only thought I did." He looked for Elizabeth, but she, too, had disappeared. In her place there was a red smoldering ember, and the light was dying out of it.

"Wait, Elizabeth— Wait. Tell me where my father is. I want to see my father."

The dying ember answered him.

"Your father is happily dead. He was afraid to test even death."

"But Merlin, then— Where is Merlin? If I could only find him."

"Merlin? You should know of him. Merlin is herding dreams in Avalon."

The fire went out of the ember with a dry, hard snap. There was no light anywhere. For a moment, Henry was conscious of the deep, mellow pulsation of the Tone.

THE STORY OF PENGUIN CLASSICS

Before 1946 . . . "Classics" are mainly the domain of academics and students; readable editions for everyone else are almost unheard of. This all changes when a little-known classicist, E. V. Rieu, presents Penguin founder Allen Lane with the translation of Homer's *Odyssey* that he has been working on in his spare time.

1946 Penguin Classics debuts with *The Odyssey*, which promptly sells three million copies. Suddenly, classics are no longer for the privileged few.

1950s Rieu, now series editor, turns to professional writers for the best modern, readable translations, including Dorothy L. Sayers's *Inferno* and Robert Graves's unexpurgated *Twelve Caesars*.

1960s The Classics are given the distinctive black covers that have remained a constant throughout the life of the series. Rieu retires in 1964, hailing the Penguin Classics list as "the greatest educative force of the twentieth century."

1970s A new generation of translators swells the Penguin Classics ranks, introducing readers of English to classics of world literature from more than twenty languages. The list grows to encompass more history, philosophy, science, religion, and politics.

1980s The Penguin American Library launches with titles such as *Uncle Tom's Cabin* and joins forces with Penguin Classics to provide the most comprehensive library of world literature available from any paperback publisher.

1990s The launch of Penguin Audiobooks brings the classics to a listening audience for the first time, and in 1999 the worldwide launch of the Penguin Classics Web site extends their reach to the global online community.

The 21st Century Penguin Classics are completely redesigned for the first time in nearly twenty years. This world-famous series now consists of more than 1,300 titles, making the widest range of the best books ever written available to millions—and constantly redefining what makes a "classic."

The Odyssey continues . . .

The best books ever written

PENGUIN (🐧) **CLASSICS**

SINCE 1946

Find out more at www.penguinclassics.com

Visit www.vpbookclub.com

CLICK ON A CLASSIC
www.penguinclassics.com

The world's greatest literature at your fingertips

Constantly updated information on more than a thousand titles,
from Icelandic sagas to ancient Indian epics, Russian drama to
Italian romance, American greats to African masterpieces

•

The latest news on recent additions to the list, updated
editions, and specially commissioned translations

•

Original essays by leading writers

•

A wealth of background material, including biographies
of every classic author from Aristotle to Zamyatin, plot
synopses, readers' and teachers' guides, useful Web links

•

Online desk and examination copy assistance for academics

•

Trivia quizzes, competitions, giveaways, news on
forthcoming screen adaptations